Suddenly Snow

ISBN: 979-8-6362-7376-9
ASIN: B086ZZ3G2K

Cover photo by Susanne Bacon
Author photo: Donald A. Bacon

Susanne Bacon

Suddenly Snow

A Wycliff Novel

Also by Susanne Bacon:

Wycliff Novels

Delicate Dreams (2015)

Wordless Wishes (2016)

Telling Truths (2017)

Clean Cuts (2018)

Haunted Homes (2019)

Other Fiction

Islands in the Storm (2020)

Non-Fiction

Home from Home (2019)

Preliminary Remark

The town of Wycliff is entirely fictitious. So are all characters in this novel. Any similarities with living or late persons and operating or former businesses, except those mentioned in the acknowledgements, are totally coincidental.

Susanne Bacon

To Sandra Windges
and Marianne Bull,
both of whom inspired this novel.
And to Donald,
the love of my life …

Chapter 1

December 22, 09:00 a.m.

When the first snowflake tumbled from the sky, Abby was closing her suitcase with trembling hands and sank back onto her bed. She suddenly doubted whether her idea of traveling to Seattle was as great as she had thought it would be twenty-four hours ago. Maybe it was exactly the opposite of what she should do. Maybe it only meant that she was running away from her real life. She had thought making the trip would mean she would be catching up with it. Or get it back.

She stared out into the leaden grayness that was huddling over the roofs of Wycliff and the mysterious depths of the Sound beyond, the islands that started slithering into a silvery fog-like density, nothingness. At other times, she would have enjoyed the coziness of her bedroom with its cheerfully blazing gas fireplace, shabby chic furniture, a dried lavender bouquet on her dresser, a collection of driftwood and glass baubles on the mantlepiece. Not today. Not for a while.

She sighed. Could she have seen what was coming? She had felt as if hit by a train when Hank had left her. It had been so suddenly, so overwhelmingly painful. They had had dinner at *Le Quartier*, that cozy French-style bistro restaurant downtown, the place where they had always had their date nights. Only, this time it had felt differently as soon as they had found their seats at a corner table. And when the wine had come, Hank had casually said that they needed to rethink their relationship and that for him it was not working anymore. Just like this. He might as well have stabbed her with a steak knife. That had been four months ago. Since then no phone calls, just a couple of emails announcing that Hank would move his stuff out of *her* home. He didn't even call it *theirs* anymore.

Home. That was a beautiful Bed & Breakfast business she had taken over a couple of years ago. It was called *The Gull's Nest*, a cozy old Captain's house with big picture windows affording views across downtown Wycliff and the water. Wycliff had been the town in which Abigail Winterbottom had grown up. The quaint Victorian town somewhere on the shores of South Puget Sound between Seattle and Olympia was in her blood. There had been Winterbottoms in this town ever since its founding. First, they had lived in quarters above their haberdashery in the part that was called Downtown with a capital "D" because it was below a steep bluff. By the end of the 18th century they had obtained a lot in Uptown and built a fine old home there.

Abby had met Hank while she was still working with a paper company in Tacoma. She had been claiming the last empty bar stool at the *Harbor Pub* that late Friday night at the same time he had been doing so from the other side. It had been love at first site. They had laughed and offered the seat to each other, then moved it out of the way to stand side by side at the bar. Later that night they had walked up Main Street, both presuming that the other one needed to head that way when Abby's direction was towards Uptown and his only to *The Ship Hotel* a block away from the pub. When they realized their mistake, they laughed and hugged. They ended up in their first kiss. That had been eight years ago.

"Eight years," Abby mused. "Why this? Why now?" She rose from her bed and walked over to the window. Outside the first single snowflake had been joined by a multitude now. It was really pretty. Unless you were packed for a trip out of town. "Eight years…"

Hank had been working for Microsoft up in Seattle even back then. He had been visiting Abby every weekend until he said he would like them to move in with each other. Abby hadn't wanted to move up to Seattle though. Small-town girl that she was she felt bewildered by the city's size, its speed, its many different town parts. Hank had offered to move in with her. So, they had started living together. And it had felt good and natural. Hank was easy to have around. He took over half of the household chores; he helped maintain the house and garden. He was tidy. He was fun. He was affectionate.

The day came when the paper factory had to lay off people because the Chinese competition had grown stronger in the market and their prices needed to become more competitive. Abby had received a pink slip because at age 30 she was one of the employees who had been there the shortest amount of time. Coming home, Hank had just taken her into his arms and comforted her. That had been three years ago. Unfortunately, her attempts to find similar work – that of an accountant with secretarial skills or the other way around – had failed. Her despair had grown. Hank had stopped trying to console her and told her to try something different then. Meanwhile, his working hours had extended, and sometimes he had come back home from work so late that she had already been lying in bed, fast asleep.

Then, one magic day, when she had been racking her brain during a walk through her Uptown neighborhood, she had come across the "For Sale" sign outside *The Gull's Nest*. She had been thrilled. She was good with people. She knew she could do this. Maybe this was what she had been meant to do all the time. Save an old business in her hometown. *Stay* in her hometown. As to financing the business – she would find a way.

"You don't expect me to shell out anything, do you?" Hank had asked cautiously.

"No," Abby had said and then added reluctantly, "I might sell the house and invest it into the B & B."

"Sell your family home?" Hank had asked surprised.

"Why, yes!"

And that was what she had done. She had spent days and weeks at the place to refurbish it. She had made contracts with the Chinese dry-cleaner below the bluff, with *Nathan's* bakery department, with *Dottie's Deli* for cold cuts, even with *The Flower Bower* for fresh bouquets for the reception desk. She and Hank had moved out of the big family home and into two rooms on the

B & B's first floor, marked off as "Private", a master bedroom and a sitting room. The rest of the house had been declared business area.

Maybe this was when it had begun. Hank had never complained about their smaller space for privacy. But she had felt him become tenser. If he had been quite familiar with the house guests in the beginning, he made himself less and less seen. Their date nights had become scarcer. And when Hank had called her to take her out to *Le Quartier* the weekend before Labor Day, it had turned into their last date night. He hadn't made big excuses.

"I have met somebody who lives in University District."

"A student?"

"A docent. She isn't much older than the students though."

She had felt her bile rise. "Why?"

"I cannot say," he had said, lifting his hands in a shrug. "Things just happen sometimes."

"How long has it been going on?"

"Half a year. Maybe longer?"

She had swallowed hard. That long. "Is she worth it?" Hank hadn't answered. Instead he had taken her hand. She had snatched it away from him. "Don't! Don't you ever dare touch me again."

He had looked startled. "We are not married, Abby."

"And thank God for that," she had spat. "This saves me a lot of trouble."

They had called dinner off after that. Hank had walked back to the B & B in silence. He had packed a bag and left. Only then had Abby permitted herself to crumble onto the bed and cry. The next morning, she had served breakfast to her guests with a cheerful smile and a heart that felt as if it had bled out. Life must go on.

But, oh, how she had been missing Hank ever since. You couldn't eradicate eight years from your life and pretend they had never happened. Well, they said that it was always easier for those who finished a relationship than for those on the receiving end.

The picket fence around her garden started collecting little caps of white fluff now. Abby turned away from the window. Snow was never good news here in the South Puget Sound area. People were not used to it. They hardly ever got more than a few flakes. Half an inch in the roads meant traffic chaos. Because nobody ever thought of buying winter tires for their cars, half an inch of snow was sufficient to strand you on level ground. There was no way of trying to drive up any slope. Also, Wycliff didn't have any snow ploughs – it was not worth the one or two days of snow every three or four years that the weather was like this. The snow would have melted before the ploughs would be ready for deployment.

Abby stared into the mirror on the dresser. She didn't look too bad for her 33 years. Her face was a little more haggard than it had been four months ago, and there were a few very faint lines on her brow from worrying. Her eyes were a dark gray with some green and brown flecks, her small nose was dusted with a few freckles, and her mouth was not ugly either. Her sandy hair was pulled back into a short ponytail. Her hands were still looking soft and smooth, her fingernails were kept very short for practical benefits. In short, she was looking down-to-earth. Not spectacular. Not terrible either. Somewhat simply average.

Only yesterday night, shortly after dinner, she had climbed up the stairs and knocked at door 24. All the rooms on the second floor had numbers preceded by a "2". The Gull's Nest certainly didn't have 24 guestrooms, just a very practicable seven.

"Come in," a strong male voice had answered, and she had slipped into the dusky room.

Her eyes had had to get used to the darkness inside. She knew where every piece of furniture was standing, and she had known where the voice was coming from.

"Good evening, Dave," she had said softly.

"Abby," the voice had boomed out of the dark.

"Mind if I switch on a light?"

"Not at all," the voice had chuckled. "It won't make much of a difference to me though."

Abby had found the switch, and the soft light had illuminated a nicely-sized room with a gas fireplace and a rocking chair. It was very sparsely decorated, and the furniture was kept to the bare necessities.

The voice belonged to a big old man who looked like Santa Claus with his white hair and well-kempt white beard, a slightly bulging stomach, and an air of benign amusement. "What brings you here, my dear?" He had turned his face into her direction, his blind eyes dark and impermeable.

Abby had hesitated for a moment. "I am thinking of going up to Seattle over Christmas," she had finally said.

"Are you thinking of it, or have you already decided?"

Abby had bitten her lips. "I have already decided."

"Are you sure this is a good idea?"

"Do you think it is a bad one?"

"I'm not the one who is making the decision," Dave had said. "Are you trying to see your ex?"

Abby had taken a deep breath. "I have to see him. I need to make sure he doesn't want to come back and is just too shy to ask."

"Pffff…," he had made. "You really think that he is that kind of man? Too shy?"

"Well, he was the one to finish our relationship. He might think I wouldn't want to take him back."

"And why should you indeed?" Dave had wondered.

"I love him," Abby had said.

"Do you love him? Or do you love the idea of loving him?"

"What's the difference?"

"What indeed?" he had said and chuckled to himself. "Child, you are so young … and there are many, many fish in the sea."

Abby had frowned. "I don't care for the others."

"How do you know that? Have you even tried?" He had listened for an answer and, as none had come, he had shaken his head. "This one proved to be a very slippery one, you know?"

"We were together for eight years."

"Not all of it, as far as you told me."

"No," she had said meekly.

"So, your decision is made?"

"It is."

"Well then, safe travels. But…"

"Yes?"

"Don't come back creating the same episode all over again."

Abby ignored him. "I'll have Dottie see to you whenever she goes to work in the morning and when she returns in the evening. She offered it so you would not be all alone in the empty house."

"Kind little German woman," he had said softly.

"How do you know she is little?" Abby had wondered.

"Whenever she visits, her voice is not that far up. Yours comes from a little higher – so I guess you are a little taller than she is."

"Hmmm," Abby had said. "You sure are clever."

"Not as clever as I wish."

"How so?"

He had tilted his head and grinned. "If I were, I'd be able to keep you from taking this trip."

Abby had almost smiled. "Good night then, Dave."

"Good night, Abby."

And now it was December 22, the day of her departure, and it had started snowing. What at first had been a soft hovering of single flakes that almost couldn't decide whether to dance upwards or fall to the ground, had developed into something more consistent in the last hour. It didn't look good. Taking the car was no option in this weather. The train might have to do. More inconvenience on top of an already aggravating mission. Backing down was no option though. Abby changed her shoes for some sturdier boots. The bus to the train station it would be.

Let's face it – maybe the snowfall was to her advantage after all. The tiny boutique hotel she had booked in Belltown didn't have a parking garage or parking lot, but it was affordable. So, it would have been a crazy feat to find parking space in Seattle. At Christmas at that. And if she did, it would be outrageously overpriced. Maybe public transport would take away from her stress that lay ahead. It wouldn't be easy to go to Hank's apartment and talk to him. Her stomach roiled just at the thought of it. But she needed to open him the door back to her and their life together. These eight years, well, almost eight years couldn't have been for nothing.

Abby pulled her suitcase off her bed and carried it outside her door. A quick dash upstairs to see that Dave had eaten the breakfast she had brought him earlier and to say good-bye. The old man smiled at her with unseeing eyes. "Be safe, child," he said. "I smell snow in the air."

"It *is* snowing," Abby confirmed. "I'm not taking the car, so don't worry. And I'll call Dottie as soon as I have arrived. So, she can tell you." Downstairs the phone at the reception desk rang. "Got to go now," she said and gave Dave a hug. Then she rushed out of his room, closing the door a bit louder than she would have if not in such a hurry, and flew down the stairs. What if it was Hank?

By the fourth ring, Abby reached the phone. "*The Gull's Nest*, good morning?" she said.

"Hi Abby, it's Dottie."

Abby's heart sank. "Good morning Dottie. What's up?"

"Have you looked outside the past few minutes?"

Abby spied through the curtain next to the reception desk. Outside was a white-out. "Ooops," she said miserably. "Doesn't look good."

"You weren't going to take your car, were you?" her friend said with ever the slightest German accent.

"No way," Abby laughed nervously. "Not with summer tires and our slopes. Bad combination."

"Well, Luke just got a call from BNSF," Dottie said. She was married to Wycliff's Chief of police, and often received news earlier than the mayor. "It doesn't look like you are going anywhere near Seattle today, dear."

19

"What?!" Abby sank down on the chair behind the reception counter, feeling a little wobbly on her knees all of a sudden. "Why?"

"There has been a landslide a bit up north, and it has the road covered as well as the train tracks that are running alongside it. With the weather seeming to get worse, clean-up crews can't move in there and work. They need to wait until the snow lets up and then start."

"But when will that be? What does the weather forecast say?"

"No chance until Christmas Day," Dottie said dryly. "Poor guys who are supposed to leave their families and work on that mess. No fun at any time. Even less so on Christmas Day."

Abby's vision blurred, and all of a sudden, a big tear rolled down her right cheek. "I had been relying on going to see him and spend Christmas with him," she whispered.

"But he didn't know you were coming, right?" Dottie asked, ever practical.

"No," Abby sniveled.

"Just as well, hm? He also might have *not* wanted to spend it with you..."

"I'd prefer to hold a little hope," Abby said very softly.

"Oh, Abby," Dottie replied. "Dear soul. Don't waste hope in the wrong place."

Abby nodded, which Dottie, of course, wasn't able to see. Then she swallowed. "I guess I better let Dave know that I'll be staying after all. And you won't have to come and look after him either, of course."

"It wouldn't have been a problem," Dottie replied. "Well, I have to go. I just had to let you know about the landslide." She hung up.

Abby shut off her phone as well and let it sink into her lap. Christmas was going to be a very dreary affair this year.

Chapter 2

December 22, 11:00 a.m.

La Strega had almost finished her West Coast concert tour. She was tired and bored. The same program every night, not even changed up a little like a rock band would have. Always the same process of building suspense to her final aria. The usual three curtains and encores. Then the endless signing of autograph cards and meets and greets with people who all seemed to gush the same words at her. Interchangeable.

She hadn't even been able to see anything of the cities she had been touring. Manfredo – what a silly artist's name for her impresario! – had seen to it that there would always be rehearsals with whatever orchestra or pianist she was appearing with, that the food she received before a performance would not affect her voice, that the hotel rooms were quiet and close to the venue. He made sure that her evening gowns were dry-cleaned and returned to her in time for the next stage show. He saw to advertising and newspaper articles. In San Francisco, she had had a radio interview, and she would be on a radio interview near Seattle the day before Christmas Eve. At least that had been the plan. But now it looked as if nothing was sure anymore.

La Strega's real name was Florence Piccolini. "La Strega", Italian for "the sorceress", had been the description of her in some music critic's concert review decades ago, and it had stuck. Indeed, her high, full soprano lent itself as easily to the lyric notes of a Mozart aria as to the more dramatic ones by Puccini. And she had a secret affection for Handel coloraturas even though she felt the composer had shortchanged her with so many glorious pieces for deeper voices.

Florence Piccolini was not so much to look at when not on stage. She was rather on the stout side with dark Italian looks, a longish nose, and a chin tending to double and triple when she was laughing. But on stage … oh my! She was as much a believable Pamina as a tragic Tosca, and her Solveig performances, when singing Grieg, were legendary. She became the characters; she looked haggard when the role demanded it, outsized when she was meant to be furious. But today, she was not La Strega. Today she was simply Florence, with Manfredo already up in Seattle and her retracing childhood days.

She had stayed at a dingy motel near the Dome District in Tacoma, as every single hotel room or Bed & Breakfast accommodation in Wycliff had been fully booked. That's what you had to deal with when you decided spontaneously to go somewhere privately and ditch the impresario's services. But the people who ran the motel had been friendly, and the room had been clean. It had been just for this one night.

Now, Florence was riding on the shuttle bus from The Harbor Mall – with the harbor nowhere near – past some housing project with a high-and-mighty name towards Main Street. Florence had lived in Wycliff when she had been a child. She

23

remembered the man who had raised her and her mother, who had pretended that man was her father. Until one day there had been that final straw that had severed the marriage that had been built on that pretense. She didn't remember much about before, just that her mother had obviously loved her. And not much of how she came to live with who turned out to be her real father, John Piccolini, and his wife, *not* her mother. Oh, so very much not so. At first, Florence had received loving letters from her mother, but her father's wife had demanded that stop, as the constant reminder of Florence's physical presence had been enough to bear already. She hadn't needed to have John's former lover in her face on top of that. So, the letters had stopped.

Florence had tried to fit in as best as she could. She had even taken her father's last name to make things as unobtrusive as possible. She had known she was not a natural charmer, so she had put herself to work like an invisible house elf. And she had discovered the radio – all the beautiful arias that half-goddesses belted out while telling about their anguish, their love, their longings. Ah, to be one of those people one day! To slip from the dreariness that seemed to follow her wherever she went, even though it was not of her making. To step into this fairy-tale of a stage career and forget who she was, but become the focus of attention if just for a few hours.

A music teacher of hers had discovered her gift, and as her parents had been doing alright but hadn't been able to finance all the extra-lessons somebody with an ambition for the stage needed, that same teacher had started a fundraiser for her protégée. Florence had felt embarrassed and delighted at the same time. She had felt indebted, almost legally bound to make it big time from there.

The rise in the musical world hadn't been pleasurable all the time. There had been groping opera producers and male opera singers who already had built a successful career. She had gritted her teeth because it was obviously taken for granted that any female star had been through a stage like that. Ogled, pawed, seduced. It had been bearable with a few. Then, one night after she had managed to escape another see-through offer of a drink in a seedy bar behind a midsized town's opera house, she had lain awake in her hotel room and decided that this kind of life had to stop. She had known she was good at what she did. She was young to boot. She had wanted to have a career, but she wouldn't pawn her body for that anymore.

Life had dealt her one of these rare serendipities the very next morning when she had opened the newspaper that had been slipped underneath her door. Last night's performance had made it to the top of the cultural pages, and there had been a photo of her singing the title role of a Verdi opera. That had been the article that had gained her the artist name "La Strega" – and from now on half of her musical audience had been believing that was her real name. Announcements for concerts bore her new epithet, and her name had started to draw public attention more than the more seasoned male co-singers. Her fame had started building her a safe distance against all too bold colleagues and bosses. She had been able to choose now. But she hadn't chosen anybody.

Her mother' misfortune had made her suspicious of legal bonds for any relationships, and to be honest, there had hardly been any time for her to make friends beyond the backstage. So, she had stayed alone. Of late, she had begun wondering whether she had missed the boat somewhere in her life. Was a musical career really all she wanted? Would she have to live and die alone in the end?

She had decided to step back into her childhood when her concert tour brought her near Wycliff. And now, as she stepped off the shuttle at the ferry terminal, she was wondering whether it had been such a good idea after all. The town hadn't changed so much in architecture and lay-out as in businesses. It was beautifully decorated for Christmas, and the shop windows were beckoning with their warm lights and sophisticated displays. This was not the childhood Florence remembered.

It had started snowing a while ago, and now, Florence was sitting in front of a bowl of razor clam chowder at *Le Quartier*, a stylish bistro restaurant with very young staff, apparently. Soft Christmassy background music added elegance to the room, and the fragrance of French cuisine wafted on the air, making her suddenly feel ravenous. Why not try one of these wonderful looking salmon quiches she had spied in a glass display next to the bar?

The young waitress saw her frown over the crackers and approached her quickly. She had introduced herself as Hannah earlier, and her face expressed real worry something might be wrong for her guest. "Is everything okay?" she asked.

"Absolutely," Florence answered with a quick smile. "Except that I feel like eating more than I should." She held up her hands as if in defense. "No, don't say anything. I don't need false flattery; I keep getting my share of that." Hannah blinked. "Just have me reheated some of this delicious looking salmon quiche. There's a dear."

Hannah smiled and turned around to comply with her customer's wish.

"Uh, one more thing – how long will the busses to the train station run tonight?"

Hannah turned around again. "Oh, didn't you hear? There was a landslide on the train tracks north of town. There won't be any trains tonight. Neither direction."

Florence's face fell. "No trains?"

"No, Ma'am. As a matter of fact, I have my doubts any busses will run for much longer either. Just have a look outside the window. It's a complete white-out."

"But you will have snow ploughs coming through, right?"

Hannah shook her head slowly. "This town doesn't have any, and it will take a while till any will come through. Besides, ploughing makes no sense with the amount that is coming down. We'll simply have to wait it out."

Florence started looking really worried now. "But … I have to be in Seattle tomorrow."

Hannah shook her head. "I have not much experience with snow in the lowlands, but I hear that once you have a snowfall like this, you better get ready to dig yourself in. Do you have a hotel room in town?"

Florence shook her head. "Everything was booked last night. I didn't intend to stay longer."

"Well, you better be prepared to do so and check for a room. This snowstorm might be bigger than what was expected in the forecast even."

Florence sighed. The chowder was suddenly less flavorful, and her appetite for the quiche was gone.

Hannah saw all light from the lady's face vanish. "You still want the salmon quiche?" she carefully asked.

Florence shook her head. "If it's getting as bad as you say, I better start my search for accommodation tonight …"

Hannah nodded and smiled, pity in her eyes. "I'm so sorry."

Florence shook her head impatiently. "None of your doing, no need to be sorry."

Hannah smiled weakly. "Would you like your check then?"

Florence just blinked her okay.

Ten minutes later, she was struggling through the snow towards *The Ship Hotel*. If she was lucky, nobody else would have heard of the landslide, yet, and have landed a room before her. But when she entered the hotel lobby, she saw a couple at the reception desk who had just been turned away. They passed her with looks of worry on their faces.

"Let's at least call the kids and tell them we are not going to make it tonight," the woman said.

"But they will have heard it on the news by now," her husband replied.

"Don't be such a bear!" she scolded. "They want to hear it from us, too."

"As if that changed anything", was the last that Florence heard of the exchange.

She stepped towards the reception desk. The man behind looked up at her with a worried face. "Don't ask me for a room, please," he said in mock misery.

"I won't," Florence said. "But do me the favor – are there any other places in town that might still have a room?"

The man frowned, then nodded. "The motel near the Harbor Mall is fully booked. That much I know. But there might be some ... why don't you check with the Tourist Information at the ferry terminal?"

Florence nodded resignedly. "Back into the snow again."

The man behind the desk shrugged his shoulders. His eyes said, "what can I do?!" And Florence retreated.

Half an hour later, she was still on Main Street, realizing that it was not a good idea to get herself all wet through during such a snow storm, and that it wouldn't help her get a room either. The Tourist Information had called six different Bed & Breakfast establishments, all of which were fully booked till after the holidays. After that they had left her in the lurch, just suggesting that she might want to wait out the storm at the ferry terminal. Florence dreaded the atmosphere of such a shelter, and rather decided to walk towards Downtown again.

She walked past the cozy bistro, and a gust of snow and wind almost blew her into the German store next door. *Dottie's Deli* was crowded with customers this morning, in spite of the snow outside. There was a long line in front of the deli counter, and it twisted like a snake through the aisles towards the door. She gasped with astonishment.

"Is it always like this in here?" Florence asked nobody in particular.

"Especially before Christmas," a cheerful voice answered next to her. She turned around and found herself looking at a very petite lady in a red sweater covered with white polka dots. She was busily packing rolls into a paper bag. "I'm Dottie. Do you need anything specific with which I can help you?"

"A room," Florence blurted. Then she laughed. "I know, wrong business."

Dottie shook her head and smiled. "Lucky you! I might actually be able to hitch you up with someone who has got one."

"No!" Florence gaped and felt a wave of anticipation and doubt run through her. It almost hit her physically.

"Let me make a call," Dottie said, waved to a staffer to take over her place at the cash register-cum-bakery-counter, and walked into a back office. A moment later she returned and pressed a notepaper into Florence's hand. *"The Gull's Nest* in Uptown. I have scribbled down directions – I hope you can read my writing." Then she returned to the crowd lining up in front of the cash register, not expecting as much as a thank you.

Florence was stunned. Suddenly, she felt ravenous again. But the line was insanely long, and she wanted to make sure that her room for the night wouldn't fall through after all. She looked at the paper and committed the directions to her memory. Then she walked back into the snow storm.

Two hours later, Florence was sitting cozily wrapped up in her upstairs room overlooking the front yard of *The Gull's Nest*, sipping a cup of tea while gazing into the merrily dancing flames of a gas fireplace. Her landlady, Abby, had welcomed her warmly though somewhat curtly. She had explained she hadn't planned to open her Bed & Breakfast over the holidays and needed to get some groceries yet. But she had given her the keys, shown her the room, number 23, and pointed out the coffee and tea making tray on a corner table next to a big arm chair. The twin beds in the room were both full-sized, so she knew she would be fine for the night. It all could have been so much worse.

The only thing that she had to do, yet, was to call Manfredo and tell him about her misadventure. She knew he'd be upset, perfectionist that he was. She sighed. She might as well get

31

it done and over with. She went through her handbag and found her cell phone. She clicked the fast dial button and listened for the buzz tone on the other side. The receiver was picked up after the very first ring. So Manfredo. He must be having his phone ready for a call at all times of day and night.

"Flo, where are you at?!" he asked without any greeting.

"I'm still in Wycliff, Manfredo," she answered calmly. Over all these years they had been working together she still called him by his full artist's name, never finding him cute enough to abbreviate it or to give him a nickname.

"Wycliff?!" he was yelling now. "I thought you were going to stay in Tacoma."

"I did, but I decided to explore this quaint little town this morning."

"It's long past morning!" he said, and she heard irritation and despair creep into his voice.

"Don't I know that," she answered. "And, listen, Manfredo ..."

"When will you be here?" he interrupted.

"Listen," she repeated. "I won't make it to Seattle tonight."

"But you said you'd be there. We were to dry-run the radio interview. And there is the TV gala on Christmas Eve in the morning."

"Well, yes." Florence sighed. "There was a landslide between here and Seattle. So, there won't be any trains running today. Probably longer. And with all this snow, buses aren't running any longer either."

"Can you take a plane?" Manfredo asked irrationally.

Florence laughed, then said: "I doubt even a helicopter would find a landing patch in this blizzard. We will simply have to go without the dry-run."

"So, you promise you will be at the radio station in time for the interview tomorrow?"

"I will try, but I can't promise."

"Why did you have to go to Wycliff *before* all these important appointments? Couldn't it have waited until everything was accomplished?"

"Should have, would have, could have ... Manfredo, it is what it is."

"I don't have to tell you that publicity like radio and TV shows are getting more important the older you get, right?"

"You don't have to rub in my age, Manfredo," Florence said dryly. "I know that any kind of PR is helpful, but this situation can't be helped."

"What if you can't make it to the TV gala? They will have us pay a hefty contractual penalty."

"First of all, it's *I* who'd have to pay up, Manfredo. Second, what if I were sick instead of being deterred by a landslide that interferes with our plans?"

Manfredo sighed. "One day you will be the death of me, Flo."

Florence shook her head though he couldn't see her. "Hardly, Manfredo. You are 15 years younger than I am. You have plenty of time left long after I'll have left my stage life behind."

Chapter 3

December 22, 03:00 p.m.

Starlene, Darlene, and Charlene Williams were used to people staring at them open-mouthed and starting to whisper. They had grown up with it. Born on the very same day with only a few minutes between each other, their similar looks were striking sometimes even to themselves. Only their parents had been able to discern them by minimal differences such as a tiny mole behind Darlene's ear and a double dimple at Charlene's mouth. They had been assigned different colors by their mother at birth. Starlene was always wearing red, Darlene green, and Charlene blue. Not that it helped people later in their life – because the brunette, blue-eyed triplets sometimes pulled pranks on them switching wardrobe colors.

Now, they were not as mischievous anymore as they had been as teenagers. They were in their early fifties after all. But they still loved to have their good fun, and they still wore the colors their mother had once chosen for them. Starlene preferred a warm burgundy or a dramatic fiery red over pinks and magenta these days. Darlene sometimes chose pastel greens, sometimes a dark luscious Russian green. And Charlene went with any shade of blue. Even their winter coats today were kept in those hues. And it was good they had chosen to wear winter coats at all.

Yesterday, when they had gathered at Charlene's home in Steilacoom, where they intended to spend Christmas because it was Charlene's turn to play the host, it had been just raining heavily. But this morning had taken on a definite chill, and by the time they had enjoyed a big breakfast, taken Starlene's car – because it was the biggest –, and driven to Wycliff, it had started snowing. Staring through the windows, they had already discussed returning to Steilacoom, as the snow had started lying on the ground. The roads had been turning treacherous.

"I'm not going to turn around," Starlene insisted. "I have been looking forward to our Victorian Christmas shopping all year long. Besides we are half-way there anyhow. So, we might just as well keep going."

In the end, Starlene had had some serious difficulties, steering the car around some steeper bends, and when they had reached the outskirts of Wycliff, her knees had felt a bit weak. "Surely, it will stop snowing later and melt away," she had murmured to herself.

They had left the car in the Park & Ride at the Harbor Mall, which was nowhere near Wycliff Harbor and even north of the wharves and housing projects. They had taken the free shuttle bus into Downtown.

Now, four hours later, the heavy snowfall was nowhere near letting up, and the three sisters were looking at each other as they were feasting on some stunning looking slices of buttercream cake at the *Lavender Café*. Next to their chairs and under their

36

table was an abundance of shopping bags. They had entered store after store, delighted by their imaginative Christmas displays. Lunch had been an array of small dishes at *Le Quartier*, Wycliff's renowned French bistro. Last year it had gone steeply downhill and only barely recovered around Christmas, as they had been direly short-staffed after Chef Paul had been shot in the back and had had to leave the kitchen. But these days, his former prodigy, Chef Finn, was doing the finest of jobs, and they had truly enjoyed what they had been served. *La Boutique* had been their first massive shopping stop-over. After that they had hit *Main Gallery*, and Charlene had bought a mid-sized abstract seascape that she would pick up on their way back to the shuttle stop. A beautiful lacy breath of nothing had lured Darlene into *Naughtical Lingerie*, where, in the end, all three of them had indulged themselves.

"Though I don't even know for whom I'm going to wear this," Starlene had muttered.

"Oh, but you will know that you are wearing something sexy underneath," shop owner Lee Anne Minh had smiled. "And that sometimes makes all the difference."

The next stop had been *The Treasure Chest*. And on and on they had walked through the ever-thickening layer of snow gathering on the sidewalks. When daylight had started turning murkier, they had entered the cozy little café on Back Row with their loot and dropped into the last window table. Coffee and cake in Wycliff were also part of their annual Christmas tradition.

They must have started this about ten years ago. Their father had passed away, and their mother had followed him shortly after. The triplets had always been close, but this made them close ranks even tighter. Charlene had lost her husband due to cancer only a year before. Starlene, who had never married, and Darlene, who had been through a divorce five years before, had thought of a way to support Charlene in this extreme period of grief. As their parents' home had stopped being the venue of any family fests and had been sold, they had decided to descend on their sibling shortly before Christmas and help Charlene spend this especially emotional time of the year. It had been a great success for all of them. So much so that they had made it an annual event and rotated in hosting it.

"This is the first time in years that we will actually have a white Christmas," Starlene observed and pronged another bite of amaretto buttercream cake with her fork.

"I'd like it much better if we were able to observe it from the safety of home," Charlene said.

"Ah, come on!" Darlene smiled. "I wouldn't want to miss all the fun around here. Isn't Wycliff simply stunning around Christmas? All the decoration in the shop windows. And the lights. The special events they have going on in the shops. I can't believe that we even get snow on top of it all. I feel like in a Christmas story by Charles Dickens."

"Umh, I should hope not," Starlene argued, who was teaching literature and creative writing at a college in Tacoma.

"Dickens uses rather drab characters and surroundings in order to create more empathy in the reader. It's all these Victorian pictures that you see on praliné boxes and old advent calendars that make you think it were Dickensian."

"You cannot create empathy," Charlene countered. She had read some books on psychology lately. "It's inherent. Either you *are* empathetic or not."

Darlene looked from sister to sister. "May I just find it simply beautiful? Dickens and empathy or not? Thank you."

They laughed and proceeded eating their cake. Outside the wrought-iron street lanterns turned on and created puddles of yellow brightness in the street. The bluff behind was hardly visible in the white flurry.

"I am a bit worried about the drive back home," Starlene suddenly admitted. "I had a hard time for the last five miles while driving here. I don't know whether it would be wise to try in this onslaught of bad weather."

"So, what do you suggest? Walk?" Darlene laughed.

"Maybe the train."

A middle-aged waitress with tattoos showing under the cuffs of her sleeves was passing by their table with some empty, dirty dishes. She stopped in her tracks as she overheard the remark and shook her head. "Sorry, no trains for a few days to come," she said.

"What?!" Darlene said. Why?"

"Haven't you heard?" the waitress wondered. "There was a large landslide up north. It almost hit a freight train on its way south. The train tracks and the road to I-5 are both buried under tons of earth."

"Oh no!" Charlene said. "No trains at all?"

"None." The waitress walked off.

The sisters looked at each other. The buttercream cake on their plates had disappeared, and suddenly sitting here seemed to be the wrong thing to do in the wrong place at the wrong time.

"I have started defrosting the turkey," Charlene said darkly.

"If it's the same size as the bird you made three years ago, it will still be frozen next week," Starlene winked.

"Not funny," Charlene said. "I ate left-overs for weeks after."

"You could have shared them with us," Starlene said.

"She couldn't," Darlene said. "Remember you were on a diet at the time and the only day you didn't stick to it was Christmas Day? And I had to leave for home early because I came down with the flu and didn't have any appetite whatsoever."

"True," Starlene said.

They sat in silence for a few minutes, and the waitress came to their table to remove the dishes and present them with the check.

"My turn," Charlene said and picked it up.

"So, what do we do now?" Darlene asked, slipping into her lime green winter coat.

"Go to *Dottie's Deli* for some German Christmas treats as always," Charlene said cheerfully, putting on her dark blue gloves.

Starlene shook her head, while pulling up the collar of her maroon redingote. She always looked the most stylish of the three. "I don't think this was about which *store* next," she said dryly. "We are stuck. Since no trains are running and us driving through this snow is out of the question, we better look for a place to stay for the night. Maybe tomorrow it will be better and we can drive back."

When they opened the door, they were struck by the icy late afternoon air outside.

"Half a foot of snow already!" Darlene exclaimed. "That's so beautiful!"

Starlene checked her sister's face whether she was serious. Indeed, Darlene looked enchanted. Starlene sighed. "Well, let's go to *The Ship Hotel* right now," she said. "I hope they still have a room left."

They started walking through the snow. Traffic had come to a halt almost entirely. The only cars that were around were headed to other Downtown destinations. Nobody tried to venture up the slippery sloping thoroughfare that connected Uptown with the southernmost part of Downtown. Shoppers tried to get inside businesses as fast as they could and became fewer and fewer. The sisters' breath rose in white vapor, while the snow kept falling incessantly.

Finally, they reached the big doors of *The Ship Hotel*, stomped the snow off their boots in the entrance area, and went in. It didn't look good. There was a line at the reception desk, and while some guests triumphantly returned, room keys in hand, to ascend the wide carpet-covered stairs, it quickly became clear that the few keys that were still available would be long gone by the time it was the sisters' turn to ask for a room or two.

"Dang," Charlene said. "That doesn't look good."

"No," Starlene said and put her gloved hands into her pockets. Charlene and Darlene knew that this was a defiant stance she always took when she was at a loss.

Darlene suddenly smiled. "We could still go to *Dottie's Deli* now."

"But that's a *deli*, not a hoteli," Charlene joked lamely.

"Right," Darlene said. "But Dottie always has some good advice. She might know of a place that is suitable."

Starlene raised her hands out of her pockets. "Then what are we waiting for?"

Back outside, they found that their foot prints in the snow were almost covered up again. They looked up Main Street, then trudged back the same way they had come, and then a little.

"Why is it that snow is so much more fun when you look at it from inside a home?" Darlene asked nobody specifically. She didn't receive an answer.

42

"Just as well that I forgot to switch on my slow cooker this morning," Charlene suddenly burst out. "Imagine what the food inside would be like when we come back tomorrow if I had."

"You might want to toss it anyhow," Starlene said.

"Why?"

"Well, it's been out there unheated and probably drawn all kinds of contaminating germs."

Charlene sighed. "What a waste."

"What were you making anyway?" Darlene asked.

"Hungarian goulash soup. Remember when Dottie gave me her recipe?" Darlene nodded.

After what felt like an eternity, they reached the entrance to *Dottie's Deli*. One of the windows was decorated in a fairy tale theme and held all the sweet delights with which a German deli could lure young and old, the other one was dedicated to savory delicacies that would elevate any holiday dinner. The store was crowded, especially at the deli counter where people bought German cold cuts and sliced cheese by the pound. All the staff were busy, but they still had a cheerful word for everybody.

"I have to have one Christstollen," said Charlene. "Even though my favorite kind always is out by the time we make it here."

"You could have called me to save you one!" Tiny Dottie with her five foot two had overheard her sigh and approached the sisters. "It's really no big deal. I could even mail it to you."

"Really?!"

"Anything that is packaged and cannot go bad in the mail," Dottie confirmed and smiled as Charlene packed the two last Stollen into her basket. Darlene returned from a display of Ritter Sport Christmas chocolates with an entire collection of this season's special flavors. She was beaming. Dottie wanted to return to what she had been doing – replacing stock on the empty shelves. But Starlene, ever practical, put one hand lightly on her arm to stop her.

"Listen, we have a problem today. We know that trains have stopped running due to a landslide up north, and there is no way we will drive back home in our car."

"Oh my!" Dottie said. "You mean you have come here for the day only?"

"Right," Starlene said and smirked at their fate. Snow had been in the weather forecast after all, but who took such forecasts all too serious in the lowlands?! "We are stranded. We haven't got a place to stay."

"*The Ship Hotel* is all booked, it seems."

"Indeed, it is no option. We saw the line."

Dottie gave them a wide smile. "I think you might be a heaven-sent to a friend of mine who got herself in a pickle." Starlene looked at her nonplussed. "She's kind of stranded herself. She has a beautiful Bed & Breakfast in Uptown. Because she had intended to leave town over the holidays, she has taken no reservations whatsoever. Nor would she have been able to spread

44

the word she's open at such short notice. Which means that she probably has room enough for all of you."

"Uptown?"

Dottie shrugged. "I know – not much fun climbing the stairs in this weather. Therefore, let me make sure that you don't do it in vain. I'll give her a call." She quickly walked over to her office, and Starlene watched her dial a number on her business landline. A couple of minutes later Dottie returned with a big smile on her face. "She's expecting you. She asked whether it was okay to pack the three of you into a family room with a queen and two full beds. It has a bathroom ensuite." Dottie looked almost pleadingly. "I said it would be okay because with this weather there might be more people looking for a room tonight. So, if the three of you were willing to share …"

Starlene sighed with relief. "Sharing is no problem at all, Dottie. Thank you ever so much. Darlene was right."

"Right about what?"

"That you would know what to do." Starlene gave her a hug. "That means that I can do my German food crave shopping now. Without a hurry." She winked and joined her sisters in their fun.

Half an hour later they were carefully climbing up the stairs at the bluff. Somebody had started clearing them a while ago and salted them, but the snow had started to cover the barely melted spots again. And now the steps had become even more treacherous with black ice developing underneath the snow.

45

When they finally reached the little plaza at the top, next to the lighthouse, they were breathing hard. "Turn around," Darlene finally managed. "Look at this!"

"This" was the illuminated snowy downtown area, the yacht harbor in which some boats were lightly swaying on the leaden water, their topmasts festively decorated with Christmas lights. The snow was steadily falling and dimming the sounds from below.

"Beautiful," said even Starlene, who was the most stoic when it came to expressing emotions.

"How far did Dottie say it is from here?" Charlene asked.

"Just a few yards. Next to this pretty little house."

"*The Sound Messenger*," Darlene read out aloud. "So that is where it is at home. I had somehow always pictured it in one of the business blocks in Downtown." They passed the quaint building with its wintery garden. "There's the sign!" Darlene exclaimed. Her shopping bags had become heavy after all, and she was glad they were at the end of today's journey.

The Gull's Nest was tastefully illuminated with white Christmas lights. There were candles in the windows and a big beribboned wreath at the front door. The garden path had been cleared from snow very recently, and walking the final yards towards the Bed & Breakfast suddenly became much easier. An automatic light came on, and the front door opened.

"Welcome to *The Gull's Nest*," the young landlady called out to the colorful trio coming up the stairs, carrying dozens of

46

paper bags and cloth totes. "You must be Starlene, Charlene, and Darlene." They nodded. "Dottie announced you already. I'm glad to be able to help you out. Come inside and warm yourselves. You will have room number 22 on the second floor. I hope you will enjoy your stay."

The lounge behind her was glowing invitingly in the reddish gleam of a fire place. An old gentleman sat in a rocking chair by its side.

"Why, it's Santa himself," Darlene exclaimed.

A good-natured chuckle was the answer. "And Merry Christmas to you, too," he said.

Darlene blushed as she crossed the threshold. Maybe she was just about to step into a story by Charles Dickens after all.

Chapter 4

December 22, 03:00 p.m.

Aaron White was watching his nine-year-old baking away. Her tongue was clinched in one corner of her mouth, her cheeks were glowing, and her pig tails were coming askew. She was placing her cookie cutter at as many different angles as possible to make the most of what dough she had rolled out in front of her. At one point she had looked at him with gleaming eyes; then she had re-immersed in her work.

Heather reminded Aaron so much of his late wife, Olivia. It hurt. He saw Olivia in so many tiny movements of Heather's. How she wiped her brow. How she walked. How she frowned. Her eyes were her mothers, and so – thank goodness! – were her mouth and nose. She had inherited his dark hair color, though, as well as his lankiness.

It had been only ten months since Olivia had decided to leave them. He had known she had been feeling depressed every once in a while. Then he had taken her for long hikes and deposited Heather with his parents, who were living near their home in Eatonville. Olivia had usually liked their hikes and perked up again. They had done the entire Wonderland Trail at one time, and friends of hers had cached food at all their camping destinations. It had been rough and tough – not necessarily something he was into. But they had been together. And he had never thought it would be that serious. How had she managed to cover it up? He knew that she had been taking pills every once in a while. But more often than not she hadn't. She had said they made her dizzy and bloated.

That day when he had driven Heather to one of her soccer tournaments taking place in Graham, she had said she'd meet some friends for a scrapbooking retreat. Only she never did. Instead, when he and Heather had returned – Heather all happy adrenaline after a goal she had scored just before the referee whistled the game over –, they had found Olivia lifeless in the living room. She had been lying on her stomach half on, half off the sofa, her long reddish-brown hair fallen over her face. Aaron had managed to move himself into Heathers field of view quickly, but not fast enough to keep his daughter oblivious of the fact that something awful had happened. An empty jar of pills was lying on the floor right next to a glass that probably had contained water.

Aaron had felt bile rise in his throat. With a pressed voice he had told Heather to go to her room and stay there. For once she had not tried to argue and gone upstairs quietly, her eyes huge with worry. Aaron had called an ambulance at once. But when he had knelt by his wife's side and felt for her pulse, he had already known what the medics would confirm half an hour later. Olivia was gone. And Aaron's world had crashed.

He had moved through the first days after Olivia's suicide like a robot. He had tried to keep Heather's world normal, but there had been no way. As soon as they sat across from each other at breakfast or lunch or dinner, the unspoken question had hung between them: Why?

Hadn't they been loving and caring enough? Had they missed any signals of distress? Should they have insisted that Olivia come to the soccer game along with them? Should they have checked with her friends beforehand whether there really was a scrapbooking bee that afternoon? Should Aaron have controlled her intake of pills in a regular manner? If he had, would she still have been able to collect a number of pills that facilitated her suicide?

In school and at his desk in a construction company, people had obviously had a tough time to express their sympathy. A suicide – what was wrong with that family? At least Aaron thought that was what they were thinking.

Heather's little friends had been a bit more open about it.

"She really did it herself? Wow, that takes a lot of grit!"

"Will she still go to heaven?"

"Did you give her a hug before you left her?"

Heather and Aaron hadn't been able to talk about Olivia's suicide. Both had felt raw about it. Both had been feeling at fault. But life had gone on relentlessly. And after the funeral, Aaron had insisted that Heather go back to school and pick up her soccer club again and perform as "before".

It had been easy enough for him to insist that Heather continue to live normally. As to himself, he had felt he was drowning in a sea of guilt and questions. If it hadn't been for his daughter – who knows, he might have simply done away with his life as well. But instead he had gone through the motions. He had come to a high school theater recital in which Heather had been performing. He had driven her to her soccer games. He had learned how to cook her favorite dishes with more or less success; mostly less. He had had her friends visit for a sleep-over with pop-corn made on the stove top and giggles in Heather's bedroom until after midnight. He had seen Heather heal. And he had envied her.

Heather had been watching her father fall apart. His gait had become listless. When he had thought himself alone, he would stare into space, his face twisted in pain. She had known that she was just a child. But she had wanted to help him in her little ways. So, she had become docile and had suppressed her former temperament that had needed to balk and argue. She had taken up soccer again, though the game would forever stay connected to that dreadful afternoon when they had found her mom dead on the living room sofa. She used to almost choke on the food that her father prepared, but she hadn't had the heart to tell him that he had overcooked and burnt the veggies again or that she hadn't felt like eating at all in the first place. She had even gone along with his idea of inviting her friends for a sleep-over; her friends had been having a glorious time, while she had been lying in the dark on her mattress, tears silently running down her cheeks.

That school year's certificate hadn't shown the greatest marks, but for once nobody had asked Heather how this could have happened. Everybody knew. Everybody had been tiptoeing around her and tried to nudge her into a more positive direction. But how could anybody feel positive when their mother had decided to take her own life?! There had been no scolding, no wondering, no strange looks why a straight A and B student had suddenly become one with more Cs than anything?

Summer vacations had been tough. Usually, they had gone camping and kayaking, all three of them. Now, each and every time Heather and Aaron had looked through their camping gear and gazed at the kayaks hanging from the garage rafters, they had pushed any activity including these off to another time. Instead, Heather had hung out a lot with her grandparents, her father's parents, and been involved in how to harvest a garden and to can or make other use of the picking. She had grown up a lot during those weeks, and her father had tried to treat her like a little woman. But she still was a child after all, and they both had felt bewildered as to what role she should take after the summer vacations, when she turned nine and entered fourth grade.

Time had gently started to blur the edges of their nightmare. As the new school year had begun and fall mornings were dawning later, Aaron had taken more care of preparing a nutritious breakfast for his little girl, and he had been able to choke down some bites himself again. His hollow cheeks had begun to regain a fuller shape once more, and when Heather had returned home one afternoon with an A in a math test, they had celebrated with some great Chinese food at *Chopstix*. For the first time in a long while they had enjoyed their food again, and Heather had managed the smallest smile when her dad told a friend at a neighboring table that his daughter was a rockstar when it came to math.

They had known they would have to deal with setbacks every once in a while, of course. Olivia was missed badly. They had begun to realize how quietly she had stepped in whenever there had been a need – a quick trip to the body shop for car maintenance, picking up clothes from the dry-cleaner, baking cupcakes on teacher appreciation day, cutting the roses in their front yard, cleaning house, packing their lunchboxes. They had started to take over for her, but had realized that they were just handling chores. The soulfulness was missing.

Thanksgiving had almost been a disaster. They had decided to brave it at their Eatonville home and invited Aaron's parents for dinner. Aaron had packed a frozen turkey into the oven, forgetting to remove the plastic bag with the innards from the carcass. And as the beast was still far away from being done after four hours of slow roasting, they had been at a loss. When Heather's grandparents had shown up, there had hardly been anything on the table, and they had simply been relieved that Aaron's mother had wisely foreseen the disaster and brought some ham that could easily be heated and eaten with the canned gravy she had also brought along. The turkey had been rescued from its ordeal, and grandmother White had managed to shave off at least some of the meat that would be edible yet, in spite of the plastic stuffing.

Now, it was almost Christmas. Aaron had decided he needed to do something special for his little girl. When he had heard of the Christmas bakery that Wycliff's well-beloved Chef Paul was setting up at the Wycliff Community Center on December 22, the Wycliff advent calendar with one business after another revealing a specially decorated window and hosting an event or activity until Christmas Eve, and when he remembered that he had done no Christmas shopping at all so far, he had decided that it was time to gather some Christmas joy for his kid and drive out to the Sound with her.

Heather hadn't been as enthusiastic about the trip as Aaron had hoped she would be. But good kid that she was, she had played along. She had even pulled on one of the Santa caps that they had used to wear during Christmas shopping when Olivia had still been around. The trip to Wycliff had been mostly quiet.

"Will we be able to get home again?" Heather had asked at one point.

"Why? Because of this bit of snow?" Aaron had asked in return and suddenly felt that she might be right with her worry.

"Well, let's face it – it's becoming worse. And if it is this bad down here, where we are almost in the lowlands, how will we manage to reach the hills later on our way back home?"

Aaron had pondered this and then answered cheerfully, "You know, we are almost there. Why not simply enjoy Wycliff and go from there?"

Heather hadn't answered and just raised her brows. For a nine-year-old she was really reacting in a pretty mature way.

The road into Wycliff had become slippery, and when they had reached the Harbor Mall, they had left their car to continue their trip Downtown with a shuttle bus. "It looks like this might be one of the last runs for a while," the bus driver had announced when they had reached the Community Center by the harbor. "In this snow, even a bus cannot maneuver safely. As soon as the roads are clear again, we will resume our service."

Heather and Aaron had slithered across the parking lot to the Community Center's main entrance. And now they were inside along with dozens of other parents and their kids, who were rolling out dough and cutting cookies into different shapes, adding sprinkles and glazes, a crowd of red-cheeked, gleamy-eyed little cherubs in aprons and paper chef-hats. Chef Paul was walking between the tables in his exoskeleton and lent a helping hand, encouraging a little girl here, soothing a little boy there, whose cookie sheet had just fallen face-down to the floor. Aaron closed his eyes for a moment. If he tried very hard, would he be able to make himself believe that all was right with his world?

"Aren't these smells heavenly?" a woman by his side asked him and startled him out of his thoughts. "I wish I were that young again and could participate in this fun."

Aaron didn't know what hindered her to make some dough at her home that very moment and have that very fun she was talking about instead of standing and waiting around. Olivia

55

would certainly have created half a dozen of different kinds of Christmas cookies and some beautiful pies to boot by this date. And their home would have smelled of cinnamon, vanilla, and apples up to the rafters. But ever since she had passed, their home had been just a normal house, and all of its usual spirit seemed to have drained away. He gave the woman a pained smile and walked over to Heather.

"Having fun?" he asked softly. She nodded vigorously. Maybe a little too vigorously, but at least she gave the annual Christmas cheer a try.

An hour later, Heather had wrapped her beautifully glazed cookies into a paper bag and presented her dad with it. "What are we going to do now?" she asked.

"How about some Christmas shopping at the toy store?"

"Oh Dad, really? I'm too old for toys."

"Really?" Aaron looked at her and suddenly realized that she might be right. His daughter had been catapulted forward in maturity by her mother's suicide. And toys were certainly the last thing she would feel comfortable around anymore. "Then what would *you* like to do?"

"Could we go to *The Owl & The Book*, please?" she begged.

"The bookstore?" He was positively surprised by her request. "Sure. Maybe I'll find something for myself, too."

Outside, the snowfall had picked up in intensity, and their feet sank into the snow ankle-deep. The buses had indeed stopped running, and the few cars that were still around crept along Main Street at snail-pace. The lanterns had come on early, as daylight had turned murky.

"I don't think that we will make it back home today," Heather said suddenly.

Aaron scratched his head under the woolen hat he was wearing. "I'm not all too sure about it either. How about we go to the bookstore and take it from there?" She looked at him doubtfully, but then she thrust one mittened hand into his and tugged him on.

The Owl & The Book was crowded with Christmas shoppers. The shop kitty had retreated to a shelf way in the back and was watching them all distrustingly. The section with youth books held a number of grown-ups looking for appropriate literature for their children or their grandchildren. Heather went to the adult section instead.

"Are you sure you want to look over there?" Aaron asked her.

"I am," she said. And then she went to the science section of the store. Aaron watched her perplexed. Then he turned towards the shelves with biographies. There were some pretty interesting new ones out in the market that had been discussed on the radio lately. Why not try one of those? He started pulling books from the shelf and reading their back covers, then opened one or the other and read the first couple of pages. He lost himself between the covers and was startled when Heather appeared by his side after a while, holding a thick paperback in her hands.

"This one?" he asked and read the title. He frowned. It was a book on the basics of psychology. "Aren't you ..." He left the sentence hanging in mid-air, as he recognized his daughter's determination.

"I'm not too young," she confirmed his premonition. "I want this book. And if I have any questions, I will ask you. It's that easy."

"Only, I'm not a psychologist," he answered seriously.

"But you are a grown-up," she insisted.

Aaron sighed. With all her prematurity, Heather still was a child. He'd have to see them through this difficult period of searching for scientific answers as well.

When they stood in line for cashing out, they overheard one of the sales associates talking to a customer in front of them. "No more trains until the snow stops; and the road to I-5 is covered by the landslide as well. Unless you want to brave the hills south of town and drive to the interstate that way, you better try and find a place for the night here in Wycliff."

All of a sudden, Aaron didn't feel as confident anymore. When it was their turn, he asked the associate whether it was really going to be as bad as he had just said. "I thought that here in the lowlands you never had snow. Or if there is snow, it will melt within an hour."

The young man shrugged as he was bagging Heather's psychology book and Aaron's biography. "Once it is as bad as this, it is serious. Honestly, man. This your little girl?" He nodded towards Heather.

"She is," Aaron said.

"Well, if I were you, I'd see to getting yourselves a place for the night right now. There will be more people stranded than we have hotels and motels in town."

"*The Ship Hotel* just put out a sign that they are out of rooms," a woman behind them said.

"Great," Aaron muttered.

"Try *The Gull's Nest* up on the bluff," she suggested. "Abby Winterbottom might still have rooms. She wanted to leave town for Seattle today. But I guess in this weather she is as stranded at *her* house as you are stranded away from yours."

"Thanks for the tip," Aaron said. "Is it far?"

"Up the stairs by the lighthouse and then a block."

Aaron looked at Heather. "Seems like we are having an adventure, hm?"

Heather looked at the sales associate. "Would it be possible to borrow your phonebook, please?"

The man smiled and dug around under his counter. "There you go, young lady." He handed her the Wycliff Chamber of Commerce's telephone book. "Your dad sure can be proud to have such a partner in crime in you."

Heather started going through the booklet, then handed it to Aaron. "I guess it's better you make the call," she said very seriously. "She might not want to have me."

Aaron stroked over her hair lovingly. "Anybody would want to have you, sweetie," he said, but took out his cell phone and started to dial the number she pointed out to him.

Half an hour later they arrived at the Bed & Breakfast, puffing with the effort of having climbed the stairs in the snow. *The Gull's Nest*'s front yard was a winter wonderland already, with bushes and trees turned into huge white puffs and the lawn covered up in thick white fluff. The warm light from the windows shone invitingly into the snowy dusk.

"It looks like a beautiful home," Heather whispered.

Aaron swallowed hard. She hadn't said that once about their house back in Eatonville since Olivia had gone.

Chapter 5

December 22, 05:00 p.m.

When Roger and Kathy Johansen had piled their boxes with yarns and needles into their car parked in front of their Lakewood store, *The Sock Peddlers*, this morning, the first soft flakes of snow had started descending from the wintry sky. Roger had looked up with a slight frown, snowflakes hitting his glasses, but closed the trunk with a decisive "Thump". They had committed themselves to a two-hour sock knitting event at *Ultimate Crafts* in Wycliff later in the afternoon. And they would pull it through, as this was owner Marylou Webster's day of special activities and revealing a Christmas window at her store.

"I like snow," Kathy had pondered as she had gotten into the car. "I only wish it had started *after* the event when we would have been home gain." Her cheeks had been glowing with the cold, her dark shoulder-length hair made a pretty contrast to her otherwise fair skin, and her green eyes exuded excitement. She had been blowing into her hands to get warm again.

"Everything will work out," Roger had said. "It's good that we packed an overnight bag last night just in case anything was going to happen."

They had left Lakewood around ten in the morning. Traffic had started slowing down within half an hour. The snow had started settling on the ground as they had been nearing

Wycliff. Some cars had already been stranded by the roadside as they had passed by, very, very slowly. When they had finally reached the back alley behind Marylou Webster's craft store on Back Row, Kathy had exhaled with relief. "That was not something I'd want to relive any time soon again."

Roger had only smiled. "Neither would I," he had said in his usual quiet way. "But we made it."

They had carefully gotten out of the car. The alley had already been slippery with snow, and they hadn't wanted to risk hurting their ankles and ruining their event. Cautiously they had walked around to their trunk and started unloading. The backdoor of *Ultimate Crafts* had been flung open, and Marylou Webster had appeared in the doorway. She was a midsized woman in her sixties, with merry brown eyes and short hair bleached to a golden-blonde.

"Let me help you guys," she had called out and energetically stepped into the snow in her heeled pumps. She had promptly slipped and been able to catch hold of the wall barely in time before she would have gone down. "Ouch!" When she had straightened up herself again and tried to walk towards Kathy and Roger, she had winced and stopped again. "Bummer! I think I sprained my ankle!"

Kathy had dumped her boxes back into the trunk and glided to Marylou's side as quickly as possible. "Let's get you inside," she had said. "You need boots to walk outside in this weather." She had put an arm around the other woman's waist.

"Put your weight on my shoulder," she had offered. "It will make it easier for you to get inside." As the two of them had somehow made it back into the store, Roger had unloaded box after box and carried them into the warmth of the big, but cozy craft store.

Marylou had plumped down on a chair next to her cash register. Kathy had knelt down and inspected her ankle, which was already swelling. "It's just as well that you have booked us for today," she had said cheerfully, her big green eyes full of sympathy. "Imagine it had happened while you were opening up and nobody would have found you for a while out there in the back. Let me find something to put on your ankle, and then you just sit and relax. We'll see to the rest."

"But I cannot ask you to run my store for me!" Marylou had said desperately.

"Shhh," Kathy had smiled. "Friends are helping out friends whenever they can, right?" Marylou looked at her with doubt. "Right?"

"You are such good people!"

Kathy had risen and talked quickly to Roger, who had nodded and kept on removing ball after ball of yarn from one box.

That had been hours ago. Kathy and Roger had helped customers find items since then, brought in some hot food for Marylou, seen to rewinding her bandages, set up their knitting corner amongst the needle crafting items of the craft store, and spread holiday cheer to whoever came in. And now, they were surrounded by a dozen of women in their fifties and sixties, but also some young girls concentrating on their needles and their most beautifully colored sock yarns.

"I can't get over it that this yarn creates the most regular pattern all by itself, while I'm just knitting one stitch after the other," one younger woman exclaimed.

"Isn't it fun?" Kathy nodded. "They have an entire collection of these yarns. And it doesn't matter where you start. These days socks that don't exactly match are absolutely in fashion."

"They do have the same color scheme though," Roger remarked quietly, himself knitting busily at a heel that one of the knitters had handed him. "See? This is the trick!" He handed it back to her.

"Did you know that knitting is really healthy for our brains?" Kathy asked.

"Because you have to keep counting stitches and rows?" a young girl asked who held the needles very awkwardly, as she had only just learned how to cast on.

"You've got a point there," Kathy said. "But what I was going to refer to was the wonderful impact motor skills have on the brain. Knitting somehow makes the brain process analytic tasks more easily."

"Now that makes sense," an elderly lady said as she was holding up her half-finished sock for inspection. "Miss Marple is always knitting, while solving another case."

"Who is Miss Marple?" a young girl asked and earned good-natured laughter.

"She's just a fictional character," Kathy said. "But it's true. Besides, it probably kept her hands dexterous when she was picking up clues."

"Come to think of it," added the same lady who had brought up Agatha Christie's protagonist. "Have you ever read about anybody planning bloody murder, while they were knitting? I think knitting makes you benign as well."

"I heard it lowers your blood pressure and reduces stress hormones," another woman interjected. "Planning murder must be quite stressful. So, you better don't get hooked on these needles if you plan to remove some adversary for good."

"Talking of removal: I've lost ten pounds ever since I started knitting a while ago," a middle-aged lady said.

"You must have knitted a lot then," another said.

"Not that much," the lady replied. "But I cannot snack while I knit. So, when I'm watching TV, these days I always have some yarn and needles at hand. Saves me calories and keeps my household budget healthier, too."

"I think it has done my daughter immeasurably good as to self-esteem," another knitter said. "You know, she was that shy little mouse who got startled whenever anybody talked to her. I was worried that she might never make any friends. So, one day I showed her how to knit. Next thing you know, she has finished her first little sweater and wears it to school. And everybody finds it so cool. She has found some friends now, and they knit together. And she has lost her shyness almost entirely."

"Look how it's snowing outside now!" Marylou exclaimed suddenly. "As if somebody was dumping a bag of down feathers all at once."

"I still don't get it," one woman said. "This landslide up north – that wasn't caused by the snow, was it?"

"No, that was the hard rain these past days," another knitter answered. "Happens all the time on the coast. But I cannot remember it happened anywhere near Wycliff in decades."

"You will probably have to stay here in Wycliff, right?" Marylou asked Roger and Kathy.

"We haven't really made any plans yet," Roger said calmly. "But we are prepared for anything."

"Oh good," Marylou said. Then she frowned. "Did you make reservations anywhere already?"

Kathy shook her head. "No, we didn't. We will be alright though, I hope." She gazed through the shop windows. Outside it was dark, but the snow was bright enough to see, and the lanterns threw a warm light onto the sidewalks. The flakes were falling densely, thick, and large.

"I heard that *The Ship Hotel* is completely booked," one knitter said.

"It is not the only hotel in town though, right?" Kathy asked.

66

"Pretty much," Marylou answered. "There is one motel when you enter the town limits. And we do have a couple of Bed & Breakfasts. But I know for a fact that the one on my street is totally booked, too."

"Maybe we should look into finding something then," Roger said. "I prefer not to try and drive home in this weather. The snow seems to be almost knee-high already."

And indeed, knee-high it was. The few passers-by outside were having a hard time lifting their feet and making advance. They were ducking their necks into collars flipped upward. Their tracks were soon filling with more of the white stuff from above.

"Would you like me to make some calls?" Marylou asked. "I wish I could take you in, but my children and grandchildren are staying with me over Christmas."

"A call would be great," Kathy said, her eyes filled with hope.

Marylou nodded and grabbed a Chamber of Commerce brochure from a display on her counter. She started leafing through it, stopped at a specific page, and began to dial. Everybody in the knitting group held their breath. You could have heard a needle drop.

"Hello?" Marylou said. "It's Marylou from *Ultimate Crafts*. I was wondering whether you still have a room for two people." She listened into the receiver, her face not betraying anything. When she hung up, everybody's face was filled with curiosity.

"Nope," Marylou said. "Let me try another place." She dialed again. "Hello?" she called. "This is Marylou from *Ultimate Crafts*. I was wondering whether you still have a room for two people. They are teaching a class here this afternoon and …" She listened intently. "Oh, okay. Thank you!"

"Was that a yes?" Kathy asked cautiously.

"No," Marylou sighed. "But I got a tip from her where else to try. Hang in there. You won't have to stay on the floor anywhere tonight. I'm pretty sure of this." She grabbed her phone again and dialed. "Hello? This is Marylou from …"

At that moment the lights flickered and went out.

"Oh!" everybody said. "Oh my!"

Outside, the street lanterns went out as well. Marylou let her phone sink. "No more reception," she said. "Great!"

"Well," Roger said calmly into the darkness that everybody started adjusting to only slowly. "I guess we will have to finish these socks some other time."

The snow outside reflected some diffuse light into the store. Marylou tried to rise from her chair. Kathy got up and helped her. "It will be best you just lock up as it is and see to your store tomorrow when it's light again," she said.

"I have a torchlight somewhere," Marylou muttered.

"Forget that torchlight," Roger said. "I'll bring everybody to the door." He lifted a knitting needle with an inbuilt light. Everybody gasped. "I never thought that these would come in this handy sometime," he joked. By the quirky light of the needles the knitters packed their yarns and unfinished socks, thanking The Sock Peddlers profusely all the while. When the last one of them had left the door, letting in a bit of the cold each time the door opened, Roger and Kathy stared at each other.

"This doesn't look good," Kathy said finally.

"Whom did you try to talk to with your last call?" he asked Marylou.

"*The Gull's Nest*," she said. "The owner was supposed to travel to Seattle today, but somebody said that she is still in town. That was the last resort I had for the two of you." She looked a bit lost in the semi-dark.

"Is it far?" Roger asked.

"Not far, but a little tedious in the snow," Marylou said. "You'll have to go up the bluff to get there."

"But there are stairs, aren't there?" Kathy asked.

"Right. Still, there is no guarantee that the Bed & Breakfast is open."

"We can at least try," Roger said. "I'll get our overnight bag, and then we'll go."

"I'm so sorry that your class has ended this way," Marylou wailed.

"It wasn't your fault," Kathy consoled her. "And I guess nobody will ever forget it. What an event!"

They all laughed; then Roger dipped out into the back alley to get their small baggage. The store started cooling down. With the power outage the electrical heating system had gone down as well. Kathy suddenly shivered. She was glad to slip into her coat and wrap her shawl around her throat.

"I had hoped for a hot shower tonight," she admitted, as she and Roger went outside and left Marylou to close the store behind them. Marylou would be picked up by her kids later, as they had planned on dinner at *Le Quartier*. "Probably not much of a chance for that when nobody has power."

"I wonder what happened," Roger answered. "Their power lines are all underground. This looks like something with the town's transformer station went wrong."

They carefully made their way towards the stairs at the bluff. The post office had some light left, so had the *Soup Cellar* in their basement from where a wonderfully fragrant steam was rising from a vent into the snowy night.

Kathy sighed. "I wish we could go in and have a bowl of soup and a roll right now. But I know we have to find a place for the night first."

Roger nodded. "Let's go. Everything will turn out alright."

"How do you know?"

"It's just a hunch."

They climbed the stairs. The snow was blowing in gusts; the flakes had become smaller, but were needle-sharp now. It stung their faces, and they were glad when they reached the top of the bluff and could see the sign spelling out *The Gull's Nest*.

As they walked towards the quiet big house in its wintry garden, they saw a reddish-yellow light from inside its windows, almost luring them towards the entrance. Kathy pressed the bell button, but there was no sound.

"Of course," Kathy said. "Electric…" She knocked on the door instead.

A little while later they heard firm light steps, and then the door opened. A woman in her early thirties, holding a burning candle, opened the door.

"Hello," she said with a warm smile. "Come in quickly so the warmth stays inside. You must have been sent by Marylou."

"How do you know?" Roger asked, surprised.

"The last number I saw on my phone display was hers, and when I was picking it up, the phone went dead. So, it's just a guess actually."

"Spot on," Kathy beamed. "Now, please, please, please say you have a room for us!"

"In fact, I do," the landlady said. "I'm Abby by the way. And there is one more double that I can give to you. It's here on the first floor, room number 1."

"Oh good!" Kathy sighed with relief and now let her eyes dart around the front room. There was a big fire in the fireplace, and the toasty warmth reached all the way to where they were standing. An old bearded gentleman sat in a rocking chair, and a little girl was sitting by his side, chatting away.

Abby handed a key to Kathy. "Unfortunately, the teakettle in your room won't work, of course. Neither will the hot water in your bathrooms. I hope that this is only temporary, though."

"As long as we have a roof over our heads and some warm place to stay …" Roger smiled and carried their baggage down the hallway. Kathy was unlocking their door and vanished inside their room.

"Oh, as to breakfast," Abby said.

"Yes?" Roger turned around.

"I won't manage anything fancy. Because of the power outage, I won't be able to provide you with any cooked breakfast and no tea or coffee either…" Abby lifted her hands helplessly. "But you would have guessed that already anyhow, right?"

"No problem," Roger answered. "As long as we are warm and dry, what's a power outage?! Let's make the best of the situation." He smiled and followed Kathy into their room.

Abby smiled back into the dim hallway. Nice guests, she thought. But before she got anywhere further in her contemplation, there was another knock at the door, and she needed to see to it. Just imagine if she had already left for Seattle yesterday! Where would all these people stay?!

Chapter 6

December 22, 05:00 p.m.

Pippa Jensen was serene. Her small rambler on Anderson Island was a Christmas fairytale smothered with decorations inside and in the front yard. All her Christmas mail had left just in time for the Christmas delivery cut-off date. And she had received Christmas mail in return from all the people who counted and even some who were a surprise to her. Maybe the latter counted even more. But Pippa didn't want to discuss that with herself – she had strung each and every card onto a long clothesline stretching from one end of her hallway to the other. And now she was giving herself one of her favorite Christmas treats, a shopping spree in Wycliff.

Even as she had gone onboard the ferry at the Anderson Island dock the first snowflakes had sailed from the winter sky. She had smelled the snow in the air yesterday already. She had hoped that it might snow – if just for the sake of making Bing Crosby's song, which was one of her all-time favorites, sound a little less cheesy. The trip on the ferry had felt even better when the snow had begun to fall thicker and she almost slid on the deck before she headed for the canopied passenger bridge at the Wycliff ferry terminal.

It had been so much fun going from store to store, exploring their last-minute gift ideas in special displays, looking at their festive window decorations, and having a decadent hot chocolate with a scoop of vanilla ice cream, topped off with whipped cream at *Fifty Flavors*. Her eyes had gleamed like a child's when she had bought birdseed Christmas ornaments at *Birds & Seeds* for her wild front yard visitors and some colorful macaroons at the *Lavender Café* for herself. Lunch had been at *The Soup Cellar*, which hadn't been there last winter, and the two African-American owners did a great job obviously, for their place was teeming with locals who were enjoying their hot creations. She could have licked out her bowl if it hadn't made her look odd – at home she wouldn't have hesitated for a second. Pippa had bought herself a fashionable brooch at *La Boutique* and stopped by *Main Gallery* to have a look at their current Christmas-themed painting exhibition and to chat with the owners, Harlan Hopkins and Mark Owen. And after having enjoyed a plate of charcuteries at *Le Quartier*, she had started walking through the winter dusk towards the ferry terminal again.

Pippa was glowing with Christmas joy. It had been a trait of hers ever since she had been a little girl. She knew that some people thought her a little over the top because of it, but – hey! – it didn't hurt anybody, right? And during the Christmas season her house was the one that most visitors of Anderson Island searched out to get their share of Christmas anticipation and then some.

Sometimes she felt a bit wistful about not being able to share her dreams and her little joys with a partner. She felt as if she had missed the boat at one point in life, and looking back she kept wondering where she could or should have made a different decision. Should she have given in to the photographer who had been courting her in her early twenties? But then she would have had to deal with his constant road trips and have led a life pretty much as the single she was now anyhow. Or she would have been on the road with him, but would have missed having a home. Or would the fire fighter who had asked her to marry him in her early thirties made her happy? But then she would have worried about losing him whenever he was called on a fire deployment; and by now she would have been a widow anyhow because he had died of cancer ten years ago. Had she missed any signals sent from some other man? She didn't think so. If any of them had been serious, they would have made it clearer, she was sure. And with a little sigh she kept settling back into the spinsterhood she was used to. She was a strong woman after all. She was able to look after herself. So why would she need anybody?!

Fumbling with the door and a dozen bag handles at the same time, she finally entered the warmly lit ferry terminal. The waiting room was crowded. A few children were running around, laughing happily. A decorated Christmas tree in a corner by the front windows turned the otherwise sterile atmosphere of the place into something vibrating with anticipation. More people were coming in. Pippa sank onto a chair that enabled her to look at the tree as well as into the white flurry outside.

"It doesn't look too good for any ferry service tonight, does it?" she said to the person next to her without looking at him.

75

"Highly unlikely," was the short reply.

Pippa's head flew around. Oh no! She had inadvertently seated herself right next to one of Anderson Islands weirdest characters. That came from all her Christmassy thoughts and making her point in having a seat with a view. So much so that she had totally ignored her chair's vicinity. And now she was stuck because it would have seemed rude if she rose and walked away. Unless... She scanned the far corner of the waiting area where the restrooms were. There was a line outside the Women's already. So, that excuse would have been a poor one as well. Though ...

"They will probably have to make an announcement soon," the man next to her said.

Pippa squirmed. Ronald Hoffman was one of those men who usually kept to himself. He looked rough with his shoulder-length hair and a grizzly beard, and he usually walked around with a face that dared you to even utter as much as a greeting. If you did, the answer was monosyllabic and gruff, and you'd think twice about it the next time you ran into him. So, what more of a surprise that he actually spoke another entire sentence without having been prompted by her! She looked at him askance.

What did she know about this man, who must be pretty much her own age? When he had moved to Anderson, he had come alone. There were no visitors to his home that anybody ever noticed. Well, let's face it – his home was so out of the way that only the mailman drove over. Would anybody really have noticed? Somebody started the rumor that he had once been married, but that his wife had died under mysterious circumstances. Was it that which made people on the island so wary about him? The assumption about his late wife (had there really been one?) and the gruff and rough outer appearance? Add to that that Ronald Hoffman was an outsider, one of those people not born on the island. Add to that that nobody ever saw him go to work. How did he make a living?

Suddenly there was a loud yelp from a child, which ended in a roaring howl. A couple of minutes later, two other overtired toddlers picked up the bawling and joined the chorus. Some adults raised their brows and stared at the parents as if it were their fault. Pippa noticed now that the festive flair of the ferry terminal had only been of her perception and that everybody else in fact seemed to be pretty tense. Except herself and maybe Ronald Hoffman, who didn't seem to be upset by the noise or the uncertainty of another ferry departure tonight.

"What if there is no ferry back home tonight?" Pippa asked. She was not sure whether it was more to herself or whether she was actually addressing her island neighbor.

"Something will come up," Ronald replied calmly.

Now Pippa turned her head and looked at him. She was seeing him for the first time really. His hair showed that somebody had tried to cut it and managed to do so only clumsily. His beard, if combed, would not look so very dreadful. And his brown eyes actually wore more of a sad than a grumpy expression. There were tiny wrinkles around them that made her think that at some time he must really be laughing hard. Or maybe had done so. She needed to stop her assumptions. Wasn't she any better than this?!

There came a short screeching noise from the loudspeakers that hung from the ceilings, and everybody was startled from what they had been occupying themselves with.

"Good evening, this is a message from Washington State Ferries to all passengers outbound from Wycliff Harbor. All ferry services tonight have been canceled due to weather impact and will stay discontinued until further notice. We apologize for any inconveniences." The loudspeakers crackled once more, then were switched off.

At first there was a numbed silence. Then people started to stampede for the tiny windows of the ticket offices.

"Poor ticket vendors," Pippa sighed. "As if it were their decision."

"Well, we might as well try and find a room for the night then," Ronald Hoffman said calmly. "I'm Ronald Hoffman by the way."

"I know" Pippa wanted to say. "Because everybody on the island knows you." Instead she said, "I'm Pippa Jensen. Nice to meet you." They shook hands.

At that moment the lights flickered and went out, but flickered on within a few seconds again. "Emergency power," Ronald said. "We better be headed outside now before the crowd gets the hint and beats us to our mission."

Pippa nodded. "But how do you know it's the generators that kicked in and not just simply a short power outage?"

Ronald pointed outside and rose. It was pitch-black. All the streetlights had turned dark. "No more lights out there. I guess that means something major went wrong with the town's electricity."

"Bummer," Pippa said, grabbing her bags and getting up as well. "Will we be able to find our way around in the dark?"

"I guess that most downtown businesses do have generators as well," Ronald said. "At least if they are in the food industry. There will be light enough."

"It never occurred to me," Pippa said as she followed him to the terminal doors. "You must think me pretty naïve."

He chuckled. "I'm rarely judging anybody that quickly."

Pippa blushed as if she had been caught red-handed. Outside their feet sank into the snow, and Pippa bit her lips, as her ankle boots proved too low-cut. Snow seeped into them and wet her feet after only a few steps.

"Try to step into my foot prints," Ronald said gallantly. "You might get your feet wet otherwise."

"Too late," Pippa said. But funny enough she didn't feel too disturbed about this. Actually, she started rather to enjoy this unforeseen adventure. The snowflakes were thick and fell densely. The sounds from town were muffled already. A few people were rushing home from work. Some cars were rolling up Main Street really, really slowly, their red tail lights disappearing into the falling snow like specters.

When they reached *The Ship Hotel*, Ronald stopped at the front entrance. They peered inside through the glass doors. There was a long line in front of the reception desk in the lobby.

"Not an option, it seems," Ronald said.

"No," Pippa said and suddenly felt way less adventurous. "We better return to the terminal then. At least there's light and warmth in there."

Ronald looked at Pippa. Her short black pixie hair was glistening with melted snow flakes, and her gray eyes were looking worried. She was flapping her arms to stay warm. "No option," he decided.

She looked at him almost with relief. The thought of spending the night, sitting in a stiff waiting room chair, surrounded by strangers and cranky children wasn't very enticing. What would he come up with? Why did she throw her fate in with his anyhow? He was only another stranger. Just his being from the same island didn't mean he was trustworthy. Pippa was stomping her feet.

"Where else could we try though?" she asked.

"I know a small Bed & Breakfast in Uptown," Ronald said. "My wife and I stayed there once, and I have ..." He bit his lips, and his eyes became very dark for a few moments. "Never mind. I know it is still there and doing business."

"But will they have room for us?"

80

"We will see when we get there."

"Why don't we call there first?"

"My cell phone has no reception."

"Oh."

"Probably some antenna service down in this storm as well." He turned around and looked over his shoulder. "Ready to go and give it a try?"

Pippa nodded bravely.

"What if they only have one room left?" she asked.

"We will make it work," he said and trudged on.

She had to make big steps as his gait was way longer than hers. "I don't know you at all."

"Neither do I know you," he replied.

"This is not a Hallmark movie, you know?"

"I'm very much aware of it, thank you."

"Are you snoring?"

"Not that I am aware of," he answered. "But then people who do snore are not the ones who are disturbed by it, right?"

"True," Pippa conceded and almost slipped as her right foot hit some black ice underneath. "Would you mind making smaller steps, please?"

"Am I too fast?"

"My legs are too short to step into your prints."

"My apologies."

"Accepted. – What have you been doing in Wycliff today anyhow? I don't see you carry any bags – so you haven't been doing Christmas shopping, right?"

"Right."

"So?"

"Christmas visits," he said.

"Oh, how nice!"

"At the hospice."

Pippa's face fell. She was almost lost for words. "Anybody of your family?" she asked cautiously.

"No," he said. "Playing some Christmas music for the people there."

"Oh." Now she really didn't know what else to say. Might as well shut her mouth before she put her foot in it again. They were reaching the stairs at the bluff now, and she would need her breath anyhow. They climbed up in silence. When they arrived at the little plaza by the lighthouse, they looked back. Downtown Wycliff was blotted out almost entirely by the snow. A few brave lights were piercing the dark and the snow storm where businesses were still open and had a generator running. Otherwise no sounds, no views.

"Magic," Pippa breathed.

"That's a way to put it," Ronald replied dryly.

"Well, how would you put it?"

He shrugged. "Power outage in Wycliff during a snow storm."

Pippa burst out laughing. "Now, I call that romantic!"

"I try to see things for what they are."

"But that is so … sad."

He shook his head. "Not really. That way that which would really seem sad becomes just another fact."

"But the really nice things in life … they won't touch you either, right?"

"It's not that important."

"But how can you bring Christmas joy to others and not feel all the joy and magic of Christmas yourself?"

"I see their need and I bring my capability. That's all there is to it." He stared into the darkness. Then he looked at her. "Let's go. The B & B is just a block from here."

"I don't believe you," Pippa stated and fell into step.

"I told you I know it's still in business."

"No, about just taking down the facts in life and not feeling anything."

He gave her a long look, and she shut up. They walked the rest of their way to *The Gull's Nest* in silence. The tracks in the snow showed that other people had come up with the same idea earlier on. There was candlelight in the windows and a reddish glow that showed that somebody had lit a fire inside.

Ronald's knock on the door was answered almost immediately. Abby looked at them and stepped back. "Come in," she said cheerfully, and Pippa eagerly followed the invitation. "I have to warn you though," Abby said. "No hot water, no coffee making facilities, no fancy breakfast, and … I only have two single bedrooms left."

Pippa's frozen face started beaming. Ronald was grinning. "That is even better."

"Oh, you don't belong together?" Abby asked.

"No," Pippa and Ronald said at the same time.

"Well, then – it's rooms 2 and 3 on this floor," Abby handed them the keys. "We are going to toast some marshmallows later. Come and join us if you like." She pointed to the fireplace in the front room where a little girl was leaning her back against an armchair, talking to an old gentleman who could have been Santa Claus himself.

"This is like a Hallmark movie after all," Pippa said as they were walking towards their rooms.

Ronald looked at her. "An old man and a child in front of a fireplace don't make for much of a plot, don't you think?"

"Maybe not," Pippa admitted. "But maybe we are all just the backdrop and the real story is somewhere yet to come…"

Chapter 7

December 22, 7:00 p.m.

After Dottie had called Abby to tell her about the landslide, Abby had slowly pondered her options. The snow outside had been falling more and more densely. By noon the ground had been covered with almost three inches of it, and more had kept coming.

Abby had talked to Dave about her change of plans. She had been devastated.

"I feel betrayed," she had sobbed out to her blind guest.

He had chuckled. "Snow is entirely impartial, I'm afraid. It comes with no purpose in mind, as it doesn't have a mind. Neither does a landslide, by the way."

Abby had had to laugh. "I know! Still, it comes at the worst time possible. I was going to bring Hank home. I know it! And now there is no chance, and I will be all alone over the holidays." She had realized what she had just said and had blushed. If she had left, Dave would have been the one all alone. "I'm sorry," she had whispered. "I know I sound selfish."

Dave had sighed. "The worst time possible … how do we know about any of that?! Sometimes we have to go through a valley of misery in order to become more aware of the good things in our life. To be more compassionate. To grasp opportunities and not dismiss them because they aren't screaming loudly enough."

"I don't know what you mean," Abby had pouted. "There is less opportunity in staying here than in trying to get Hank back."

Dave had chuckled, and his belly under his long white beard had been dancing. "I don't know about that, Abby. You know my opinion about trying to win back the man you think you are in love with."

"I don't just think it, I know it!"

"Fine, suit yourself. But this man has betrayed you and left you. And you are still thinking that you need to have him back! No, don't say a thing. If he had wanted to come back to you, he would have done so already. In time for Christmas, too. It is *you* who hasn't let go yet. You are clinging to an image you have created of him. That's not healthy, to say the least. But you also think your life is less meaningful without him. And that's the truly sad thing. Just think how much it means to me to have you in my life. I know, I know, I'm not Hank. But just give it a thought. I have a beautiful room that is taken care of. You give me lovingly prepared food three or four times a day, depending on my whims. You share your thoughts with me. I won't be alone here over Christmas."

"You were one of Dad's best friends," Abby had said. "You always supported me when I was a kid. How could I not care what happens to you when I have a business with room enough for an old friend?!"

"Anybody else might have just put me into assisted living or a nursing home."

"I'm not anybody else," Abby had protested.

"That's the spirit! – Now think of the opportunity that lies in not being able to travel to Seattle and of being stuck here in Wycliff ..."

Abby had frowned. "That means that everybody who has arrived here this morning or whose stay was planned to be over this morning is also stuck."

"There you go!"

"Which means I need to see that all the rooms are tidy and ready for guests." Abby had suddenly set herself in motion. "Oh my, and I need to get breakfast items. I barely have enough for the two of us!"

"See, that's what I mean by opportunity."

By noon, Abby had dusted the already clean bedrooms again, checked the bathrooms, seen to it that the coffee trays had all been refilled. She had even received the first guest of the day, a stout, Italian-looking lady who had seemed vaguely familiar. But Abby hadn't paid the thought any more attention and set out for doing groceries on foot. Nathan's, the local supermarket, was half a mile away at the Harbor Mall. It had taken extremely long to walk there through the slippery snow. Nathan's had been crowded with customers hunting for the last Christmas items, for special deals on anything turkey or ham, and for delicacies to elevate their Christmas dinners. Abby had grabbed bread, butter, cereals, milk, two different kinds of juices, and some extra jars of jam in case somebody didn't care for the kind she had opened for Dave. As an afterthought, she had bought a turkey roll for her and Dave's Christmas dinner, a can of mushroom cream soup for a bean casserole, and a couple of slices of raspberry cheesecake. Lugging home the groceries had been exhausting, and by the time Abby had made it, she had been a steaming mess.

When she had stowed away everything, her dreary thoughts had pressed in on her again. What would Hank be doing? Would he be thinking of her at all? Somehow, Dave's words had reverberated with her. No, Hank probably wouldn't ponder her situation at all. If she had meant anything to him, he would have stayed with her or told her their relationship was over before he had started another one. But he had chosen to hurt her, to betray her.

Abby had banged a fist on her kitchen table. Then she had kicked a sideboard. It hadn't changed much, except that she had broken one of her nails, stubbed her toes, and had achieved to place a black rubber mark on the sideboard that she had needed to clean off. Great!

Abby had finally sat down in her lounge and stared out of the window into the slowly sinking dusk. Maybe Dave was right after all. Maybe they were each other's blessing and she just needed to become more aware of it.

When Dave had entered her life, she had been a toddler. Or rather, she probably had entered Dave's life, as he had already been a family friend before she had even been born. He and her grandfather had gone to college together. He had been a family friend for decades and extended that friendship to Abby's father. While Abby's grandfather had turned his back on a career in Seattle and stayed in Wycliff to work at the bank and to found a family with his high school sweetheart, Dave had become a renowned heart surgeon who had been searched out by people from all over the world. Although very famous, he still had made time every once in a while, to visit his old friend and his family in the quaint town of Wycliff. Abby's father had been growing up with this fatherly friend, married a girl from Steilacoom, and moved from a rental into the family home in Uptown after his parents had passed. And when Abby had been born, Dave had taken to her as if she were his own grandchild.

Dave had told her stories about the countries his patients came from. He had later brought her exotic gifts from places he had flown to, to attend conventions or perform surgery on patients who were too sick to fly to him. He had consoled Abby when her mother had died of breast cancer way too early. He had sat with her when her father had followed his wife only two years later and encouraged her to continue her studies. He had even helped her finance the rest of her college semesters and find her the job at the paper mill, so she could stay in Wycliff and keep her family home. Dave had stopped visiting after Hank had moved in with Abby.

Then, a year ago, Abby had heard that Dave had fallen seriously ill, and that his eyesight was failing. Hank, who had been wary of the old family friend all the time, had balked at taking Dave into their Bed & Breakfast place.

"I don't see why his own family won't take care of him," he had growled.

"He doesn't have any," Abby had said.

"Then his bad!"

"How can you be so hard-hearted?!"

Had she really said this? And why hadn't it hit Abby back then that she had just voiced what Hank had turned out to be? Because she had wanted to stow away the thought that Hank was a selfish person into the "one-time-only"-drawer. He had said this one time only. He wasn't really that bad, right? Stupid! Stupid!

Well, when Dave had been released from rehabilitation, Abby had picked him up and brought him home with her. He still had had a little eyesight left. He had been able to see what she had made of *The Gull's Nest,* and he had loved the room she had set up for him. He had always had a thing for attic rooms, and this one would have offered a most beautiful view across Downtown and the Sound over to the Olympic Mountains if he had been able to see that far anymore.

Hank had been aghast about the new, permanent houseguest. One night he had icily told Abby what he thought of Dave.

"He is going to exploit you, and he will constantly breathe down your neck. He will soon be blind, and then he will have you at his beck and call. Are you insane? Where does that leave me?!"

Dave might have overheard the argument. He had never let on. Abby had tried hard to make up for it. Then, all of a sudden,

Hank had left Abby, and their relationship had been over. Looking back, Abby had found that she had suddenly felt as if a burden had been lifted. She didn't need to go upstairs secretly anymore to slip Dave a treat or just to see whether he was alright. And she had been able to ask Dave to join her in the front room in the evenings ever since Hank had left. Why hadn't she realized how much Hank's dislike of Dave and her haunted attempts to make up for it must have hurt her old friend?

And now she had done it again. Really?! She had almost left Dave alone over the holidays just to be with a man who was self-centered, hateful, and unfaithful. The blind person all this time had not been Dave – it had been herself!

Abby had started to bake cookies. Baking had always been a way to take her mind off troublesome thoughts. A batch of coconut macaroons and one of snickerdoodles later, she had gone upstairs again and invited Dave down for tea. He had gone entirely blind during the past few months, but he didn't seem to have any misgivings about it.

"I'm old, and the human body is only meant to be working for so long. Basically, it is a repair station. And sometimes the best mechanics cannot help when the material has worn out. I've had my share in seeing the world. Maybe I'm meant to use my other senses more now."

Abby had carefully guided Dave downstairs and towards his favorite seat, a rocking chair by the fireplace. She had started a crackling fire a bit earlier on. The smell of it was mingling with that of the freshly baked cookies from the kitchen and the cup of steaming tea she had placed onto the table next to him. Abby had slipped outside to clear the garden path to the house just in case any more guests would find her B & B. Then she had quietly returned inside, cheeks all ruddy, and huddled up near the fire to get warm again.

"This is what Christmas feels like," Dave had said quietly.

"Like what?" Abby had asked.

"Being warm and cozy on the inside," he had replied, and his blind eyes had seemed to gaze to where the fireplace was spreading its cheerful warmth. "On the outside, too, of course, but mostly inside. To have found a home where you are loved and people don't mind taking care of you. Thank you, Abby."

Abby had given him a hug. "You are my family. You have always been family to me."

Dave had chuckled. "Maybe I finally really am." Abby had stayed silent. "You know, I fell in love with your grandmother around the same time as your grandfather did."

Abby had been taken aback. "Really? What happened?"

He had laughed. "Well, we all know whom she chose, and all I could do was to keep adoring her as a friend."

"All these decades? It must have been incredibly hard!"

"It was. At least at first. But you cannot force love. I could have tried harder for her, of course. But would that have changed her heart? And would your grandfather have stayed my best friend? I doubt it. The best I could do was to move on, to keep in touch, and to try to find another woman who would measure up to your grandmother."

"And?"

"It never happened. So, I kept returning to Wycliff just as a visitor. And when your dad was born, I imagined he was the son I never had. And now my old friends' beautiful granddaughter is taking over and gives me a place at her table and a room to stay." He had sighed.

Abby had placed a hand onto his shoulder. "Don't get too wistful on me. I might get tearful otherwise."

Into that moment of silence the phone had rung, and Abby had taken the call. It had been Dottie again. "I'm just about sending three real nice ladies to your place. You still have room, don't you?"

"Sure," Abby had answered. "Send them on. All my rooms are empty, except one. Might as well take in more guests, right? I'm stuck here over the holidays anyway." She had thought she'd feel worse over it. Just as she had felt this morning. But to her surprise, she hadn't lost another thought about Hank. And she had been looking forward to filling her house with guests.

"Well," Dottie had said cheerfully. "You are even 'stucker' than you think. Luke just called me. There was another landslide down south. Wycliff is cut off by rail and by road, both ways, north and south. Not that it mattered much with this snow fall."

Abby had sharply drawn in her breath. "Another landslide?"

"Prepare yourself for some longer-term guests," Dottie said. "Luke is in an emergency meeting in town hall right now. They are trying to figure out how to take care of all those who will be stranded in town over the holidays."

They had exchanged some more words, and then Abby had hung up.

"Another landslide?" Dave had asked from his rocking chair.

"We are cut off from the outside world," Abby had said. "What a strange feeling!"

"I don't feel a change," Dave had chuckled. "We are still warm and safe. What's the difference? We wouldn't have gone anywhere in this snow anyhow."

"True," Abby had pondered. "But now it seems so much more inevitable."

A while later, she had heard laughter outside and realized that the automatic porch light had come on. She had risen from her seat next to Dave and opened the front door. Three ladies dressed in red, green, and blue had been coming up the path she had shoveled open earlier. To her fascination they all looked exactly the same. It had almost been as if she had triple vision. But then she had caught herself quickly again and ushered her guests in. They were easy-going, all three of them, and Abby had taken an instant liking to them. They would be great upstairs neighbors to Dave, that much was for sure.

More guests had arrived at her house. The next ones had been a father who had tried his best not to look mournful for his little daughter's sake. But Abby had sensed anyhow that they were carrying a burden in their hearts. What bliss that the child had discovered Dave in his rocking chair by the fire and, over Snickerdoodles and a mug of hot hibiscus tea, had struck friendship.

Then the lights had flickered and gone out, and all of her guests but one had emerged from their rooms upstairs, wondering whether it was only their room that was affected by a power outage. A quick check by Abby, and she had been able to tell them that the entire town must have lost power, as the streetlights on Jupiter Avenue had gone out, and Downtown lay in the dark as well, except one or the other business that seemed to be running on a generator now.

In the darkness there had been a knock on the front door. "You must have been sent by Marylou," Abby had said to the couple outside. And they had wondered how she knew. Well, though her cell phone had died mid-ring, she had recognized the craft store owner's number. And she had made a wild guess. It turned out that the couple owned a yarn store in Lakewood and had been stranded after their class at *Ultimate Crafts*. Abby had given them her last double room.

A bit later there had been another knock on the door, and she had quickly let in a man and woman in their fifties. They had looked frozen; the woman had had a desperate look in her eyes. Abby had been bewildered whether they were a couple or not. It had turned out they were not, but there was that vibe of trust hanging between them. Interesting.

And now, everybody was settled in. The little girl, Heather, had begun to toast marshmallows on a big fork she was holding over the fire, and she made sure that Santa Dave, as she had begun to call him, got his fair share. Dave obligingly tried a couple, though Abby knew he was not much into marshmallows. But how could he disappoint the little sprite?! Her father had settled in another corner, all by himself, holding a book he was not reading. From the rooms above came the soft laughter of women. Only the first and the latest arrivals were quiet and kept very much to themselves in their respective rooms.

Abby was stretching in her armchair by the fire. She was feeling strangely serene after having been so upset about her failed trip this morning. This was what she was living for – the shared comfort of a house that became home for people of all sorts for a limited time. The laid-back calm that ensued from people having arrived at a place that asked nothing of them. The joy of seeing people letting go and simply being themselves.

"Do you think we will stay here long?" little Heather startled her father out of his thoughts.

"Why?" Aaron asked back.

"Because I wish we could," the nine-year-old said. "I like sitting next to Santa Dave. And we never toast marshmallows over the fire back in …" She hesitated and swallowed. Then she hopped away from where she had been standing, leaning the fork with the marshmallow against the chimney screen, to place her hands at her father's knees. "I know, because you'd have to clean up all the mess after me, right? But if I promised not to drip melted marshmallow over the floor …" She looked at Aaron's face hopefully.

He smiled and took her little hands into his big ones. "It's not that, hon. It simply never occurred to me."

"Oh!"

A moment later there was another knock on the front door.

"More people!" Heather called out excitedly, turning her head to the entrance.

Abby looked worried. She did the math, and shook her head. All of her rooms were booked. There was no more space at the inn.

Chapter 8

December 22, 5:00 p.m.

Ramón Desoto was a student of mathematics at the University of Portland, Oregon. He was diligent. He had to be. He had a scholarship, but that wouldn't last him forever. He was feisty. He had to be. Latinos still ran into a lot of prejudices. Quite a few people kept asking him whether he was in the US legally. Well, his family had come to the Pacific Northwest only a decade after the Mexican-American War, and he was proud of that. Others made fun of his last name and called him "risotto". He found them just too stupid to honor them with a reaction.

Ramón kept to himself a lot. There were a few people he liked in his year. There were a few with whom he went out every once in a while. Not often though, because that cost money. Money that he needed elsewhere. He wore his straight black hair neatly cut. And he bought clothes only when he found that his old ones didn't look good on him anymore. For Ramón was a tidy person. But there was also another reason: Ramón was in love.

Unfortunately, the girl whom he admired didn't even know he existed. And while he was watching her with yearning brown eyes, she was giggling with her girl-friends from her art classes or sassily flipping her blonde ponytail at one of the football players who seemed to have found favor with her. Ramón sometimes wished he had the physique to be a football player just for once, but Nature had meant him to be rather on the too medium-height and too light-weight side of any game that demanded size and weight on a larger scale. He felt non-descript whenever he compared himself to any of the guys she used to talk to. At least he had found out her name after leafing through the yearbook they had received after Freshman Year: Michelle Taylor.

Ever since that moment, Ramón's entire existence seemed to have changed. He had started imagining himself with her in spite of his invisibility. Whenever he had passed her in one of the hallways, he had felt a thousand butterflies rise in his stomach. The air around her had seemed to be electrified. It had even smelled differently. Yet, she had never seemed to see him. Not a single moment. Because he was non-descript. Because he was not a football player. Because those were the kind of guys she seemed to care for.

"All brawn and no brain," Allison, a nerdy math student, had called them once when she had caught his wistful glance toward Michelle. But Ramón had known that Allison would have loved to catch the attention of one of those jocks herself. Only once! And here she had been, doomed like him, to be invisible to the sports stars. But at least they could watch their fill. Ah, the perks of being a wallflower …

The jock Michelle had fancied had been one of those toothpaste advertisement type guys. Square-jawed, huge smile, blue eyes, blond hair, tall, wide … everything that Ramón wasn't.

In their third semester, those two had been seen everywhere on campus together, and rumor had had it that they were not just discussing football either. Ramón hadn't wanted to imagine the two of them together. And yet ...

By October of their third year, it had been more than obvious that Michelle was pregnant. It had also been more than obvious that the football player had dropped her like a hot potato. Michelle had confronted him a few times in the dining hall. But the guy had denied he was the father and had accused her of probably having slept around during the summer vacations. There had been opportunity enough for her after they each had gone to their respective homes. Ramón had cringed at the accusation. There hadn't been proof to any outsider, of course. But he had watched how Michelle had behaved during the semesters before, and she had been one of those coveted girls who went out with only one guy at a time.

One evening, Ramón had had a ticket to a concert at the Wonder Ballroom – Allison had been down with a nasty flu and given him hers. "You could always sell it to somebody else," she had said hoarsely and looked at him with feverish eyes.

"I'll go and tell you about it," he had insisted. And gone he had. Though he hadn't been able to tell Allison much about the concert at all when she was back in class again.

It had been an uncommonly mild night, and the Ballroom building had slowly been filling with people. Ramón hadn't wanted to stay inside where the DJ music from the loudspeakers had already been pretty loud. So, he had walked outside – and there she had been sitting. Michelle. All by herself. Red-eyed, tears rolling down her face. He had sat down next to her.

"Do you need help?" he had asked very softly. She had only shaken her head without looking at him. "I am Ramón."

"I know," she had said.

He had been floored. "How…?"

"They say that you keep looking at me. They call you puppy-eyed."

He had swallowed hard. "Who is 'they'?"

"My ex-boyfriend's friends." She had finally looked at him. "Is it true?"

"What? Me looking at you?" He had blushed. "I guess." He had chuckled nervously.

"Why?"

"Because I find you beautiful." He had wondered where his courage came from. "And because I find you interesting. And I have been wondering about you, too."

"Wondering?"

"Yes. I mean, you are an art student. That means you have subtle interests. And here … You went out with one of those football players."

"Yeah," she had smiled bitterly. "Right?! And see how it has turned out?" She had pointed at her belly.

"You are pregnant," he had stated. "Will he take care of you?"

"He claims it's not his."

She had started to cry again, and Ramón had softly laid one arm around her shoulders. Michelle had been startled at first, but after a while she had settled into his arm and even leaned into him. And Ramón had been on cloud number nine. Meanwhile the band had arrived on stage inside and begun to play. It had been incredibly loud even outside, and it had become a bit chilly.

"Let's go somewhere else," Ramón had suggested.

Michelle had looked at his face. "Where?"

"Anywhere we can talk in quiet. If you like."

"You *do* have nice eyes," she had said.

Ramón hadn't known what to answer. They had left the Wonder Ballroom though and walked around. There were beautiful old houses in the area, and lots of old trees. And there, on the sidewalk, had been a few tables and chairs. Light had been streaming out of a building. It had looked cozy somehow, and Ramón had pulled her inside. Michelle had been hungry, and they had shared a serving of Mac and Cheese with pretzel crumbs. Ramón had tried one of their beers whereas Michelle had ordered a soda. They had talked and talked, until they had realized that they would have to take a cab back to their dorms, as they had probably missed the last bus.

After that night, the two of them had kept meeting. Michelle's ex-boyfriend hadn't seemed too happy about this turn in Michelle's life. He had started taunting Ramón, who took it with a grain of salt. Only losers taunted other people. He hadn't even responded to any of the insults flung into his direction. And though some people had wondered why Michelle had suddenly chosen the Latino guy who was on the scrawny side in comparison to the jock, they silently applauded his guts to take his stand against the bully.

Over the weeks, some deep trust had developed between the two young people. But another crisis had come up when the Christmas vacations had been around the corner.

"I cannot go home," Michelle had said to Ramón one evening after dinner.

"Why is that?" he had asked.

"My parents won't have me."

Ramón had been appalled. "Are you sure?"

"Pretty sure," Michelle had said and turned her face away. "My father told me I shouldn't even think of entering his home with a bastard."

"Wow," Ramón had blanched. "But did he really mean it?"

"After he called me a slut and somebody dragging his name into the mud? Oh yes, he meant what he said, believe me!"

"That's pretty harsh. What did your mom say?"

"Nothing."

"Nothing?!"

"Yes. Nothing." Michelle had shrugged. "I've always been left to my own devices when it came to having a different opinion from his. Or in this case falling short of his expectations."

"That's tough."

Michelle had nodded, then shrugged. "I'm almost used to it. Only … this time it's a lot harder," she had whispered, and her eyes had filled.

"Christmas and all that."

"And the baby coming at the end of the month …"

Ramón had nodded quietly and pondered her words for a moment. "What if you came with me?" he had suddenly suggested.

"All the way to Renton?"

"Yes."

"But what would your family say?"

"Just one mouth more to feed in a huge big, cuddly Latino family," he had laughed.

"But wouldn't they think all the wrong things?"

"We would tell them all that matters."

"I can't do that …"

"The telling?"

"That. Going to your family over Christmas. Pretending everything is okay."

"But we wouldn't be pretending," Ramón had said and squeezed her hand. "I'd be bringing home a dear friend who happens to be pregnant. So? Everybody will pamper you. You will love our food, and you will love my family."

"I'm sure about *that*," she had laughed helplessly.

"So?"

"Okay. I will go with you. Even though it feels all wrong." She had sighed. "Thank you, Ramón. You are a real friend."

He had blushed. And he had been wishing that he were so much more.

Christmas vacations had started this morning. Ramón had packed a duffle bag and some Christmas gifts for his family into his rusty old pick-up truck. Then he had hoisted in Michelle's baggage.

"Sorry it's not a fancier car," he had said. Especially after Michelle's ex-boyfriend had just driven by in one of the latest Ford Rangers and given him the finger.

"I couldn't care less about car models," Michelle had said and carefully climbed inside. "What you are doing for me is what counts." She looked at him with the sweetest smile. "Thank you, Ramón."

He had just nodded brusquely. Then he had started the truck, and off they had driven, towards I-5, into the snail-paced traffic across the bridges towards Vancouver, Washington. Traffic had been bad all the way. By the time they had reached Centralia it had started snowing. And it had become worse pretty quickly.

"I'm not sure we will make it in this snow," Ramón had said nervously.

"What do you mean?" Michelle had asked, her face pale.

"I don't have such good tires, and I don't want to risk an accident. Especially not with you in the car."

They had continued up to Olympia and then some. At the first of two I-5 exits to Wycliff, Ramón had decided to turn off the interstate. The road into Wycliff had proven treacherous enough with its slopes and curves. And when they had reached the Harbor Mall, they had both exhaled with relief.

"Let's wait it out here," Ramón had said. "Snowfall in the lowlands usually lasts only a couple of hours and then lets up. We'll drive the rest when it's stopped snowing and is melting again. Probably it's just a matter of another hour. And we need to eat something anyhow."

"We could explore the town since we are here anyway," Michelle had suggested.

He had looked at her doubtingly. Her belly was looking heavy, and if she slipped and fell what could happen to her and the baby?

"You sure?"

"M-hm," she had nodded. "It will take my mind off some things …"

So, they had taken the bus downtown and walked around. They had shared a burger at the *Harbor Pub*. They had looked into some stores. But the weather hadn't let up at all. If possible, it had turned even worse, dumping snow down on them as if it had to make up for all the past milder winters.

"This is crazy," Ramón had finally said. It had been half past four, and they had been warming up at the *Lavender Café* with a cup of hot chocolate for each of them. "I better call my mom and let her know that we might have to stay." He had fumbled out his smart phone and dialed a number. "My mom says never to text her. She wants to hear my voice so she knows that I'm alive."

Over the phone he had quickly explained their little ordeal. It was then that he had heard about the landslide that had cut Wycliff off from the northern access to I-5. When he had hung up, he had frowned.

"What's the matter?" Michelle had wanted to know.

"Landslide up north," he had said. "That's not good."

A few moments later the lights in the Lavender café had flickered shortly and then gone out. "No worries," a voice in the dark had said. "Our generator will pick up in a moment." And sure enough, the lights had come on again.

"Wow," Michelle said. "What was that?"

Ramón pointed outside. "Apparently Wycliff has just lost its power." The streetlights had gone dark, and there was only the twilight of the snow outside the windows.

"This really doesn't feel good," Michelle said, and her face betrayed worry.

"Let's take it at face value," Ramón replied calmly. "Today, we wouldn't have been able to go anywhere anymore. Not with this kind of snow piling up on us. That's why we better pay now and check in at a motel or hotel or whatever place they have down here. By tomorrow it will have stopped snowing, and

I'll drive back to the interstate exit where we came from. And the rest will fall into place. No worries." He patted her hand. "Okay?"

"Okay," Michelle said with a wan smile.

They paid for their hot chocolates and struggled back into their winter coats. Then they stepped outside into the wintery cold.

"Apart from the fact that we are stranded," Ramón suddenly remarked, "isn't it truly beautiful?" He put out his tongue and caught a snowflake.

Michelle laughed with desperation. "Apart from it being really cold and us being stranded, we should truly go look for a room now!"

They started walking. Their feet sank into the snow ankle-deep, and what was only a short distance to *The Ship Hotel* seemed to stretch into an exhausting hike. By the time they had reached the hotel entrance, Michelle was panting hard, and Ramón looked at her anxiously.

"Are you alright?" he asked.

Michelle nodded. "It's just tough walking with this watermelon of a belly *and* snow…"

They went inside. The lobby was warm and crowded. There was a long line at the reception desk.

"This doesn't look good," Michelle whispered.

"No," Ramón admitted. "But you never know. We should give it a try …"

They waited in line, but little group after little group of people ahead of them were turned away, and only very few people passed by to the huge staircase, key in hand. Finally, it was their turn.

"Sorry," the receptionist said at their request. "Our hotel is completely booked."

"Are there any other hotels in town?" Ramón asked.

The receptionist smiled, pity in her eyes. "Unfortunately, I have heard earlier on that the motel at the other side of town is totally booked too."

Ramón turned to Michelle. "Looks like we are out of luck."

"Are there any other places in town where we could stay?" Michelle asked the receptionist, panic in her eyes.

"I'm not sure," the young woman replied. "I'm new in town, but I know definitely that there is only one hotel and one motel in town."

"Any Bed & Breakfasts maybe?" Ramón asked.

The receptionist shrugged apologetically. "As I said, I'm new in town. Maybe you could go to the Community Center and ask there. They might have some idea."

"Is that far to walk?" Ramón wanted to know.

"Just two or three blocks. By the yacht harbor."

"Thanks." Ramón turned to Michelle. "Might as well head there now. Maybe we could even stay there for the night."

Michelle's face fell. "I'm not sure I will be able to do this."

"Come on," Ramón said. "You can, and you know you will. Sometimes it gets a bit tough before it gets better." He nudged her into her arm. "Let's walk. Once we are there, I'm sure everything will fall into place.

Ten minutes later they stood inside the cozy lobby of the Community Center. A fire was blazing in the big fireplace. The building was filling up with stranded people like them. Ramón found a seat for Michelle and walked to the reception window. When he returned to Michelle after a while, his face was quite serious.

"This is it," he said to her, and all of a sudden, he felt the burden of responsibility for her. "I wish I could have done better than this."

"It's not your fault," Michelle said. "What's going to happen now?"

"We'll sit here and wait until it's over," Ramón shrugged. "They said that we can stay. They will keep the fire and the generator going. We will be warm and dry." Michelle hung her head. "Hey! It could be way worse, right?"

Chapter 9

December 22, 5:00 p.m.

Hope had been the one to smell snow in the air when she and her sister Destiny had walked from their apartment near the Wycliff ferry terminal to their restaurant this morning.

"I believe it when I see it," Destiny had laughed. "Snow in the lowlands? I can't even remember what it feels like." But her voice had sounded hopeful.

"Wouldn't a white Christmas be wonderful?" Hope had replied.

Actually, there had been a special nip in the air, and the sky had displayed a different shade of gray as they had passed Town Hall and the yacht harbor across from it. They had halted for a few seconds to catch some breath. The two robust Afro-American ladies had grown up in Seattle, but as the city had become less and less affordable for them, they had started looking for another place to reopen their business. When water damage after a first-floor fire had ruined their basement restaurant in Seattle, they had been lucky to find the former location of the Historical Museum of Wycliff in the basement of the post office building on Back Row available. Ever since they had moved in, *The Soup Cellar* had become a favorite with Wycliffians and tourists alike. Their menu was small but eclectic – three different soups or stews a day, accompanied by rolls and diverse toppings.

"Yes," Destiny had agreed. "But that would also mean that we can't drive up all the way to Seattle to visit with Pa and Ma over Christmas Day."

"True," Hope sighed. "Well, maybe it won't snow after all."

But it had started soon after they had climbed down the steps into their basement restaurant and stirred up the first batch of soup, a carrot-tomato bisque with orange juice. As the sweet and sour fragrance wafted through the kitchen and flavored the air in the front of the restaurant, the first flakes had sailed past their windows that rose about two feet above street level.

"Look!" Destiny had exclaimed. "You were right."

Hope had stepped next to her sister and laid an arm around Destiny's round waist. "You know what this also means?"

"An extra flow of customers for some hot soup," Destiny had laughed. "Let's get going!"

A couple hours later, a solid layer of five inches of snow had been pressing against their kitchen windows and changed the light inside. Hope and Destiny had started clearing the outside stairs with a broom every half hour in the hope their customers would not be deterred by the treacherous nature of snow on a rather steep decline. Indeed, so far, they had been lucky. The snow had driven in a lot more people than usually, and it had been one of their patrons who had told them about the landslide across the road and the train tracks up north.

"We can still go around it and simply take the south-entrance to I-5," Destiny had said cheerfully, while ladling some spicy Caribbean seafood chowder into a bowl. "Where there is a will, there is a way."

"And where a door stays closed to you, you better not try to open it by force," Hope had countered with a mischievous smile. "Not that I don't believe in opening doors for yourself at times. But if this snow keeps falling like this, we won't be going anywhere."

"It will stop and melt," Destiny had said. "You just wait and see. We'll have our family Christmas in Seattle just as every year."

"What if not?"

Destiny had frowned. "You *are* serious, aren't you?" Hope had nodded. "Hmmm, I guess then we will figure a way to have our own little Christmas right here in town, and that's that." She had shrugged and stirred the big kettle of green lentil soup.

By noon, they had had to set up two more batches of soup, and they had scrutinized the level in the third kettle. "Better make a second batch of this as well," Hope had decided. "Just as well that we have soaked enough of these lentils last night."

They had worked quietly alongside each other. Hope had stepped into the sitting area of *The Soup Cellar* every once in a while, to see whether new guests had arrived and whether she would be able to retrieve some of the used dishes. By one o'clock the din in the restaurant had somewhat subsided. A few latecomers had ordered their food and then lingered to avoid getting back outside into the snow.

When four o'clock had come, their basement windows were half-vanished in the snow. The restaurant had been empty, and Hope had reported to Destiny that the snowfall had even gained in density and strength.

"So much for my prediction it would let up," Destiny had stated dryly.

"It might still melt by tomorrow," Hope had encouraged her sister. Finally, they had had time to sit down and enjoy a bowl of their own food in quiet.

But it had not lasted long, for they had heard steps come down and then the ruckus of somebody stomping snow off their boots. They had turned their heads towards the door as it opened.

"Good afternoon, ladies," a tall man in firefighting uniform had greeted them.

"Good afternoon," they had replied.

Hope had risen from their table. "We are about to close," she had said apologetically, "but for the heroes of our town we always have a bowl of soup."

The man had smiled. His dark fine curls had been glistening from the wetness of melting snowflakes, and the dark eyes in his dark face had been taking in the restaurant and the gorgeous woman talking to him. "I didn't come in for food," he had said.

"Oh!" Both women had looked surprised.

"It's about the staircase of yours – it's filling pretty fast with snow."

"I know," Hope had wailed."

"We've been trying to keep it cleared all day long," Destiny had said and slumped in her chair. "We simply cannot keep up."

"It's dangerous for your customers," the man had said. "I'll help you clear it, if you want."

"You would?" Hope had said. "But you are fire department, not ..." She had lifted one hand to her mouth and giggled. "Don't I sound silly right now?"

Destiny had been catching that strange vibe that had suddenly been electrifying the room between her sister and the firefighter. She had risen and taken her empty bowl to carry it to the kitchen. "Well, while you are talking, I better fix a bowl of soup for you, Mr. ..." She had raised her eyebrows, waiting for him to state his name.

He had caught the hint. "Nouveau. Pascal Nouveau," he had said. He had stayed, rooted in his place. So had Hope. When Destiny had reentered the kitchen, she had almost burst out with laughter. She had never seen her sister as if struck by lightning before. She had taken her dear time to stir the seafood chowder, to get an extra-large bowl, and to fill it with the fragrant, chunky mixture. She had taken her time to fix some tiny bowls with cilantro, chopped peanuts, and a slice of lime. She had been extra-slow in getting another flatbread and cutting it up on a plate, then

115

arranging all the bowls and the plate on a tray. When she had finally finished, she had carried everything outside into the front room.

"What took you so long?" Hope had asked, bewildered.

"Where has your eye-candy gone?" Destiny had countered.

"My eye-candy?!" Hope had gaped. Then she had closed her mouth and blushed. From outside, they had heard the noises of someone shoveling the snow from their steps.

"That him?" Destiny had asked, and Hope had nodded. Destiny had started cleaning the tables with a wet cloth, and Hope had gone into the tiny office to work the balance ledger.

"He's a good man," Destiny had said to herself but with the benefit for Hope to overhear. "Lending your neighbor a hand unasked when they are in need is just one of the signs."

"What did you say?" Hope had asked.

"Nothing."

They had kept on working in silence, and after a few minutes the noise outside had ended. The restaurant door had opened again, and Pascal had stuck his face inside.

"It's all done for now," he had said cheerfully.

"Oh, but you need to come in and warm yourself up," Destiny had insisted. "We have fixed you a nice tray of our extra-special Caribbean seafood stew." She had pointed at a table set next to the office. "It's on the house." Then she had simply vanished behind the kitchen door.

116

A few moments later, Pascal had been able to hear the clanking of metal and china, as if somebody willingly created more noise than necessary. He hadn't felt the will nor the strength to resist such an invitation. There was something to be said for hot food on a cold day and with such a beautiful woman to glimpse through the office door, too. He had pulled out a chair and then begun eating.

Hope had looked up from her books and over her shoulder. She had smiled at him with shy eyes. Pascal had smiled back broadly.

"This is good soup," he had said, breaking off another bite of his flatbread.

"You can have more if you want to," she had offered.

Pascal had wiped his mouth with a paper napkin. "No thanks. I have to go over to town hall in a few. We have been called in for an emergency meeting."

"An emergency meeting …" Hope had echoed.

"Well, with the landslide up north we won't see a snow plough any time soon. And as the snow keeps piling up, we have to make some plans in case anything worse is going to happen."

Hope had nodded pensively. "I see. Well, I hope you will stay warm, Mr. Nouveau."

"Just call me Pascal."

Hope had blushed. "Pascal," she had repeated. "We will have some nice squash soup tomorrow. You might want to come by and try it."

"I won't be able to resist," he had said. Then he had lifted his hand as in a small salute and walked towards the door. "I'll see to it that you will find your door shoveled clear tomorrow morning – so don't bother to get up extra early."

The door had closed behind him, and Hope had buried her glowing face in her hands. "Oh my…" she had whispered.

"Mmmmm-hm," Destiny had made. "That guy has really fallen for you, let me tell you."

"You think?"

"Yep. He has." And Destiny had laughed deeply.

They had continued to perform all the little tasks that needed to be done for closing the restaurant for the night. And just as they had put away the vacuum cleaner and folded the last laundered towel to put it away, the lights went out.

"Dang," Destiny called out. "Did you just switch off the light on me?"

"No," Hope said from the front room. "It went out on me, too. It must be a power outage. I cannot see any light from the streetlamps either."

The sisters carefully made their way to their office to grab their coats and bags. Then they slowly fumbled their way through the restaurant to the entrance door. It was just as well that the snow from outside was reflecting a somewhat eerie light into the basement. Otherwise it would have been pitch-dark.

They stepped outside into the cold, and Destiny took out her keys to lock up.

"This is unreal," Hope said. "The steps are already covered with snow again, and Pascal has only been gone for an hour."

"Pascal, huh?" Destiny teased.

Hope ignored her. "It doesn't look as if it would stop tonight."

Destiny held her face up into the tumbling snowflakes. "Be-au-ti-ful," she said, eyes closed.

"It means that it will be still on the ground tomorrow," Hope said.

"We will have a white Christmas," Destiny said dreamily.

"We won't be able to travel to Seattle to celebrate with Ma and Pa."

"Which means you get some more opportunity to maybe meet your hunk of a firefighter." Destiny escaped a sisterly slap with a peal of laughter.

"He's not *my* firefighter," Hope said.

"Girl, you should see your face when you say this!"

Hope threw a chunk of snow at her sister. Destiny bent and quickly shaped some snow into a soft ball to fling it back. It became a snowball fight in the wintery silence of Back Row, and the sisters left off breathlessly and with glowing faces after a little while. Then they cheerfully walked towards Main Street.

The streetlights on Main were off, too. So were the lights of quite a few businesses. People were struggling through the snow, while stores were getting locked up.

119

"I wonder what caused this power outage and how long it will last," Hope said.

"I guess it's something at the transformer station," Destiny replied. "After all, Wycliff *does* have all its powerlines underground. So, it must be something out there."

They were passing *The Ship Hotel* where people were standing in line at the reception desk inside and others were just pouring out of the door, discussing what they ought to do now.

"It looks like there are people stranded in Wycliff and don't know where to stay for the night," Hope pondered.

"That must feel awful," Destiny said. "I just hope they will find a place."

"I'm pretty sure that the Community Center and the ferry terminal might be able to stay open all night."

"Hmmm, that sounds like only half the solution," Destiny said and looked at her sister whose eyes had taken on a far-away look. "Do you think the same thing that I think?"

Hope nodded. "I guess. Let's take a look how many people there are and talk to the people who run the Community Center."

It was a struggle through almost knee-high snow by now to get to the yacht harbor and then cross the parking lot to the Community Center. The lights inside were shining brightly, and there were groups of people flocking to the building ahead of the sisters. Inside, a big fire was crackling in the fireplace of the lobby, and there were throngs of people already who had found themselves a seat or were huddled on the floor or against a wall.

"Dear me," Hope sighed. "This doesn't look comfortable."

"All the more reason to bring them some comfort," Destiny agreed. They wound their way towards the reception desk where an exhausted volunteer was answering questions. When it was Hope and Destiny's turn, her eyes lit up.

"Hi! Nice to see some familiar faces tonight. What can I do for you?" The elderly lady suddenly seemed to have shaken her weariness.

"Hope and I were wondering whether you'd like us to help feed the crowd dinner tonight," Destiny said.

"What?! You would really do this?"

"Well," Hope said. "You can't have all these people here sit and wait out the snowstorm without food. Something warm will fill their tummies and keep them relaxed."

"You are really serious about this?" The lady looked from face to face and shook her head. "You two are something else indeed. And who would say no to such an offer. Will you need any help?"

"That would be marvelous," Destiny said. "We would also want to let the people inside the ferry terminal know that we are offering food here."

"What happened anyway?" Hope asked. "Do you have any idea?"

"Well, someone from town hall came over here a few minutes ago. Apparently, there was another landslide south of here. It must have knocked out one of the power lines providing our substation."

"Oh," Hope said with a worried face. "That might mean a cold night for a whole lot of households…"

"It also means that Wycliff is cut off from any outside support," the lady said. "The tracks and the road to the southern Wycliff I-5 exit are covered up with debris. Even if the snow lets up, it will take a couple of days to get through to us."

Destiny raised her brows. "All the more reason we Wycliffians close ranks and help each other out as well as those who are here against their plans. Let's grab some people from the crowd and go back to our pantry. We need somebody to help us lug over some food."

As Hope and Destiny approached the crowd in the lobby and in the dining room, they started looking for able-bodied males and began talking about their plans. They soon had a handful of volunteers for carrying food from *The Soup Cellar* to the Commercial Kitchen of the Community Center and their wives and girlfriends for assisting with cooking and feeding the crowds.

Just as they were about to leave the lobby, Hope spotted a young couple. The girl was sitting on a chair, the young man was kneeling in front of her, talking to her softly. She was heavily pregnant and had her eyes closed.

"Wait a second," Hope told Destiny. "I need to talk to those guys over there. They seem to have a situation."

Destiny scanned the crowd, and her eyes, too, found the young couple. "Not good," she nodded. "I'll walk over to our place and get the stuff. See to those kids meanwhile." And she headed out with her recruits.

Hope grabbed a map from the reception desk and approached the young people. "Excuse me, please," she said softly. The young man looked at her with a pained face. "Are you okay?"

The young man looked at the pretty, tired girl and slowly shook his head. "My friend is exhausted, and I wish we had a place where she could lay down and rest."

Hope took a ball pen from her handbag and drew two crosses on the map. "Here," she held the map out to the young man. "I know that the hotel is booked out. There is another place close by, though it means a climb up the bluff. It's right there," she pointed to one cross. "And we are here," she pointed to the other. "Will your … friend … will she be up to it?"

"Michelle?" the young man asked the girl softly. She nodded, opening her eyes.

"Then just go there and ask whether Abby will take you in. Tell her that *The Soup Cellar* girls send you."

"What's the place called?" the young man asked, his dark eyes gleaming with hope.

"*The Gull's Nest*," Hope said. "Abby is a wonderful hostess. I'm pretty sure she will be able to help you out."

A few minutes later she was on her way over to her restaurant to help her sister and their team haul food to the Community Center. Looking over her shoulder, she saw the couple emerge from the warmly lit building and trudge their way towards the bluff.

Chapter 10

December 22, 7:00 p.m.

Another knock on the door. Abby rose from her chair. She passed Aaron who still wasn't reading, but just held his book.

"I thought all rooms were booked by now," he wondered.

"And they are," Abby said. "Maybe it's just one of the neighbors in need of a candle. If these are new guests, though, I will simply have to turn them away."

Abby opened the door and looked into two very young, desperate faces staring back at her from the dark cold. The young man was holding up well enough and seemed only slightly out of breath from the walk up the bluff. But the girl was visibly exhausted; her eyes were watery, and her peaked nose was red from the cold.

Abby silently held the door open. The two young people heaved a sigh and stepped inside. Only then did Abby notice the large bump under the girl's coat. It is just as well, she thought. She hadn't been able to send these kids away. It didn't matter that one of them was pregnant. Highly pregnant if she was guessing right. She had put herself into an impossible situation. There was no room at her guesthouse.

Little Heather came over from the fire place with a fork load of toasted marshmallows. She held out the treat to the young woman. "Would you like some?" she asked.

"Heather," her father admonished her from his seat, noticing the predicament Abby had put herself into.

Heather turned around and smiled at him, unperturbed. "They must be so much colder than we were when we came here. It's really dark now, and the snow storm seems to have picked up even more." She still held the fork out to the young woman. "I made them for Santa Dave, but I can toast some more for him later. He has already had some."

"Thank you," the young woman said with a sad little smile. "I'm not really hungry."

"We have been sent by a lady," the young man, obviously of Latino descent, said shyly. "She was down at the Community Center. She didn't say her name, and I forgot the business she owns …"

"*The Soup Cellar*," the young woman stepped in. "She said you'd find a way to help us."

Abby bit her lips. A fine kettle of fish she had been served by either Hope or Destiny … But then she shook her head. It didn't matter that they had been sent or by whom they had been sent. They had been standing at her door. She had taken them in. They were her task now. She couldn't turn them out into the cold again.

The young man realized that Abby was looking torn and helpless. "You don't *have* a room for us after all, do you?" he asked cautiously.

Abby shook her head. "Sit down on the sofa by the fire," she said. "I'll try and find a solution."

126

"You've got a garden shed," Heather suddenly chimed into the ensuing silence.

"Heather!" Aaron said, and this time he really looked upset.

"But I saw it through our window before all the lights went out," Heather insisted in a half-whisper.

"This is none of your business. Let the grown-ups handle this, okay?"

"But ..." Heather faltered.

"Can I offer you something to eat?" Abby asked the young people.

"Are you going to turn us away after that?" the young man asked warily.

"No," Abby said because she knew she wouldn't have the heart to do so. "I won't, though I still have to think how to accommodate you."

"In the garden shed ..." the young woman said very cautiously.

Abby suddenly burst into unexpected laughter. "I wonder what you must think of me. Of course not!" She rose. "I'll make you some sandwiches, and maybe in the meantime I have an idea. My name is Abby, by the way."

"Ramón," the young man said and rose politely. "And this is my friend Michelle."

"Nice meeting you," Abby said friendly. "Though it's sad that it's under these dire circumstances. – It can't be easy for you," she turned to Michelle.

Michelle just smiled wearily.

"We were on our way to my family in Renton when the snow started and kept coming," Ramón explained. "We had hoped it would let up. Instead we are stranded here in Wycliff."

"It could have been worse," Dave suggested from his rocking chair.

Ramón looked over to him and frowned. "It feels bad enough as it is."

"Imagine you'd been stuck somewhere in the middle of nowhere. No food, no warm beverages, and gas running low because you'd have to keep your engine running for some heat."

"True," Ramón conceded. "That and with Michelle being with child …"

"Oh," Dave just said and stroked his beard.

Ramón wanted to say something, but then he realized that the old man in the rocking chair was blind and swallowed down what he had wanted to counter. "That's the only reason why we went away from the Community Center – because it became so crowded, and Michelle would have had to sit in a chair all evening."

"Well, at least here she will be able to lie on a sofa, I guess," Aaron looked over the seating area in front of the fire place pensively.

"That would be a lot better than down on the floor," Michelle said softly. "And it's so cozy in here, too."

They all fell silent again. The fire was crackling merrily. Abby returned from the kitchen with a plate filled with sandwiches and half an orange for Ramón and Michelle each. "Would any of you others want something to eat as well?"

"No, my dear," Dave said.

"No thanks, Ma'am," Aaron said. Then he suddenly became alert. "Where is Heather?"

"Oh, she went upstairs a few minutes ago," Abby said. "I saw her walk past the kitchen door."

"But I have the key to our room," Aaron said. "Oh my! What is this child up to now?!"

Dave chuckled. "She's sure got a bright head on her little shoulders. You should be proud of her."

"Too bright for her own good sometimes," Aaron replied. "It's not always good to pipe up when you'd better kept your manners."

"She hasn't misbehaved here," Abby pointed out. "In fact, she has helped me welcome our latest guests, and I'm sure she has been a wonderful little companion for Dave."

"Excellent," Dave confirmed.

There was a little commotion on the upper floor, and then they heard steps on the staircase. But as the hallway angled off where the stairs were, they were not able to see what was going on. A moment later they heard somebody knock on a room door

129

and the light squeaking of a door opening and closing. Then it became quiet again.

"I wonder what Heather is doing right now," Aaron rose. "I don't like her roaming around in a stranger's house all by herself."

"But I told her earlier to make herself at home," Abby tried to calm him. "She just took me at my word. Why don't you sit down again and share a glass of sherry with us?" Aaron sank back into his arm chair. "Michelle, may I get you some juice instead?"

Michelle smiled. "That would be lovely. And thank you for these delicious sandwiches." She took a tiny bite.

Abby busied herself with glasses and a carafe on the side board. Then she poured some juice from the bar fridge into a bigger glass. She handed everybody their drinks. "Here's to being safe and warm on one of Puget Sound's rare real winter nights," she toasted.

They drank in silence.

"Do your parents know where you are?" Abby broke the silence again and looked at Michelle.

"No," Michelle said and clammed up.

Ramón took one of her hands and caressed it tenderly. "Mine do. Sort of. We were talking on the phone and decided that we'd look for a room here in town instead of traveling any farther today."

"Which was wise. And Michelle's parents?"

Michelle looked warily. Ramón shook his head. "Let's say it's a mutual agreement that Michelle decide where she wanted to celebrate Christmas." He questioned her with a look, and she nodded with resigned eyes. "They didn't want her to come home."

"Didn't want her back home?" Dave asked. "Now why would that be?" He didn't get an answer. "Because of a little one on its way, isn't it?" Still no answer. "They don't know how badly some people wish to have grandchildren of their own at any price and won't ever really have them." He sighed.

Abby went to his side and laid an arm around his shoulder. "But you have me, Dave. And I'm as good as your grandchild. Right? You said so earlier today."

Dave patted her arm and smiled. But he didn't answer.

Michelle and Ramón ate their sandwiches. Aaron was sipping his sherry with his ears pitched in the direction of the hallway. And indeed, a few moments later the sound of a door opening could be heard, and a lot of commotion between upstairs and downstairs ensued. Abby felt curious herself now, as she could make out the steps of grown-ups as well as Heather's lighter tread. But she pretended to be calm and disengaged in order to keep Aaron from bearing down on his daughter.

Five minutes later, Heather returned to the front room with glowing cheeks and a beaming smile.

"Where have you been? What have you been up to?" Aaron wanted to know.

"I've just been making friends," Heather said and plopped down on a foot stool by Dave's rocking chair.

Now, the stout lady from room number 23 – Abby still wasn't quite sure where she knew her from – and Pippa appeared from the hallway as well. They were also smiling widely.

"Room number 2 is available now," Pippa announced.

"What ...?!" Abby was totally bewildered.

Aaron stared at his daughter, who was giggling behind her hand. Her mirth was contagious to the lady, who was Florence, and Pippa. They chuckled, too. But Florence caught herself quickly again. Her laughter had reminded everybody of bells.

"It is true," she said. "A Christmas elf knocked on my door a little while ago and told me about what she called a 'predicament'. And I was all ears." She winked at Heather who sat up a little straighter. "Long story short, we went to Pippa's room and asked her to move in with me – who needs twin beds when they are all alone, anyhow?! And now room number 2 with the queen bed is free."

"Heather ..." Aaron was not sure what he wanted to say to his daughter. She looked a little smug for sure. But she had also helped solve a situation in a way only a child would have been unconcerned enough whether it was proper or not.

Abby had found her speech again. "Why, Heather?! That was incredibly sweet of you to help me out!"

"It was also incredibly uncalled for," Aaron said. "You cannot go about and ask other paying guests to vacate their rooms!"

Heather shrunk. "But it hasn't caused any damage to Miss Abby, Dad. They have just moved, not vacated as in 'left'."

Aaron rolled his eyes. Having his child act in unpredictable ways was tough enough. Her being a wordsmith was an added difficulty. Abby bit her lips to stifle some merry laughter.

"Now, now," Pippa interfered. "We were only told about the situation. We were in no way asked or advised to taking any particular action." She smiled at Heather.

"Right," Florence added. "Heather only reported to me about the young couple that arrived here and was told that there was no room at *The Gull's Nest*. I think, she saw that nobody downstairs had come up with a solution so far and figured that my room was a double with a single occupant. Quite clever, don't you think?" She looked around the room.

"Still, it was none of her business," Aaron insisted.

Florence ignored him. "I asked Heather who the other guests were, and in hearing that there were two single rooms downstairs, one of them occupied by a lady, I quickly made up my mind to share my double room with her. Of course, only if she were willing."

"Which I definitely was after I'd heard the story," Pippa confirmed and smiled at Florence. "We are all grown-ups making our own decisions. Sometimes we only need a little nudge."

"You really mean to let Ramón and Michelle have your room?" Abby asked incredulous.

"Absolutely," Pippa said serenely. "Especially after I heard about the option of the garden shed that was brought up as an alternative suggestion."

"Not by us," Abby said aghast.

"I thought not," Pippa giggled. "But I simply found that too droll not to mention. Grown-ups ought to think with a child's imagination more often. We might leave the ruts we find ourselves in and discover something exciting. As to me, I haven't shared a bedroom ever since my college days way back when. And sharing it with somebody as extraordinarily generous as this lady will be certainly fun. I'm curious for the stories I might get told just because I'm in the same room with her."

"Oh, you might have to shut me up when it's getting too much," Florence smiled and her eyes twinkled. "I might regale you with stories you wouldn't believe. It truly takes all kinds of people to make a world"

"So, is it settled?" Pippa asked Abby. "May I hand these young people the key to what used to be my room?" She was already stepping towards Ramón, holding out her room key. "I didn't lie on the bed yet, and I only used the bathroom once."

Ramón looked at Abby for her approval. She nodded. Ramón took the key and heaved a big sigh of relief. "You have no idea what this means to me," he said.

"I have a slight idea," Florence smiled. "It must have felt dreadful not to know where to go. Especially in this … condition." She nodded and smiled at Michelle. "I hope it's not too forward of me to ask when you expect your little one to come?"

Michelle shook her head. Her eyes were brimming, but her smile showed that these were tears of joy. "At the end of December," she answered. "The doctor said that it could take a little longer because when they are your first, they sometimes take their time."

"Well, at least you can relax about having a bed for the night now," Dave said and smiled into his white beard.

"I'll quickly change the towels for you," Abby said. "Then you can move in as soon as you are ready." She moved toward the hallway.

"As to you, young lady," Aaron said to Heather, "you've had your big moment for now. It's bedtime for you."

"But Dad …!"

"You heard what I said."

Heather pouted and rose from her footstool. "That's not fair."

"Heather …" He handed her the key to their room.

She sighed and raised her head. Then she stomped past Michelle and Ramón. A small smile crept onto Aaron's lips as he heard his nine-year-old walk up the stairs, unlock their door, and close it again quietly. He was a bit proud of her after all. If she hadn't come up with the idea of involving other houseguests, they might have still been sitting around the fireplace wondering what to do about the young couple.

Abby returned and smiled brightly. "Your room is ready now."

Ramón had risen and shook Pippa's and Florence's hand. He was choking on words. Michelle rose heavily and hugged their two rescuers.

"Thank you," she whispered. "Thank you so much!"

Then the two of them disappeared into their room.

"All's well that ends well," Florence said and smiled. "Is this sherry you are having?" She pointed at Aaron's glass.

"Oh!" Abby was flustered. "I'm so sorry. I should have offered you some earlier!" She filled a glass for Florence. "You too?" She looked at Pippa, who shook her head.

"I'd rather take some juice, please." She dropped into the seat Michelle had just vacated.

Finally, they all were sitting. They were listening to the fire crackling in the fireplace and watching the irregular patterns it threw over the room. Nobody was speaking for a while. The snow outside was still falling thickly and densely.

"I can't get over the idea with the garden shed," Pippa suddenly said and giggled.

They all had to chuckle.

Only Abby shook her head pensively. "To think that a nine-year-old came up with the solution to *my* problem."

Chapter 11

December 23, 09:00 a.m.

The entire first floor was smelling of coffee and fried bacon. Abby was glad that somehow at least the electricity was working again. A mug of hot coffee always started her day just right, and she had dreaded that she'd have to go without one this snowy morning.

Very snowy indeed. After looking outside her kitchen window an hour ago, she had been taken aback. The pretty white picket fence that marked her property borders was almost completely buried in snow. Only its very tips pointed out of the white mass. And only by approximating a straight line from the gap that marked the entrance to her lot towards her house was she able to figure where the garden path must be. In other words: *The Gull's Nest* was snowed in.

Not that it mattered much because so was every other house on Jupiter Avenue. And so was the Avenue itself. Besides, she remembered, there was no way into or out of Wycliff anymore either. All the additional snow did was to slow the usual way of life down a bit. Okay, more than just a bit. She'd have to shovel out the house later and then see whether she'd have to accommodate her guests for other meals besides breakfast. For if the bluff stairs weren't cleared and safe to use, there would be no way for anybody to go to one of the downtown restaurants. Abby sighed and took another sip of black coffee, while she was waiting for four more slices of bread to pop out of her toaster.

"Good morning," she heard a chirpy little voice from beyond the kitchen door. It was little Heather who was looking excited and all up to adventure. "Have you seen the snow?!"

Abby laughed. "How could anybody *not* see it!"

"Just imagine! A white Christmas!" The little girl beamed at her. "Do you think it will last long enough? Till Christmas Day? May I make some snow angels in your yard later on? And would you mind if Dad and I build a snowman?"

"Heather," she heard the sonorous, slightly rebuking voice of Heather's father, Aaron. "Come over here and have some breakfast. And then stop pestering Abby. I'm sure she has a lot more on her mind than answering all your questions."

"Oh, Dad …"

She heard Heather's steps move away. Then new ones could be heard, accompanied by some lively talk and giggles. The triplets were coming downstairs. Pop! went the toaster. Just in time to place a basket of fresh warm bread onto their table by one of the windows overlooking the backyard and the roofs of Downtown below the bluff.

"Good morning," Abby greeted everybody as they passed by the kitchen door. Then she carried a tray filled with little jars of jam and honey and with a bowl of fruit over to the table.

Charlene was looking dreamily outside the window already, while Darlene was filling their cups with steaming coffee, and Starlene was discussing an embroidered center table cloth with Pippa. "Did you make this yourself?" she asked Abby.

"Heavens, no," Abby laughed. "I bought that at one of the Oberlin church bazaars a few years ago. I thought it looked festive and was not as obstructive to conversation as a floral centerpiece might be."

"It's a winter fairytale outside," Charlene remarked and turned her head towards the others now.

"Hard to believe indeed," Darlene nodded with a twinkle in her eyes. "Do you think there will ever be the slightest chance to go for a walk later?" she asked Abby.

Abby shrugged. "To be honest, I hadn't figured that it would snow this much. It must be something like three feet. I will have to dig out the garden path, while you are having breakfast. But I am not sure whether you will be able to get anywhere from there. Wycliff doesn't own any snow ploughs at all. And I have my doubts that any made it into town before the landslides yesterday."

"Hmmm," Starlene said. "Then let's enjoy breakfast and see what there is to do later. If we are stuck, so be it. But maybe, we can get someplace or other in spite of the snow." She dedicated herself to breaking off the tip of a brioche. "At least we all know that we are at a wonderfully nice place, and that the electricity has come back on. That is a lot under the circumstances."

"Can I build a snowman later?" Heather piped up from the neighboring table.

"May I …" her father corrected.

"*May* I build a snowman later?" Heather repeated, rolling her eyes.

"Oh, wouldn't that be fun?!" Pippa interjected. "I can't even remember when I built my last one."

"You don't look that old," another male voice sounded from behind her. She turned around and faced Ronald Hoffman. "Good morning, Pippa."

"And good morning to you," she answered cheerfully.

But if she had expected to get more out of him, she pretty quickly decided that he was back to his old grumpy ways again. He took a set of dishes from one table and moved to a tiny table in a niche that was not set for service. Then he helped himself to some breakfast essentials and dropped into a chair, his back to everybody else, and started to read a book. Every once in a while, he guided a slice of bread or his coffee cup to his face without ever looking up.

Another door snapped shut, and Roger and Kathy entered the breakfast area. Kathy was beaming. "And isn't this the perfect day to knit some mittens, socks, and hats for ourselves?" she suggested, while Roger was smiling into the round quietly and nodded his greetings to everybody present. They walked over to a table set for two and soon were quietly engaged in conversation.

"Is knitting very difficult?" Kathy was startled, as Heather had silently stepped up to their table and used a small break in their talk to put her question.

"No, not at all," Kathy smiled. "Everybody can learn it."

"Can you knit, too?" Heather wondered and looked at Roger.

He smiled gently. "Why, yes! And it is real fun. You will have to try our circular knitting machine sometime today."

"A circular knitting machine?"

"It's a little like magic," he said mysteriously, and his eyes twinkled in his otherwise solemn face.

"Oh, I love magic," Heather said with enthusiasm. Then she looked over her shoulder. Aaron was watching her with increasing exasperation. "Maybe I need to be with my Dad now," she explained. "But I'd love to knit with that circular magic machine later."

"Well, just knock on our door. If we are in, we'll show you how," Kathy smiled.

"Your daughter is quite the talker, isn't she?" Ronald grumbled at Aaron, his head turned sideways from behind his book.

"And don't I know it?!" Aaron sighed. "I sometimes wonder whose genes she got. They are surely not mine."

Heather had overheard him and was looking down at her pants and giggled. "You are so silly, Daddy. Of course, they are not your jeans. I'd drown in them. Just imagine!" And she giggled some more.

Aaron almost choked on a bite of bagel, and even Ronald's grim face lit up with amusement for a moment.

142

"Maybe you sit down again and have the rest of your breakfast," Aaron said to his daughter. "You will need to feed all that energy well if you plan to build a snowman, do snow angels, and learn how to knit later."

Heather sat down obediently and bit in her PB & J sandwich that her dad had just made for her.

For a moment, quiet settled in the breakfast room that was filled by the bright reflection of the snow outside. The clinking of cutlery and cups set on saucers and the soft rumbling of a burning log sliding into a new position in the fireplace were the only sounds to be heard.

"I will be outside to clear the garden path," Abby announced. "If anybody needs anything, please, let me know. I'll be glad to help you."

The front door fell into its lock behind her, and a moment later there was the sound of a snow shovel on the steps of the front porch.

"Well," Aaron said to Heather. "I guess I better lend her a hand. It can be quite hard to shovel a path. What with this height of snow she might be just glad for anybody helping out."

"Well," Ronald observed from the neighboring table without even turning around, but quickly downing the rest of his coffee. "That makes two of us."

"Aren't you the perfect gentlemen?!" Pippa observed with a beaming smile.

143

Ronald rose und shook his head. "Takes more than a snow shovel to turn a man into one."

Dave, who already sat in his rocking chair by the fireplace, chortled. "I sure know that I got my fingers slapped and my hide tanned before any lady told me I was one, for sure."

Everybody chuckled. Heather tugged at Aaron's sweater sleeve. "Why do they all laugh?"

"Ah Heather, my girl," Aaron said. "It means that sometimes a lot of work goes into success. And sometimes somebody else puts in as much effort as you do to help you along."

Heather eyed him with a knowing look. "Like when I bake a cake and you clean up the kitchen because I messed it up. But the cake is really good?"

Aaron massaged his chin, trying to stay serious. "Something like that." He rose. "Ready, pumpkin? We better wrap you up warm."

Heather nodded and followed him upstairs. The other guests also left, one after the other. The smell of hot coffee and toast lingered in the air for a while longer.

An hour later, Ronald, Aaron, and Abby had managed to carve a path into the snow, creating a line from the porch towards the garden gate. The snowy masses piled even higher where it had been shoveled aside, and Aaron wasn't sure that snow angels were such a good idea after all. Heather pouted.

"How about we build a snowman instead?" he asked her.

"Will you really help me?" she asked dubiously. She knew that he had just performed some hard work.

"Well, maybe you ask Ms. Whatshername whether she is still interested in joining you." Aaron scanned the house with hopeful eyes, but nobody inside was stirring.

"You mean Pippa," Heather stated.

"Probably." He looked at her warily. "How do you even know everybody's name?"

"I ask," Heather replied and started towards the house. "And they tell me."

Ronald had overheard the conversation while he was strewing sand onto the cleared path. He chuckled. "Seems that some things are way easier for kids than we grown-ups think they are. I wonder why that is."

Abby wiped her sweaty brow under her thick woolen cap. "It's because we overthink whether it is the done thing half of the time. It's like when we are facing a piece of chocolate and start debating whether we should have it or not. Guess what a child would do!" She looked at Aaron, then winked at Ronald, and marched back to the house. "Apropos chocolate – how about I'll make us something to warm ourselves up along with some nice cookies to recover from our work?"

The men's sweet tooth didn't need any further temptation. They fell in step behind her and followed her inside.

*

Ramón had waited until the breakfast room was empty. Michelle had had a restless night and kept him awake for most of the time. Apart from not being used to share a bed with her and feeling every movement of hers on his side of the mattress, his thoughts had been wreaking havoc with him. To share a room with the woman he coveted. To share a bed with her even though it was in an entirely platonic way. There seemed to be an incessant train of thought in his brain about what his future might or might not hold and if it contained Michelle. And her baby. Because Michelle would not come alone. It was either her *and* the child or nothing. Was he ready to step into such a situation? Was his love for Michelle strong enough? In the end he must have fallen asleep.

When he left the room, Michelle was stirring slightly. So, Ramón picked breakfast for two from the breakfast room. He scanned the kitchen and found a tray on which to place juice, coffee, some bagels, butter, jam, some – now cold – fried bacon and some hardboiled eggs, a cup of fruit yogurt, and a bowl of mixed fruit. He carried it back to their room and found Michelle sitting in bed, very pale and slightly upset.

"Are you alright?" he asked, setting the tray down on a nightstand, and felt like an idiot immediately. Very obviously she was not alright.

"I'm not sure," she said. "I'm feeling quite weird."

"As in sick?"

"Not really. Different."

"Is it the baby?"

"I guess."

He nodded. Of course, how would she know? She had never had a baby before. And even if she told him any details about what felt wrong with her – how would *he* know what that meant?! He wasn't a doctor.

"Do you need to see a doctor?" he asked nervously. And in the next moment he held out a glass of juice to her. "Want to drink some?"

Michelle laughed, then winced. "Ouch, that hurt."

"Is your baby coming?"

"I'm not sure. It shouldn't. But my back hurts like hell, and the kicking inside doesn't help a lot either."

"Doesn't sound like fun." Ramón felt helpless. He started busying himself with cutting up a bagel.

"Getting a child is not supposed to," Michelle said.

"What?" Ramón was totally out of his comfort zone. He hadn't even registered what she was saying.

"Forget it," Michelle said.

"I could go and ask Abby whether she can arrange for a doctor."

"It's way too early." Michelle shook her head.

"But how do you know?"

"Trust me, I know." Michelle looked at the fruit. "Save me some of the strawberries." She clumsily moved out of bed and waddled to the bathroom. "Gosh, I'll be glad when this elephantine time is over." She closed the door behind her, and

147

Ramón began to pick every single strawberry out of the fruit mix and arranged them onto a plate.

"In fact, we might ask about a doctor," Michelle's voice came through the bathroom door. "Just to be on the safe side." She came out again. Ramón sat in a chair motionless. "I mean, it's not supposed to come any time before New Year's Eve. But I have my doubts that babies know about calendars. – Ouch!" She dropped onto her bedside again.

Ramón pushed the plate of strawberries towards her. "Does it hurt badly?" he asked with worry in his eyes. "Are you supposed to start counting between your pains?"

Michelle looked at him and suddenly had to giggle. "How many bad movies about giving birth have you been watching?" Ramón blushed. "Sorry, Ramón! I mean, the back pain is just constant, and the kicking is more often than not, and then there is a new pain I haven't had before. And I simply cannot keep track about which is which and what it all means." She begged him with her eyes. "Maybe if you just leave me in the room for a while and do something by yourself? I don't think I will be good company today."

Ramón nodded. "Sure. But I will stay around. Just in case you need me. Okay?"

Michelle smiled softly. "Do something nice. Remember, this is entirely my own business. You shouldn't be making it yours."

"But you are my friend," he said, and his eyes fleetingly betrayed that she was ever so much more.

Michelle discovered it though. "Friends still have a right to their own private lives."

Ramón swayed his head. "You are certainly right in a way. But if it weren't for me, you'd not be stuck in a snowed-in town. You'd be ..."

"... at a dorm at an empty university campus with nobody around who cared at all," Michelle finished the sentence for him. "I'm much better off here. It's a cozy place. So, no worries. Just give me a little space and the chance to pity myself some."

"If you are sure..."

Michelle made some shoving movements with her hands, and Ramón complied. He softly closed the door. Outside in the hallway he took a deep breath.

"Are you alright, son?"

Ramón was startled. He hadn't realized that the Santa Claus-like man from last night had come up from behind. "Sure," he stammered. "It's just nerves."

"All first-time fathers are nervous wrecks," the man chuckled.

"I'm sure nervous," Ramón answered. "But I'm not the father."

Chapter 12

December 23, 11:00 a.m.

Florence had had a wonderful night of deep, relaxed sleep behind her. When her roommate, Pippa, had risen around eight, she hadn't been asleep anymore, but she hadn't been in a mood to make conversation. So, she kept her eyes closed and pretended she was still asleep. The bed was comfy, the air was smelling seductively of fried bacon, toast, and coffee, and she simply wanted to enjoy that for the one time she was not on a schedule. She guessed that, by now, Manfredo had his panties – or probably rather his fashionable boxer shorts – in a knot. It was just a dry-run they had planned, after all, and anything could happen today.

When Pippa had closed the door behind her, Florence sighed with pleasure and turned in her pillows. The first light of day was showing through the window, and it had that specific quality that snow lends to it – a somewhat bluish tinge. Wasn't it wonderful that nobody seemed to have an idea who she was? Though Abby seemed to second-guess herself, Florence was pretty sure that in giving her name as "Flo" hadn't revealed too much about herself, and the name Piccolini didn't seem to ring a bell either. Just to stay in a pretty place like this and not to be recognized …

Shortly before the breakfast hours were over, Florence made her way downstairs. She grabbed a slice of toast and a banana. The coffee was smelling thick and burnt by now, but the tea tray held some interesting options, and the hot water carafe was still filled to the top. Abby was just coming in, her hair glued to her brow under her knitted cap, her face glowing.

"Good morning, Flo," she said a little breathlessly and rubbed her hands. "The garden path is usable again. Just in case you'd like to snatch some breath of fresh air later on."

Florence smiled. "In fact, I had planned to go downtown and check out some of the places I missed out on yesterday."

"Good for you." Abby tossed her cap onto a hat rack by the door and slipped out of her boots. "I hope you have sturdy shoes?"

Florence nodded. "I came well prepared though I had forgotten what the weather would be like around here in winter. Now, I remember that the lowlands rarely see any snow. But I'm glad I thought because it was that close to Canada that I needed to take a North Pole explorer's worth of wardrobe along." She laughed, again with this bell-like quality, and bit off the tip of the banana she had been peeling while talking.

"Well, it certainly is a surprise to us, too," Abby admitted. "Would you like any bacon or eggs? I can quickly make you some."

Florence shook her head and swallowed. "My own fault to come downstairs so late. But I have to admit I really enjoyed my room and just sleeping in on a day like this."

Before she ventured out, she felt her conscience pricking her, though. She ought to call Manfredo again. Therefore, she went to her room once more and speed-dialed her impresario's number. He picked up at the first ring, as usual.

"Ah, Flo!" he exclaimed. "Does this mean you are on your way to Seattle?"

Florence sighed. "I'm sorry, Manfredo. Nowhere near. In fact, this morning looks worse than last night, although it has stopped snowing for now."

"So, did they put their snow ploughs to work in that town, what's its name?"

"Wycliff. And no, there are no snow ploughs. People are shoveling each other out. In fact, we are glad to have electricity back this morning. As to transport – I can't see even a single car driving through the neighborhood." She gazed out of her window and saw Mr. White and his little daughter building a snowman in the front yard. Jupiter Avenue was a fairy-tale in white with gardens sunk deep into the snow.

"So, no dry-run. I get it," Manfredo whined. "I guess it's not that important. You've given interviews before. Will you be here in time for the actual broadcast at the radio station?"

"That's why I'm calling, Manfredo. You will have to cancel for me. No, hear me out," she cut into the gush of protest that came through her receiver. "There is simply no way to get out of town, neither today nor probably tomorrow. So, you might cancel my appearance at the Christmas gala as well."

"You are sounding almost gleeful!" he accused her.

"I'm not," Florence lied. "I had really planned on being with you in Seattle on time for everything. But I'm simply not able to do so. So, please, convey my apologies to everybody for the inconveniences and the disappointment. I'll make up for it some other time."

"There might not be another time," Manfredo warned. "You don't simply ditch such opportunities. Being a diva only gets you this far, especially on such occasions."

"I sure hope that people don't think of me as a diva," Florence said and actually felt a little hurt.

"Well, they might about your no-show."

"Then tell them about Wycliff being cut off from the world. Maybe that distracts at least the radio station. They might even send out their helicopters for reporting on it. As to the Christmas gala – they will have me pay that penalty, and some of my colleagues will sing a couple more encores. In the end, my failure to travel with you for one single day …"

"… which has turned into more than one now …"

"Right, but it will be water under the bridge. By the end of January, nobody will care to remember."

Manfredo sighed. "Is that your last word?"

"Has to be." Florence rolled her eyes. "Now, be my saving hero and walk into the lions' dens to tell them about my situation. Will you? And dine out somewhere nice tonight – my treat." Then she hung up.

A bit later, Florence was trudging across the garden path and picking her way carefully towards the stairs down the bluff. Somebody had actually taken care of those, cleared them of snow, and strewn a new layer of salt. So, Florence found herself encouraged to venture downtown and explore what she had missed out on the day before. *Main Gallery* was a point of interest to her, and she contemplated the impressionist painting of a Washington barn. Or, maybe, she should get an abstract bronze sculpture for Manfredo? He certainly deserved a Christmas gift for all the care he took of her and all the worries she caused him.

Finally, she felt drawn to the windows of *La Boutique*, an elaborately decorated store for ladies' attires. The shop windows had all a theme of whites and light blues and were sparkling with supersized snowflakes and artificial snow on the bottom. Inside, the rich red velvet tones, chandeliers, a grandfather clock and a gilded fauteuil set a matching tone of thoughtfulness.

"Good morning," a beautiful tall lady greeted Florence. Her hair was done Regency style, and her olive skin was set off by a slim dress in a shade of muted mauve. "Feel free to browse, and if you need anything, please, let me know." Then she withdrew behind her glass counter that displayed vintage precious and costume jewelry.

Florence started going through the racks. Not that she needed anything. But if an item "spoke" to her, she was ready to buy it. She enjoyed to touch the brittle tulles and sleek silks, the knobbiness of some boucle-woolen jackets, and the unique feel of

154

an appliquéd felt coat. She loved the way the store was organized into color schemes – that made it so much easier for her to find something that matched her wardrobe.

And then she gasped. On an antique sideboard with open drawers displaying shawls, scarves, caps, and gloves, her eyes were caught by a peculiarly shaped handbag. She walked over and picked it up to inspect it more closely. It was a beautiful brocade evening pompadour in golds and greens, its silken strings serving as its seal as well as its handles. A label read "Bags 4 Choosers", one that she had never heard of before. She turned the bag upside down and found that the bottom was doubled, and a zipper provided access to a separate compartment such as for a handkerchief, a money bill, a ticket, or a credit card. Or all of these. Florence grew cold and pale. Her heart started racing.

"Could I sit somewhere, please?" she asked faintly.

Margaret, that was the boutique owner's name, came rushing towards her, worry in her face. "Are you alright, Ma'am?" she asked and led her potential customer to the Regency fauteuil near the counter. "May I bring you a glass of water?"

Florence shook her head. "No, thank you." She sat in silence for a moment and breathed in slowly and deeply. Then she held up the handbag. "This … who made it?"

Margaret smiled. "It's quaint, isn't it? It's a local company called *Bags 4 Choosers*. Basically, it's cottage industry. All the cloth totes you see around town are made by them.

Custom-printed, of course. And then they started a line of sturdier totes and individual handbags."

"I saw the label," Florence smiled weakly. "But who is the designer?"

"Oh, I can only make a guess there," Margaret said. "Because there are actually two of them. But I suppose that this is a design by Angela Fortescue."

"Angela Fortescue." Florence closed her eyes.

"Do you know her?"

"I do, in a way. It has been a while."

Margaret nodded. "I'm sure that if you brought in a fabric of your own to match a particular item of yours, she'd create something spectacular for you."

"I'm sure," Florence said. Another pause. "Is she around town over Christmas?"

Margaret smiled. "I'm pretty sure she is. After all, she and her partner, Thora Byrd Thompson, have organized a Christmas party for their staff, tonight."

"Where is it going to be?" Florence asked.

"It's at the banquet room of *The Ship Hotel*. You know where that is? But, I'm afraid, it's by invitation only."

"Oh, sure," Florence smiled. "What's her business address then?"

"I'm not sure I ought to give it to you. Let me make a call and ask her whether it's alright for you to go there. After all, she is working from home, just like her cutters and seamstresses do."

"I see."

Margaret gave Florence a curt, friendly nod and went for her old-fashioned desk phone. "Hello, Angela? ... And merry Christmas to you, dear. ... No, everything is fine. Listen, I have a potential customer here who says she knows you and would like to talk to you. It's about one of your clever pompadours, I guess. ... So, I'll just send her over to you? ... Alright. Thanks." And she hung up. "She's expecting you. Let me describe where to go."

Margaret fetched a town map from her office behind a velvet curtain and spread it across the counter. "We are here. Angela's place is also on Main Street, but way towards the Harbor Mall. It might be somewhat tough to walk there. I think shuttle services are still down." She peered outside and found that, indeed, Main Street was only for pedestrians this morning. "Don't show her that you are appalled by where she is living. It's those housing projects near the wharves. She has her pride, you know. But the outside of her home is nowhere near to what she has made of it on the inside."

"I'd never dare criticize anybody for where they live or how they live," Florence assured Margaret. "I'd hate to hurt somebody. After all, all riches in the world don't necessarily make you a mindful person either, right?"

Margaret smiled. "I hope she can help you with the fabric you would like her to work with," she said.

Florence smiled vaguely. "I'm not creative in the crafts section myself. But I sure have some design in mind." She thanked

Margaret, bought an elegant vintage brooch that would go perfectly with a summer linen costume of hers, and left the store.

Outside, she found that her hands were shaking. No, not just her hands. Her entire self was in an uproar. She wasn't sure it was right to create what would be a huge big change in her life. And in Angela Fortescue's. She was choking with anticipation. But then a sense of determination had her move in the direction of the Harbor Mall. If she had been meant to be in Wycliff at this time of year and under such circumstances, who was she to question Fate?! And that Fate had sent her across the peculiarly designed brocade pompadour was certainly more than mere coincidence. She was meant to meet the designer.

The snow was getting deeper and deeper, the farther she walked out of town. Hardly anybody cared about the sidewalks here. Who would walk to the wharves anyhow? Business there meant coming with trucks and trailers. The neighborhood became visibly less fancy. And then, there was the housing project, a collection of more or less rickety homes. They were not trailer homes – that would probably have been against the architectural policies of the Victorian town. But the cottages with their narrow front porches, flaking paint and sinking doorsteps showed listlessness as to maintenance and little caring about the people who were living there. At least they had ploughed the court from which the homes were branching off.

Florence took a deep breath. Then she approached the cottage with the number that Margaret had given her. She stomped off the snow on the porch steps and was just reaching for the bell button when the door opened as if by itself.

A thin lady with carefully coiffed hair in an incredibly deep shade of red and quite youthful clothing stood in the doorway. She gazed at Florence. Then her eyes widened. Her chin fell. Then she simply said: "You?"

Florence nodded. "May I come in … Mother?"

Chapter 13

December 23, 03:00 p.m.

"Have you seen Starlene?" Darlene asked her sister Charlene. They were both sitting next to each other on a sofa facing the fireplace, its jolly flames dancing up and down.

Pippa, who sat in an arm chair kitty corner from them, thought it was almost like looking at one and the same person talking to her mirror reflection. Only that, of course, Darlene wore green and Charlene wore blue. From head to toe in different shades complementing each other, but none the less green and blue only. "I think she went out after our lunch snack," Pippa said.

Abby had indeed provided some quickly improvised soup and sandwich meal for everybody. After that Charlene and Darlene had gone upstairs. So had Pippa. A nap on a day on which you simply couldn't do anything seemed to be in order. Only Starlene hadn't come up with them. And after a while Pippa had dozed off.

"But where would she have gone?" Darlene asked with bewildered eyes. "There is not anything remotely interesting up here."

"Except the museum, of course," Charlene stated.

"And that is closed for the season," Pippa replied. "No, I think she hinted she wanted to go downtown."

"But in this dreadful snow!" Charlene exclaimed.

"Well," Dave said from the rocker he was occupying again, holding a mug of steaming spiced cider, "apparently some people have started building snow shoveling brigades. Abby said her friend Dottie from the German deli had asked whether anybody at her Bed & Breakfast was willing to join in. Aaron, Ronald, and that young man, Raoul ..."

"Ramón," Pippa corrected.

"Yes, that's whom I mean. Ramón. Well, they went outside and met some people on Jupiter Avenue to have a go at least at all the sidewalks. Abby said that most of the males of Wycliff and all those stranded are trying to get things running within the town limits."

"Wouldn't that be great?" Pippa said and clapped her hands together with delight. "I hadn't planned to stay here for Christmas Eve, of course. But wouldn't it be wonderful to be here in time for the caroling at Town Hall?!"

"Let's see whether that will happen at all," Darlene said skeptically. "They have to clear and de-ice all the downhill paths and stairs. I don't see that happen."

"Well, at least Starlene seems to have found a way to stay away from being cooped up with us," Charlene shrugged. "I just wonder whether we are missing any fun."

The front door opened and the three women turned their heads toward it. At first, they only stared. Then Charlene gasped. "Oh no! Tell me I am seeing what I think I'm seeing!"

161

"Pinch me hard," Darlene answered, and her sister complied. "Ouch, not so hard. But yes, it is true! – Starlene, what have you done?!"

Starlene looked at her sisters and then gave Pippa a big wink. "Sometimes a girl has got to do what a girl has got to do." She twirled around. "How do you like my new look?"

"You are looking stunning," Pippa gushed.

"What happened?" Dave wanted to know. It was one of those moments when he was frustrated that his eyesight had gone. One of those moments when all the fun was happening visually, and explaining it would ruin half of it.

"I went to the hairdresser and got my bob cut into a pixie," Starlene answered cheerfully. "Also, I had her put in some highlights."

"That sounds pretty nice," Dave stated.

"And then," Starlene paused for effect. "I bought myself an entire set of new clothes – and guess what! None of it is anywhere near red."

"Ah, I remember Abby told me that you were doing color schemes," Dave chuckled. "So, you are the one in red."

"*Was*," Starlene stated, twirled around some more, and plopped into another armchair.

"You can't simply do this without consulting us about this," Darlene said almost indignantly. "This is against everything that we are used to. What people are used to."

"I don't think we need to do what people expect us to do," Starlene smiled brightly. "They have been lucky so far. But now I finally want to do what I feel like doing. I want to be myself. And that excludes the color red."

"Ever again?!" Charlene gasped.

"I don't know. Maybe for the time being."

"But red was always the color by which you were identified," Darlene frowned.

"Yes, indeed. And isn't that strange?" Starlene pointed at her sister. "Just because you have been assigned the color green at birth, does that mean you have to wear green until you die? Maybe have green flower arrangements on your coffin, so people know that it's you who is inside and not me?"

"I like my greens," Darlene protested.

"Well, good for you! But I am not wearing red because I'm Starlene and my mom found it fun to assign color schemes to us. It's just like I'm not ever going to wear baby-pink to show people that I am a woman. It's the female that makes a woman. It's myself who makes Starlene. I am fed up being labeled because somebody has seen fit to."

"That sounds like you are quite bitter," Dave dared to put in, facing in her direction.

"Well, let's say that much," Starlene answered. "I've been playing along for way too long. At first it was for our kindergarten and school teachers that we wore the colors. Later we had fun changing colors and bewildering people. But let's face it – we are way too old for such games. I feel like a circus attraction turning up with my sisters in color-schemed outfits. It's ridiculous that we have people staring at us. We are all grown-ups, and we all have our own traits. Why not live them?"

"But why now?" Charlene asked.

"You mean why not earlier or why not later?" Starlene bit her lower lip and looked pensive. "Perhaps being stuck in a place without the option of moving anywhere outside the town limits made me realize that I still have the option to push my *own* limits. That it is not a hairstyle or a color that I need to be defined by ever again. That if I want to learn to play the piano or hike Mt. Rainier, I can still go for it."

"You want to learn to play the piano?" Darlene asked surprised.

"As much as I want to climb Mt. Rainier," Starlene said and enjoyed her sisters' flabbergasted faces. Then she laughed. "Duh! You ought to know me better. But these were just examples. I have found that I have been sticking to expectations way too much and way too long. I found that I even made other people's expectations my own! Now, isn't that eerie?!"

"I'm not sure, but … would you mind if I dipped into greens and reds, too?" Charlene asked her sisters cautiously. "I *do* seem a bit tired of my blues of late."

"There you go," Starlene said triumphantly. "And I bet some accents of other colors and patterns would do wonders to you."

164

"Don't expect to dip into my wardrobe," Darlene said stiffly. "I have to get used to your ... wild ways."

Charlene and Starlene stared at their sister. Then they burst into a gale of laughter. "Wild ways!" they howled.

Dave had a hard time not to chuckle aloud, too. He just cleared his throat and said, "So the snow has been good for something at least."

Starlene became serious again. "I guess so. It's not anything that I was really aware of until I just felt the urge to go and simply change things."

"But how did you get downtown?" Pippa asked. "We thought everything was still snowed in."

"Oh no," Starlene smiled. "Town Hall has worked some small miracles. I have come across ever so many groups shoveling through snow and clearing the access to Downtown. Unless it starts snowing heavily again, we should be pretty good to go and have some nice dinner in town tonight."

"Oh good," Pippa said delighted. "I had so hoped to join the caroling at Town Hall tomorrow, too."

"It is certainly enjoyable," Dave said and nodded pensively. "You will love how every window of the building is lit with candles and the balcony is decked with fir garlands." His face turned wistful at the memories from times when he had still been able to see.

"Let us take you along," Starlene suggested.

"Ah, an old man like me would only be a burden and an embarrassment." All the ladies protested loudly. He lifted his hands. "Besides I already promised Abby to spend Christmas Eve with her. She is going through a ..." He realized with embarrassment that he had almost blabbed out a secret of the heart. He rose. "Time to get my limbs moving a little. Ladies ..." And he went towards the hallway to get to his room.

"Well, that sounded more like a retreat than anything else," Starlene wondered.

"He might have accidentally slipped into talking about something more private than he wanted to air," Pippa nodded. "He doesn't strike me as a gossip. He might be deeply worried about something because it seemed to come out of nowhere." She shook her head. "Not really out of nowhere, of course. But Abby seems to be like a grandchild to him, if you know what I mean."

The four of them sat quiet for a while, musing and staring into the flames of the fireplace. Outside it was turning dark, but the kind of bluish dark that snow and moonlight create.

A door in the hallway snapped shut, and the patter of little feet on hardwood floors was heard.

"Pippa!" Heather cried out joyfully, as she entered the lobby and approached the group. "Look at what I made!" She produced a beautiful woolen hat of different hues of pink and purple and held it out to be admired.

Pippa took it and raised her brows. "That looks pretty awesome, Heather! Don't tell me you did it all by yourself!"

"But I did," Heather insisted and beamed. "Well, of course, Roger had to get it started for me because I had no idea at all how to put the first round of the yarn into the machine. But after that it was absolutely magic! I just cranked and cranked, and the hat came together like – poof!" Her thin arms flew in the air, and her face was glowing. "And then Kathy helped me finish it off. But it only took an hour. And now I have the perfect hat to go with my purple coat!"

"That is really impressive," said Charlene. "I wish I could do this, too."

"But you could," Heather said. "You just have to go and ask. I'm pretty sure they'd show you. If you want me to, I'll go right back and ask …"

Pippa handed the hat back to Heather. "It might really be a good idea," she stated quietly. "Has anybody seen that young woman who arrived here last night? She must have stayed in her room all day, while that young man of hers was out with the shoveling crews. I have a feeling she is not happy with her situation. At least she didn't look it last night."

"Probably not. She's obviously quite near her date," Darlene guessed. "Can't be too comfortable in any position or in any company. But what does that have to do with knitting?"

Pippa smiled mysteriously. "To knit for somebody means to give them some love and thought. Most people realize that when they get something home-knit. Or anything homemade at all. And sometimes it doesn't even have to be perfection, but the love that went into the item is all that counts. I feel this young girl could use some love without the crowding in."

Suddenly Heather jumped. "I know what you mean! You don't mean to knit for her, but for her baby, right?"

"Wouldn't that be a nice project for an evening we might otherwise just be spending in front of the TV screen?" Pippa suggested.

"I don't know," Charlene said hesitatingly. "I have never been good at any needlework."

"Not true," Starlene said. "You didn't like doing it, but your stitches were as even as anybody's."

Charlene blushed. "Maybe you are right. It was because we got graded for it in school and I never got my projects finished and barely earned my Ds. Besides, some of the things we had to make were downright unimaginative, and I remember that puke-green woolen yarn grandma had left over from some wartime sock knitting bee. Ugh."

They all laughed, and Heather chirped, "Puke-green. Gross!"

"Well, it made sense back then," Pippa said. "Actually, it would have been any kind of olive hue probably. A lot of women who had loved ones in the war – fathers, husbands, sons – would knit socks for them to keep their feet dry and warm. Charlene's grandfather probably fought in World War I, right?" Charlene nodded. "It was wet in the trenches. And the war lasted for years and years."

"That long?" Heather was awed.

"It was disastrous." Pippa nodded. "And the women sent their thoughts and prayers in the shape of hand-knit items – mittens and socks, scarves even – in the hope that their loved ones would get them to keep them warm and tell them that they were loved."

"Did they get Christmas packages?"

"I don't know," Pippa said.

"I will have to ask Kathy and Roger whether they have some pretty yarns for the baby then," Heather decided. "Not puke-green!" And off she went towards the Johansens' door.

"It never occurred to me that was the reason for the color," Charlene said pensively. "I never asked my grandmother about it. And she never told."

"Well, I guess Heather has a gift about asking people the right things at the right time," Starlene smiled. "It never occurred to me either. The ugly yarn just seemed to come from an endless supply. Of course, Grandma wouldn't talk about it. It was a constant reminder that she lost Grandpa to the war."

"Was he killed in Flanders?" Pippa asked softly.

"Worse," Darlene said. "He got shot down and went missing in action."

Pippa bit her lips. "That *is* worse. Imagine you never have the certainty that he got a Christian burial. That there is no gravesite to visit."

"Or that they are still alive and you don't know where or how." Charlene wiped away a tear that had slid from her left eye.

"Happy thoughts!" Starlene said overly brightly. "Somebody is coming back, and we should talk more Christmassy topics."

Heather bounced back through the hallway. "Roger says they have some real pretty pastel colored yarns. And that he will ask at the craft store for some of their stash, too, tomorrow."

"Well, it's all set then," Charlene smiled and patted the seat next to her. "Why don't you sit with us and tell us what *you* have on your wish list for Christmas."

Heather lost her impetus almost immediately, but slid into the place next to the triplet, slumping her shoulders. Her face, so happy only a few moments ago, was frowning, her eyes had turned dark. "Nobody in the world can give me that wish," she said quietly. "And I don't really want anything else."

Starlene could have slapped herself. Here she had thought that her question would trigger a waterfall of silly little girl's dreams, such as pink unicorns and a hairdressing kit for dolls, a Barbie house and riding or ballet lessons, a date night with her daddy or a trip to Disneyland. She had envisioned bright, dreamy eyes and merry chatter. Instead the little girl had drooped like a flower and withdrawn into a zone she didn't know how to enter safely.

"What is it that you think nobody can give you back?" Pippa asked quietly.

Heather bit her lips, and tears filled her eyes. "A home," she said in a very low voice.

"But you do have a home, right? Where do you live?"

"In Eatonville."

"Is it a pretty home?"

Heather nodded vigorously. Then she hung her head again. "But it's only a house now."

Pippa bit her lips. Her heart ached for the little girl. "But your dad is such a nice and caring dad, isn't he?"

Heather nodded. "But he has changed so much," she whispered. "I just want him back as he was when Mommy was still alive."

Charlene was quietly weeping now. Starlene was choking on a big lump in her throat. Darlene rose and walked over to a window to look outside.

"He is still that same daddy," Pippa said quietly.

"He is not," Heather insisted. "He is constantly making me feel I'm doing something wrong. Even when we are having fun, he suddenly looks at me as if I'm doing something wrong again."

Pippa swayed her head. "Give your daddy a chance, sweetie. I'm pretty sure he is only worried that something might happen to you. You are the best thing he has in his life now. And he needs to guard you doubly."

"You think?" Heather asked. "But sometimes he doesn't say anything at all. He comes home and ..." She swallowed hard.

"Everything feels so empty without Mommy." And then she simply started crying.

Great, thought Starlene. Exactly *not* what I intended.

"You know," Pippa said to Heather, and it was hard for her to get the words out and to seem calm. "It must be so much worse for your daddy. He has been relying on your mommy all the time. And now he must feel exhausted what with taking over her part as well and constantly questioning himself what she would have done. Think of the last thing he has done with you that your mommy wouldn't have."

"He made a snowman with me this morning."

"There you go."

"And he wanted to give me an extra-special Christmas outing to Wycliff."

"Well, and hasn't it turned out extra-extra-special?" Heather nodded and wiped her face. "He cares, sweetie. And I'm sure he is trying very, very hard to make a home for you even if right now it might not feel much like one. But think about it – he comes back from work to a house only, too. Have you done your part to make it a home for him?"

Heather twisted her thumbs and focused her eyes on them. "I'm not sure how."

Pippa smiled at her. "With trust and love, sweetie. Trust him to try his best and give him your love even when you are not sure he feels it all the time. Maybe sometimes he will stay quiet. But believe me: He will feel it."

Nobody heard the retreat of steps in the hallway towards the stairs nor the desperate little sob that escaped from lips that had been pressed together tightly, while the little girl had been unburdening her sorrows and the older woman had been offering her solace. Ah, how Aaron wished that Olivia was back in their lives!

Chapter 14

December 23, 07:00 p.m.

Abby also had been out that afternoon, after all. She had had to leave the house. She had felt she had a bad case of cabin fever. She had thought she had seen Florence and, later, Starlene venture out. And what two of her guests were able to do was certainly not beyond her capabilities either. She had dressed herself warmly, donned an extra pair of socks, and left the house to take a stroll through the wintry neighborhood.

The trees had been loaded with heavy snow. Quite a few branches had broken off under the unusual load. One tree in a garden had actually toppled over under the heavy snow. Abby had thought it a pity. It had been an ancient apple tree that had always caught her eyes in spring when it was in blossom, a pinkish white miracle, a haven for the bees. Now it would be chopped into fire wood and never blossom again. Well, maybe it had been too old to withstand nature any longer – and if it had been rotting from the inside, it would have had to be taken down, anyhow. Still, what a pity!

The sidewalk had been cleared well enough, and even the staircase towards Downtown had been usable again. Abby hadn't picked her way into town, though, but decided she'd visit with her friend Izzy. Izzy was the custodian of the Historical Museum of Wycliff, which had only recently managed to purchase the huge old Hammersmith Villa across from the bluff stairs as the new museum location. Due to all the work that included accessioning the new museum items inside and arranging the old ones alongside them in a way that made sense, Izzy had been overly busy for the past weeks. And there was a certain gentleman who owned the "Birds and Seeds" store who had started paying her a lot of attention in ways that were leading into something that deserved the beautifully old-fashioned term of courtship. Now that Abby was stuck in town over Christmas, she might at least spend her time in visiting her friend for an hour or two before everybody got caught up in their own private holiday schedules.

Izzy had had surprise written all over her face when she saw Abby as she was opening the door. "I thought you'd said you'd be out of town and up in Seattle to celebrate Christmas with …"

"Well, I'm not," Abby had said curtly. "And I'm not happy about it, believe me."

"Want to come in?" Izzy had held the door widely open, and Abby had stepped in, then taken off her boots in the hallway of the cozy cottage Izzy had inherited from her grandmother. "Want some tea?"

"That sounds good," Abby had said. Then she had followed her friend into the kitchen. "Tell me – what would you do in my situation?"

"What situation? Is there a situation?" Izzy had asked with the tiniest twinkle in her gray eyes.

Maybe it was just the reflection of her glasses after all. Abby had never been sure when her friend was teasing her. "How do you mean?"

"Well," Izzy had turned around from the electric tea kettle she had just filled with water. "I thought that there was no situation at all anymore. You have separated, right? Hank is up in Seattle. You are down here. As far as I remember he left you for somebody else, and he hasn't been in touch with you ever since. That is what I'd call a clear non-situation."

Abby had hung her head. "And it feels dreadful."

"Sure," Izzy had said sympathetically and laid an arm around her friend's shoulders to lead her out into the living room that was overlooking a very wintry garden today. "That's what Christmas does to you when you have been dreaming of celebrating it with somebody and end up all on your own."

"But you have always been alone until now."

"Exactly. Do you think that makes you dream less and makes you feel less lonesome during 'the most wonderful time of the year'?!"

"I never thought of it that way," Abby had said and looked at her friend ruefully. "I didn't even once invite you over for the holidays. I always thought you had plans of your own."

Izzy had nodded and plopped into an armchair by the fireplace. "Of course, I always had plans. Because I made them. Do you think it would have been fun to wait until a charitable person would have come up with an invitation? Trust me, I had some of those, and I tried one or two of them, but I usually felt like the legendary fifth wheel."

"I'm sure nobody meant you to feel that way."

Izzy gave a short laugh through which the hurt of past years shone. "Of course, nobody did. But amidst family and couple bliss, there was I sitting all by myself. And everybody was so very nice to me while probably asking themselves what was wrong with me. Why didn't I have a partner? Why didn't I celebrate with a family of my own? Why did I remind them of some bleakness that they had felt way back before they had a family or a partner of their own?"

"Sounds dreadful. How did you deal with it?"

"As I said – I busied myself with making plans of my own. I planned little trips. I scheduled volunteer work around the museum and at the hospital for myself. Do you have any idea how many lonesome people there are at the hospital over Christmas?"

Abby had shaken her head. "Many?"

"Enough to fill the holidays with visits and feeling useful." The kettle in the kitchen had started whistling, and Izzy had gotten up. "I have some nice fruity tea," she had said. "It's without caffeine, so you can enjoy a couple of cups. Is that okay with you?"

Abby had nodded. A few minutes later, she had held a steaming mug in her hand, the little tea bag label dangling by a string over the rim.

"So, what would you do in my situation or non-situation?" Abby had asked Izzy.

"Honestly? Forget him!"

Abby had gasped. "It's not that easy! We have had years together."

"Right. But very obviously he has put them behind himself. And you better do that, too. He won't come back. He won't want you around, stalking him and invading him and his new life. Just imagine it happened to you."

"But it was *he* who left."

"Imagine it had been you." Abby had been gnawing at her lower lip, and her eyes had filled with tears. "For goodness sake, girl! What are you seeing in that good-for-nothing?!"

"He's not that!"

"Well, I don't see him do anything for you at all. Nothing good that is. Is it plain nostalgia that makes you hanker for him? Cut it out – you are better than this!"

"It hurts so much."

"Because you are holding on too strongly. There are more fish in the sea than this … flounder."

Abby had choked down a giggle and looked at her friend with bright eyes. "I'm just so tired of throwing out another hook."

"Well, then don't. And just don't hold on to the memories because you don't have anything better for now. Make *new* memories." Izzy had frowned, then her face had lit up. "Tell me about the guests at your Bed & Breakfast right now. Are there any interesting people? Besides good old Dave, of course?"

Abby had sighed. "I guess I have quite an interesting bunch of people there right now, that's for sure." Izzy had made an encouraging gesture with her hands. Abby had smiled weakly and done her friend the favor. "Well, there are these three fun sisters. They are identical triplets and have their own color schemes to be identified by more easily. But now one of them confided in me this morning that she intended to break the rules; and that another one might yet poke her head out of her pattern, but the third one – she was not sure she'd be happy about things being changed."

"Triplets? How exciting!"

"Quite. Then there is that very quiet and grim man from Anderson Island – I can't figure him out at all. He came with another guest, a lady from the same place. But they obviously don't belong together."

"Oooh," Izzy had winked. "Romance material!"

"I highly doubt it," Abby had said. "They hardly talk, and they keep themselves apart from each other. The lady hangs out with the triplets mostly though she is the roommate of another single lady guest who looks slightly familiar, but I am not sure whom she resembles. And she likes that little girl who is one of the guests."

"All by herself?"

179

"No. With her dad. And then there is that knitting couple – always friendly, warm-hearted, and quiet. I think they were talking about starting a knitting bee at the Community Center in order to keep people there comfortable and occupied. And they might have started one at my place as well. I'm not sure. They have these wonderful yarns, all soft and colorful."

"M-hmmm," Izzy had just said.

Abby had sipped from her mug. Then she had looked up with questioning eyes. "M-hm what?"

"Oh, nothing really," Izzy had grinned. "It just struck me that you have described every single one of your guests more closely, except 'the dad'. Interesting."

Abby had blushed and shaken her head. "You are reading too much into that. I just can't figure him out. He's a widower, and he is kind of strict with his little daughter. That's all."

"M-hm."

Abby had risen. "There is no 'm-hm' to him, Izzy. They arrived last night like the others. The little girl is darling. He is polite ..."

"And handsome?" Izzy had wanted to know.

"I don't really know," Abby had said. "To be honest, I have had to wrap my head around too many things too suddenly these past hours."

"As in what?!" Izzy had asked. She had started losing her patience with her self-pitying friend. "Running a B & B? Receiving guests unannounced? Planning a couple of days ahead, even though most of the stores will be open and you can get there without a hustle?"

Abby had winced. "You know why."

"For goodness sake, Abby! Stop moping and move on!"

Abby had nodded. "I guess I should. Thanks for the tea." She had risen and placed the mug on a sideboard. "You probably have better things to do than help a friend."

"Are you kidding me?" Izzy had asked exasperated. "I *was* helping you. I *am* helping you. Just because I am honest doesn't mean I am not trying to help."

But Abby had found her way to the hallway already and slipped into her boots. By the time Izzy had been at the door, Abby had already been trudging down the garden path. She had seen Mrs. Morgan's curtains twitch in the house across the street. That old woman was a gossip if ever there was one. Well, she was probably just lonely. Just like Abby herself would be one day. She bit her lips, but her eyes blurred.

Abby had spent the rest of the afternoon in her room at *The Gull's Nest* with a box of Kleenex, some Hallmark movies that set off a new deluge at every kissing scene, and a bag of salt caramel truffles. Life was dreary when you had reached a certain age and been betrayed by the love of your life. Abby had been sobbing until she had fallen asleep over a particularly romantic movie scene that played in front of a fireplace, the female protagonist dreaming up a wedding in December with a successful business magnate from Chicago whereas the truly good character was the lumberjack next door who'd turn out to inherit a big logging business from a long-lost relative. Abby didn't watch the story twist and turn, but dreamed about her business magnate open a door to a shining palace with marble floors and crystal chandeliers.

When Abby finally woke, it was dark outside and way past her usual dinnertime. She had no appetite anyhow. From the hallway she heard some of her guests return from their dinner downtown. She heard Heather's voice pipe up and ask for another hour of knitting before her bedtime. She heard Kathy's cheerful response and Aaron's apologetic voice. Then the house became quiet again. The snow outside reflected the moonlight in a bluish way, and some lights from Downtown shone with a mysterious warmth.

The TV screen was flickering, so was the fire in the fireplace. It could have been so very cozy an evening. She could even be in such a romantic place with Hank now, cuddled up in his penthouse apartment (she assumed he had one) with a view of Elliott Bay (she assumed it had a view), enjoying some take-out from his favorite Chinese restaurant (she assumed his tastes as to food hadn't changed). Well, his taste in women obviously had, and a new big tear collected in her left eye and started to brim over, while the right eye was following suit in production.

The Hallmark Channel didn't cheer her up anymore. Besides, she had woken up in the middle of a new story and somehow didn't connect to the main actress. Abby switched channels. "Love Actually" caught her eyes, and she remembered how she had always loved watching the all-star cast in that movie. But Hugh Grant's wassailing as the Prime Minister from door to door in a seedy neighborhood had lost its credibility. She chided Emma Thompson for searching her husband's pockets and expecting too much of a man who expected too much of an office associate. And Colin Firth seemed more wonderful as in inaccessible than ever when he bravely fought language barriers to ask a girl of no particular assets other than a golden heart to marry him.

She had these particular assets as well, darn it! Why hadn't Hank seen it in her? How could he fall for somebody else after he had encouraged her to open her business in Wycliff?! Abby sobbed loudly now, while the movie credits were rolling off.

She didn't hear the soft knock at the door nor the turning of the doorknob. She didn't see Heather peek in and close the door silently again. She only got startled by a loud knock about five minutes later. And then she didn't even have time enough to wipe her red eyes and call "Come in" because the doorknob turned almost immediately, the door opened, and Aaron slipped in.

"What are you doing here?" Abby asked aghast.

"Heather heard you cry and said you needed help."

"I never said anything to her."

"She didn't say you did. But she said you were crying heartbreakingly."

"And can't a girl have a good cry sometimes?" Abby said upset. But somehow, at the same time, it felt good that somebody had stepped in to intervene between her and her bottomless grief.

Aaron stared at her pensively. "But why would you *want* to cry in the first place?"

"Oh, it's nobody's business," Abby answered tartly. "I can deal with it myself."

"Well, then I apologize for intruding. But I still think that somebody who cries might want somebody to listen. And sometimes a stranger's ears are better than somebody's you know."

"Says who?"

"My wife," Aaron said quietly. He swallowed. "She was the wise one of our little trio. Heather is a lot like her. That is what scares me sometimes. I see her grow so wise before her years, and I can't bear the thought of losing her, too." He turned his face towards the fireplace so Abby wasn't able to see his face fight the oncoming grief in it.

"If Heather is like her, she must have been lovely."

"She was," Aaron nodded. "She was the love of my life."

"There might be second chances." Abby was surprised to hear herself say so. Only ten minutes ago she had been persuaded that her love life was finished, and here she was trying to comfort an utter stranger about the loss of his wife.

"I know," Aaron said. "That's what she told me too."

Abby swallowed. "I must seem pretty shallow to you."

"Why would that be?"

"I have just been mourning the man I thought was the love of my life. That's what Heather overheard."

"And was he?"

"What? The love of my life? I got dressed down by my friend Izzy this afternoon for clinging to the memory of him."

"It sounds like you made some good ones."

Abby looked at her hands. "At first I thought we were. He seemed so supportive. But in the end, we grew apart. He left me for a more glamorous woman in glamorous Seattle. Maybe Izzy *was* right and I should move on. These are memories *I* made; apparently they didn't count as much for him." She paused. Then she looked up at Aaron. "How do you know you have met the love of your life?"

Aaron took a deep breath and walked to the window. He stayed quiet for a long time. Then he talked very softly, almost as if to himself. "The love of your life doesn't come like a whirlwind, but like a soft, warm summer breeze when you don't expect it. You don't search for it. It happens. You find that you have lost all fear to admit your flaws, the tiny little ones and the big ones. You speak of your dreams, but your love already seems to know and to encourage you. You are not afraid of the things that might change in your life because you know this is not about your career or your looks, the places you might or might not travel to, and the things you might or might not afford. The love of your life is the person whose pain you'd like to take on just so *they* wouldn't suffer. They

185

make you stand up for them even though you know you are a coward at heart; but you become a lion. You willingly throw your coat into the mud for them so their feet stay dry. And when they leave, they make you want to leave, too, to stay by their side. But they have left you a legacy to continue. If you are a musician, they want you to keep on playing. If you are a painter, they want you to keep on painting. If you are a father, they want you to stay being a father. That's what the love of my life was to me." Abby had moved behind him and laid an arm around him. Now she was sobbing softly. "So, you lost the love of your life as well?"

Abby breathed in deeply and caught herself. She wiped her eyes. "No," she whispered. "I didn't." She realized that she had been half-hugging him and pulled her arms back to herself. She hugged her elbows closely to her and rubbed them. "No. Hank never was the love of my life. You made this obvious to me. Thank you. I finally realize."

Chapter 15

December 23, 07:30 p.m.

Abby was staring through her bedroom window into the wintry dark. It had started snowing again, but not as fiercely as the day before. The light from Downtown was a murky glow through the soft veil of snowflakes. Abby's breathing was still a little labored, racked with some dry little sobs. But they started to become more of a physical thing than something heartfelt. Aaron was standing next to her, observing her from the corners of his eyes. The flickering flames of the fireplace threw oddly shaped shadows across the walls.

"May I ask you something?" Abby finally half-whispered.

Aaron looked down at her and nodded. "Sure," he said quietly.

"Did you have to wait long to find the love of your life?"

Aaron rubbed his chin. "That's a good question," he said. "As a matter of fact, I have been asking myself something similar."

"How so?"

"Olivia and I were in the same class from the very beginning of our school years."

"Oh!"

"Indeed. We were not close neighbors over in Eatonville. She lived upstairs of her divorced mother's hair salon in town

187

center. I was living somewhere on the outskirts. But we saw each other in school each and every day of 12 school years. Well, almost. Because there was one time or another when she was sick. And I broke my leg once, falling out of an apple tree. And I was on the school's football team whereas she was more of an intellectual. I don't think she ever watched any of my games."

"Almost like a Hallmark movie," Abby remarked with a dry little smile.

"What?"

"The impossible pairing of a jock and a nerd that eventually works out."

Aaron chuckled. He sounded a bit like a coughing grizzly bear when he did so. "Maybe. Only there was no romance between the two of us at the time. I remember I asked her for help with an English composition once in eleventh grade. And at another time we were paired off in a physics class for an experiment about masses in a vacuum. That was as close we got. We were aware of each other's existence. No more, no less."

"Then, what happened?"

"Nothing," Aaron said, smiling wistfully. "If I'd known we'd have so little time when we finally got together, I'd certainly have made sure to get to know her earlier in life. Could have, would have, should have – right?"

"Well, but none of us know about …" Abby faltered. She didn't even know the circumstances that had turned Aaron into a widower. And she was sure it was not her place to ask him.

188

"I went into my father's construction business. Olivia went off to Tacoma and studied to become a teacher. I never spent another thought on her. I was busy helping people build their homes, and she was moving in different circles. A couple of times I ran into her mother at the local grocery store. One time she said how sad she was that her Olivia had decided not to take over her business and how lucky my father was that I was ready to follow in his footsteps."

"In a way she was right, wasn't she?"

Aaron swallowed. "Yes and no." He took a deep breath. "My father's business went bust."

"Oh no!"

"One summer, an outside company came into town and started underbidding every single project that my father bid on. In the end, my father told me to apply for a job with them, as he had no hope to be able to employ me and five other guys any longer."

"He made you go to the company that made him fold?"

"Sometimes you have to do what is reasonable."

"But how bitter must that have been for the both of you."

"It was a bit humiliating," Aaron admitted. "But what are you gonna do?! Dad's house was paid off. He had enough savings to tide himself and Mom over. Eventually, he went into real estate and did quite well. And the company I applied with offered me a fair job with opportunity to grow. Who knows – maybe I'm better off without the responsibilities of being the boss of a construction firm than only working for one in a rather convenient position?"

Abby sighed. "Still, I'd probably hate that company forever and ever."

Aaron chuckled again. "I have to admit that I did at first. But when I saw Dad being quite relaxed about it and telling me that bends in a road are there for a reason, I thought that maybe he was right."

"So, how did you and Olivia re-meet?"

"Construction," he said. "Her mother's home needed a replacement of the rafters, and I was there to do some paperwork with her when Olivia came in from a day of school. Boy, was I flustered!"

"She was that beautiful?"

"To me she was. Gone was all the nerdiness. This was a crisp looking beauty, and her smile was like a punch into my guts."

"That was when it started?"

"No, it wasn't. She was smitten with another teacher at her school. And I didn't have the courage to ask her out. Besides I didn't know what she thought of me."

"How long did it take?"

"About seven more years ..."

"Seven years?!"

"Well, I had a couple of girls in between as well. Nothing came of it. And one time, it was my own stupid fault, too."

"You're sounding upset!"

"I am. I mean, it's not so much that I still wish that I had married the girl. But I was a fool. Simple as that. One should know that in a small-town any tale of somebody's misbehavior won't stay only with the ones involved. The tale will spread and reach ears it's not meant for."

"What happened?" Abby had become curious now.

"I was the best man of an old school buddy of mine who had moved out to the shores of South Puget Sound. And the bride had set me up with one of her bridesmaids. She and I had been dating for a little while, and we were both pretty sure that, at my buddy's wedding, I'd drop the question to her."

"But you didn't."

"Well, I would have. But you see, the stag night had been pretty rough, and to my shame I have to say that I couldn't resist the offer of one of the generous ladies present."

"Who was *not* the bridesmaid …"

"I'd never have popped *her* the question, for sure."

"Ouch!"

"Long story short – my misbehavior became the joke of the stags, and somebody must have told his girl-friend. By the time the wedding day was there, everybody knew but the girl I intended to ask to become my wife." Abby was listening with rapt attention. Aaron smirked. "I had sent her a pink rose in a corsage to wear at the wedding. She had picked up the wedding cake for her friend and was sitting in a cab on her way to the wedding over in

Steilacoom when somebody must have given her *the* call. She never arrived at the wedding. Neither did the cake."

"What?!"

"Right. I never got to ask her the question, either. The bride looked like she'd have loved to shoot me during the entire festivity. So did her parents. Somebody managed to buy a cake that looked nice enough, but it certainly wasn't a wedding cake."

"And your buddy?"

"He laughed his head off. Said he couldn't stand my date in the first place and couldn't care less for any wedding cake."

"Come on, really?!"

"He divorced a few years later. As to the cake – I heard an elderly couple found it on their 'Adopt a Street' tour, picking up garbage by the roadside of what they call 'The Tunnel of Trees'. The corsage with the pink rose had been flung only a few yards farther on."

"Wow, they must have wondered …"

Aaron nodded. "I hurt somebody who didn't deserve it. I ruined a wedding. I certainly wasn't husband material at that time."

Abby sighed. "We learn through our mistakes."

"Well, I certainly learned to behave at later stag nights. And I tried to apologize and make it up to the bride and 'my' girl. Neither ever accepted it."

"Maybe you are forgiven by now."

"Maybe. I keep asking myself, though, whether I was the primordial cause of a bad marriage due to that wedding cake disaster."

"If a piece of cake is the making or breaking of a marriage, the marriage was doomed from the beginning already. But not through your fault, Aaron. It might have been anything for all I know."

Aaron shrugged. "Too late to find out now, right?"

"Does it really matter?"

He looked at her. Her eyes were very serious. "No. I guess not."

"So, when did you and Olivia get together?"

"That was after all my buddies had been married off and the first few of them went through their first rocky stages of their marriages. It was one of those parties where each of us knew somebody who knows somebody who knows the host. It was pretty boring, though at the same time it was loud in places. Olivia and I bumped into each other in a remote part of the garden, gazing at the stars. Sounds silly, right?"

"Not at all," Abby breathed. "How very romantic!"

Aaron's face softened. "It was the first time we really talked to each other. And we didn't even realize when the party broke up. By the time the sun rose, we had decided we were meant for each other. Boy, did I feel wrecked and elated the day after!" He laughed.

"Incredible."

"Yes." Aaron became sober again. "I had no idea what lay in store for us. We got married, and we had some pretty good years. And Heather came along and began to look more and more like Olivia." He sighed with a dry sob. "I will never understand what happened and that we didn't realize how it happened." Abby looked at him, her eyes big with questions. "I knew that Olivia saw a doctor every once in a while, when she felt stressed out. I knew that she was taking pills against anxiety. I never thought it would lead to …" He broke off and a big sob escaped his throat.

"Suicide?" Abby asked very softly. Aaron nodded. His tall frame was shaking, he was burrowing his face in his hands. Abby simply wrapped the man into her arms as he was crying out his grief. When he became a bit calmer, she led him to her bed and made him sit on it, then sat down beside him.

"She must have felt awful," Aaron said. "So awful that she thought it was her only way out."

Abby nodded. "I lost a friend that way. She was outwardly so happy. But she obviously hid her depression well inside. She never considered what *I* would feel like if she killed herself. *When* she killed herself. Or how her parents would grieve. Or her brother. Anybody."

"No, they don't. They are prisoners of their own emotions. I imagine they feel like in a dark room with the key to the door lock lost. They don't even knock anymore to be let out. And those who would like to help are either being fooled by an outwardly cockiness or resented and warded off by their anger. It

194

must have been hell for Olivia to walk through all of this on her own. Without us knowing that this was so much more than anxiety. It exploded into our faces only when we found her and it was too late to do anything."

"How does Heather bear it?"

"I don't know," Aaron admitted. "I haven't talked about Olivia's suicide with her. We just work around it, I guess."

"No therapist?"

"No." Aaron shook his head and rose again. "I don't believe in therapists. I think everybody has to deal with their own burdens in their own way. The standardized ways of a therapist will not work with an individual grief."

"I see what you mean. But talking sometimes helps, don't you think?"

"It doesn't change the facts. It won't remedy or reverse what already happened. It's a waste of their time and the person's who seeks them out."

"But it helps to be understood in a better way."

"I don't want to be 'understood' by a therapist who has dozens of so-called cases. Why would they care about *me*? It's an hour they get paid for, and after that there's another hour they get paid for by another person, and so on. How much more impersonal can it get?!"

"But maybe Heather simply needs to be able to talk to you?"

"I *am* talking to her."

Abby bit her lips. "I don't want to overstep, but I have a feeling you are pretty strict with her when you are talking."

"How do you mean?"

"You are keeping her on a short leash."

"I have to see to it that nothing happens to her. And I have to be father *and* mother to her these days."

"I don't think so," Abby ventured. "She needs to have the love of the father she knew before everything happened. And that way she will be able to heal. Not with grieving for a gentle mother who's not coming back. Not with a father who is strict because he thinks he has to be strict for two people."

Aaron sighed. "I do see what you mean. I certainly don't mean to put off my little girl. Do you think I do?"

"Not yet, I think," Abby said truthfully. "But one day the time will come when she's a teenager and she needs to experience her freedom to a certain degree. Don't try to be a father *and* a mother then. Just be her father. Now and always. That will probably be more than enough anyhow." Abby giggled. "I'm speaking from experience."

Aaron ran his right hand over his face. "I'm just worried that she gets hurt."

"I know," Abby said. "But she is hurt enough already. She needs a place to go to. A person to go to."

"She is making friends right and left as you can see."

"She is, and everybody loves her. But be honest: Dave is Santa Dave to her, and who knows how much Santa is in the package for her there? Pippa, the triplets, and Kathy and Roger are wonderful with her – but they don't replace a cuddling father or a soul-to-soul talk about what the two of you have gone through. And I am just a Bed & Breakfast owner who is playing your host for your involuntary stay over Christmas. After the holidays everybody will be gone from Heather's life, and then that will be more loss to her."

"But we might come back here."

Abby blushed slightly. "And I'd be more than happy to see the both of you again."

"Maybe we could be friends?"

"We could," Abby said quietly, but a sudden wave of butterflies told her that she had already more at stake. How had that happened?

"Maybe we could spend the day together tomorrow?"

"That sounds like the beginning of a solid friendship," Abby smiled.

Aaron nodded. "I guess I better leave you to yourself now. There's a little girl upstairs who might start getting worried about you. And don't I have good news to bring to her?!"

Abby smiled. "Give your little girl a big hug from me."

"You bet," Aaron smiled back at her and walked towards the door. "And a cuddle from her dad, too."

"That is even better."

He lifted a hand in a quiet salute to her, and she nodded at him. "Thank you for listening," he said.

"Thank you for talking me out of my ditch," she answered.

The door closed behind Aaron. Abby stared into the flames of her fireplace. An hour ago, her world had been so full of grief. And now, two grief-stricken people had ventured out to bond and try to help each other heal.

"Two minuses make a plus," Abby whispered to herself. Only, she didn't feel like a minus anymore. She felt as if a knot inside her had loosened and untwisted. She had found around the bend in her road. She had no idea where she was going to be headed. But she was sure that she had energy enough to walk the new stretch that lay ahead of her.

Chapter 16

December 24, 07:00 a.m.

For Ronald Hoffman Christmas was one of the toughest times of the year. To be stuck in a Christmassy town with Christmassy people against any decision of his made it even more awful. What would he have given to be back on Anderson Island now, in his cozy cottage in the woods, away from the hub of tourism! Instead, he was facing another day in Wycliff with people who were way too close for his comfort. Not that he disliked them. They were nice enough, he knew. And that little girl, Heather or whatever her name was, was downright entertaining. But he didn't *need* entertaining. He just wanted to be left alone.

That was one of the reasons why, as soon as he overheard Abby step through the hallway and enter her kitchen, the soft rattling of an electric kettle, the clinking noise of china, and the clicking of a toaster, he decided to have a very early breakfast today. Before anybody else would come into the breakfast room and break its quiet. So, Ronald stepped outside his room and walked towards the kitchen.

"Good morning," Abby called out, as soon as she sensed his presence. Her head was hidden behind the open fridge door.

"Good morning," Ronald replied. "Is it too early to ask for breakfast yet?"

Abby closed the fridge door and looked at him with a bright smile. "Not at all. I'm about to fix mine – so I can see to yours just as well. A full breakfast, eggs over easy?"

"That would be nice, thank you." Ronald was a bit astonished that she remembered how he had had his eggs done the day before. It was a nice surprise, and he found himself smiling as he was walking to the table he had chosen yesterday.

If he had thought he was alone in the breakfast room, though, he was mistaken. For in another corner, finger-spelling from a braille book, sat Dave.

"Good morning, Ronald," the blind man said and smiled with empty eyes. "You are up early."

"Good morning," Ronald said and decided not to respond to the unspoken question. Thank goodness, Dave obviously understood he was not in a talking mood for he soon resumed gliding his fingertips across the pages, slightly moving his lips.

Shortly after, Abby entered the room with toast and butter. She placed steaming coffee pots on the men's tables. "Bacon, eggs, and hash browns will be up soon," she announced. Neither of the men replied. "You are not exactly morning people, are you?" she teased.

"Not exactly," Dave said. "But you knew that."

"I don't mind early mornings," Ronald said. "This is just one at the wrong time of the year."

"Christmas?" Dave asked.

"Christmas," Ronald confirmed and fell silent again, turning his face to the window. Abby vanished into the kitchen. She didn't know what to say and didn't dare to pry too deeply. Dave wasn't able to see Ronald's face though, and so he blissfully ignored Ronald's obvious unwillingness to talk anymore.

"You're from Anderson Island, right?"

"Right." Wouldn't that Santa-like looking man leave him in peace, for goodness sake?!

"What brought you to Wycliff?"

"Business," Ronald said.

"That shortly before Christmas? What kind of business?"

Ronald sighed. "Listen. I'm truly not in a talking mood. And yes, you caught me out. I was not here on business. I was visiting a hospice. I'm always doing that on December 22."

Dave frowned. "Hospice, huh? That's surely no laughing matter."

"It's not meant to be."

"Mind if I take my breakfast over at your table?" Dave asked.

Ronald sighed inwardly. Now he would be the impolite, inhumane, disgusting ogre if he denied the request of the old, blind guy. "Not at all. But maybe I move over to *your* table as I realize that it's easier for me than for you to change tables." He rose and started to carry his dishes over to Dave. As he watched the old man's face, he could have sworn, if the eyes had been seeing, they'd have twinkled with glee. So what? He sat down and grabbed another slice of toast from his basket.

"You say you don't like Christmas?" Dave asked.

"I said I didn't like this time of the year."

"But this time of the year *is* Christmas."

"If my wife had died near the Fourth of July, it would be *that* time of the year."

"Oh." Dave seemed to be out of his depth, and Ronald was relieved about another moment of silence. Which wouldn't last too long, alas. "So, you have family at the hospice?"

"No." Ronald viciously cut into a fried slice of bacon, and the impetus sent the other half of the slice sailing across the table. "Dang!"

"What happened?"

"I sent some breakfast flying. – Listen, I appreciate your interest in me. But I'm not very interesting. So why don't you stop worrying about me?"

"Who says I'm worrying?"

"I know."

"You must be a psychologist or a clairvoyant then."

"Neither. I'm … I used to be a doctor." Ronald choked out the words.

"A colleague!" Dave seemed to be quite happy. "Which field did *you* specialize in?"

"I used to be a gynecologist."

"Here in the area?"

"On the East Coast. – You?"

"Heart surgeon. Maybe that's why I'm that interested in people."

"Let me guess," Ronald said. "Mens sana in corpore sano."

Dave chuckled. "You pretty much hit it there. I believe that when your soul hurts, your heart is in danger. It's like a glitch in the mechanism."

"And why is it you worry about *me*?"

"I'm not sure. But I hear … It may sound silly from a former heart surgeon. I hear a broken heart when I listen to what you say and how you say it."

"But I'm not saying much."

"Exactly. And what you say sounds abrupt, almost hostile. Like a wounded animal that wants to retreat to its den."

Ronald sighed. "Maybe I'd really like to be at my island home rather than anywhere else."

"Let me guess – all alone and somewhere in the backwoods." Ronald nodded, forgetting that Dave wasn't able to see. "And with no visitors over the holidays either. Still, that leaves the question why you are coming to one of the Christmassiest towns on the Sound and visit a hospice when you are obviously grieving and don't care for the celebrations."

Ronald leaned forward. "You don't give up, Dave, huh?" He stared into the old man's blank eyes. "I guess I'll have to tell you just in order to be left in peace."

203

Dave lifted his hands. "I'm sorry. I didn't want to make you feel pressured. You don't have to tell me. I just thought it might help a hurting person to talk. If you don't want to, of course, that is your own business entirely."

Ronald sank back. "My wife died on December 22 ten years ago. I was not her gynecologist. I wonder what would have happened if she had been my patient though. I don't know if I'd have found what was ailing her in time. I don't know if I'd have been able to help her. I saw her suffer and become less and less. And I had to let her go in spite of everything that I had learned and been so proud of." He wiped his right hand over his dry eyes. "The day she passed was the last day I ever entered my office again. I felt like an impostor." He looked up and searched Dave's face. "What would I tell my patients? My wife died of something that I should have been able to save her from? Would they have believed me, trusted me ever after?"

"They might."

"Well, we don't know that now."

"So, you moved west after that?"

"I wanted to be as far away as possible. I wanted to be as alone as possible. And believe me, there is hardly a lonelier place than as a stranger amongst strangers."

"I imagine you didn't make an extra-effort either …"

Ronald breathed in deeply and kneaded his beard. "I didn't." He realized he was sounding gruff again. "I bought a house in a remote corner of an island – I thought I'd be able to heal there."

"But you didn't," Dave stated.

"No."

Dave sighed. "My friend, I won't pretend you ever fully will. But you are too hard on yourself. As a doctor you are no God. You are maybe His tool if you choose to believe in God. If you don't, of course, you are only as good as your hands and your memory for mechanical procedures. But you are not the one who actually made something live, just as little as you are the creator of what made your wife pass away. And even if you had been able to make all the right decisions and set in motion all the right interventions – some things will always stay out of a doctor's hands."

"I know," Ronald moaned.

"I'd like to presume your patients would have known that, too." Dave fumbled for his coffee pot and almost knocked it over. "They were probably heartbroken for you."

"Some said they were."

"At the hospice – did you go there as in an anniversary-penance?"

Ronald laughed mirthlessly. "More or less, I guess. I thought that if I couldn't help anybody live, least of all my wife, I might as well help them die."

"You are quite the cynic, aren't you?"

"Comes with the situation."

"Ten years, huh?" Dave lifted his replenished cup to his mouth and took a sip of coffee. "So, your license has expired?"

"It has."

"No interest in taking up where you left off? Over here instead?"

"I'd have to requalify, I guess. I don't see myself doing that."

"You know that there is a pregnant young woman in the house, don't you?"

"I do. What does that have to do with me though."

"What if there is a medical emergency? Would you be willing to help?"

"What if any of us had a heart attack. Would you be willing to operate?"

"Different situation."

"Not all too much. I've not been practicing in a decade. I am scared that I'd make a mistake. I'm not even sure that my hands are stable enough any longer."

"You're not that old. Your voice still sounds strong."

"Maybe I'm not that old. But my confidence is not like my voice. Not anymore."

They heard steps coming down the stairs. Light steps followed by heavier steps. Then Heather came around the corner of the hallway and saw her friend Dave in the breakfast room.

"Santa Dave!" she called out. "I had hoped we could have breakfast with you. Why didn't you wait for me?"

Dave turned around and smiled, lowering his face towards where the little girl's voice sounded from. "Good morning, Heather. I had breakfast with somebody who I thought needed some company maybe a little more than you this morning."

Heather's eyes grew big, and Ronald almost blushed. Almost. In fact, he felt that he had needed somebody to air to. It was just so very hard to admit it to anybody. His wife would have wanted him to be with other people more often, too. Why had he totally forgotten that they had been so sociable at one time? That they had searched out events and talked to strangers in bars, that they had chatted to any dog owner in their little town and admired every new-born in their pram. That they had been club members and choir members and hosted dinners? That they had been a team. So much so that when he had had to watch her pass, he had stopped in his path, paralyzed. Though he knew she would have wanted him to continue what they had formerly shared, he hadn't been able to. Out of a month had grown a year, then two, day before yesterday an entire decade. He had become the grumpy man everybody seemed to evade. The man whose beard looked straggly and whose hair was unkempt. The man who barely had a word for anybody and rarely smiled.

"Then I won't complain," Heather said, and turning to Ronald, "I'm sure Santa Dave must be Santa Claus' brother in a way. Only he is for real."

Against his will Ronald had to snort, then he started laughing. Soon Aaron, who had come up behind Heather, and the two older men were laughing heartily, and from the kitchen came Abby's soft giggle.

"I'm most definitely for real," Dave finally managed to say and wiped tears from his blind eyes. "Only, I have to admit I don't have any brother. I don't even know what I look like anymore. But I assume there must be some similarities in appearance." His belly heaved with another chuckle.

Ronald suddenly gripped Dave's right hand with both of his. "I might not seem to have appreciated your company this morning, Sir. But indeed, I did. And I will work on what we talked about." He gave the little girl a brief smile. "Thank you for letting me steal your friend this morning, Heather. I needed some talking to, and now I have some homework to do."

"But it's vacations. There is no school," Heather ventured.

Aaron laid his hands on her shoulders. "Grown-ups' homework is not for school, sweetie. It's for their lives."

Heather turned her head and looked at him. "Do you have to do homework for your life, too?"

Aaron nodded. "Oh yes, sweetie. I only learned last night that I have a whole lot to work on." Abby walked out of her kitchen at that moment.

Heather tilted her head. "I guess I understand what you mean. It's when grown-ups have problems and need to solve them. Right?" Aaron's eyes locked with Abby's. "Right, Daddy?"

Abby winked at Aaron. He swallowed, then looked back at Heather. "I think you are pretty smart for a nine-year-old."

*

Abby had tried hard not to eavesdrop, but in the end the sounds of Dave and Ronald's conversation had carried over, their table being pretty close to the kitchen door. She knew about Dave's capability of drawing people out. Maybe it was because they thought he couldn't see them when they spoke. But she had been astonished when Ronald had actually taken him up on the offer to share a breakfast table and moved over to Dave's.

She overheard him state his profession, and she overheard him tell Dave that his wife had died ten years ago. After that she found herself wrapped up in a train of thought of her own.

Obviously, everybody was carrying a burden on their shoulders these days. Well, at least some of them *thought* they did. She smirked at herself. *Her* knot though had kind of gotten untied by yesterday night's conversation in her bedroom. But Aaron would have to deal with his bundle of sorrow and little Heather for a long time to come. And Ronald had become totally embittered about his. Come to think of it, even Dave had been wistful only a couple of days ago when he had let on that having her as an ersatz granddaughter was not as if she had been the real deal. Strange that this time of the year brought out all these pains to a sharper degree. Or maybe not as strange. Because when everybody else seemed to be oh so happy and everybody was cuddling up to family, those who were less blessed felt the contrast even starker than usual.

Of course, not everybody was unhappy. The triplet sisters, Starlene, Darlene, and Charlene were what you would call fireworks. Pippa carried that quiet serenity and contentment around with her like a bag of candy, willing to share it out. And Kathy and Roger were utter darlings with their creativity and warm-heartedness.

Us and them, Abby thought. And last night I stepped from one "us" to another "us", from the dark side to the light and hopeful one. Which made her try and assess the young couple – were they one or not? – in room number 2. They didn't seem too flustered about the situation. Though the young man definitely seemed to care about the pregnant young woman. Maybe they hadn't decided yet whether they would be happy or unhappy until after the baby was born. With such an event looming over their heads they probably were focusing on how to deal with what needed to be done more immediately than with the bigger picture. Ah well, none of her business. It had only popped into her head because she wondered whether they were happy or sad. And then – wasn't that some binary thinking of hers? As if there were only either light or shadow and no shades in between …

It was then that Heather called out to Dave, and Abby felt that she could step out of her self-imposed kitchen exile. When her eyes met Aaron's, her knees started trembling ever so slightly, and her heart beat in her throat. As their eyes locked, she winked at him. Suddenly, Christmas felt so full of promises again.

Chapter 17

December 24, 08:00 a.m.

Pippa had slept deeply. For whatever reason this unforeseen stay at *The Gull's Nest* seemed to be just what she had needed. Not that she had been desperate to take a vacation. She loved her work at the Steilacoom Library. She traveled over there on the ferry from Anderson Island four times a week. She helped people find what they were looking for, recommended books and films, placed books that were returned back onto the shelves, helped out with the speakers' program that they hosted in cooperation with the Steilacoom Historical Museum, joined the brown bag book club whenever they met, and in her spare time had set up a book club on Anderson Island as well.

The day trip to Wycliff had been the start of her Christmas vacation this year. She had intended to get some Christmas gifts for herself and to pamper herself at some of the restaurants – all of which she had done –, and then to return home with her treats. She'd have baked a last load of cookies to bag into those cute little cellophane bags she had found she couldn't remember where and hand those to every neighbor on her street. Not that there were that many. Well, they'd have to go without that this year. They might wonder where she was anyway. She hadn't told anybody what she had planned before she left. And now her Christmas illumination probably just sprang on and went out as timed. No footprints of hers in the snow. No snow shoveled away from her driveway. And her car was still sitting in an empty lot near the Anderson Island ferry terminal.

Everything would have been her usual Christmas routine. One that she had had for the past decade. One that she had become comfortable with. Because she was doing it all by herself again, going to Wycliff again, with the same shopping route again. And treating herself had been a lifetime routine for her anyhow, only that this was Christmastime. She had gotten used to all of this.

"Boring!" she whispered to her image in the bathroom mirror. Florence was still sleeping. She had been smiling in her dreams probably because she was pleased with something. Good for her!

Well, Pippa would have to be content that things had been changed for her without her doing. Getting stranded in as beautiful a town as Wycliff between two landslides and a millennial record snowstorm was something else. Would ferries be running again today? Pippa was almost hoping they wouldn't. How about Christmas in Wycliff? She smiled at her mirror image. "Sounds great!" she mouthed and dabbed a little more of the cold cream that the Bed & Breakfast provided in small sachets onto her face.

She wondered what she might be doing after breakfast. More shopping? "Don't be daft," she scolded herself with a frown. She had enough Christmas gifts for herself already. For herself ... Why yes, she might try and get some for somebody else. Let's see – who was the most in need of a gift? The little girl, Heather, wouldn't expect any – besides she seemed to be keener on spending time with anybody than on any material gifts. Quite unusual for such a little one. Her dad would take care of her gifts anyhow. Abby? She had been crying yesterday night, but right now she was hearing her laughing from the hallway below in such a refreshing way that, clearly, all that had been burdening her last night must have slipped off her shoulders.

Kathy and Roger, the triplets, Abby and Dave – everybody seemed to have somebody to focus on, she pondered. "Except you yourself, old girl, and grumpy Ronald." She grimaced at her reflection. She might as well get used to the thought, that she was as much a bump on a log as the man from Anderson Island. Must have to do with being an islander, she thought amused.

She carefully brushed her hair, spotting another gray thread in her otherwise thick brown mop, and pulled it out. Why was it always the sturdiest hairs that turned gray or even white?! And why did they have to stand out so much?! She wasn't that old, and she didn't want to turn gray already. "Duh, a couple of gray hairs don't mean you're old," she said.

"What?" a sleepy voice from the bedroom asked.

"Just talking to myself," Pippa answered.

"So, I'm not the only one who does that every once in a while?"

"Heavens to Betsy, no!" Pippa answered cheerfully.

"You think it's normal?"

"Absolutely. Unless you hear somebody invisible answer."

Silvery laughter came from the bedroom, followed by a light thump and steps across the floor. "Is it okay if I enter?"

"Come in, I'm done anyhow."

Florence popped her head into the bathroom and stared at her bedroom mate. "How did you manage to get all dressed without waking me?"

"I was not actually singing and dancing under the shower in the first place," Pippa grinned and walked past Florence. "What are your plans for today, by the way? I'm looking for some inspiration."

"I'm going downtown," Florence said. "Doing some more shopping, I guess. Want to come along?"

"Umh, no thanks. I got everything I need."

"I wonder how much longer we will have to wait until we are getting dug out and can go where we need to be," Florence sighed. "I mean, I love Wycliff and everything, but it's not as if we had planned this."

"I hear you," Pippa said, sitting down on her bed. "That's why I try to find something to do. Something that is fun *and* useful. And that still feels Christmassy – you know what I mean?"

"I feel you." Florence closed the bathroom door, and her voice sounded hollow from behind it. "How about checking with the people from the Community Center? I heard that Kathy and

Roger said yesterday they wanted to see whether they could help out there today. It's Christmas Eve after all."

"I might look into that though I don't feel I have it in me right now." Pippa was pulling on her boots. "I can see a helicopter over Downtown, by the way."

"Military?"

"TV rather. I guess we are a subject of interest. Imagine what we must be looking like to the outside world. Kind of exotic, cut off like this."

"Well, they are probably glad that the landslides have been harmless enough. No victims other than people stranded and trains not getting through."

Pippa heard Florence switch on the shower. "I'm going downstairs," she announced though she was pretty sure Florence wouldn't be able to hear her. "See you later."

On the stairs she almost collided with Dave, who was on his way upstairs to his room.

"Good morning, Pippa," he said friendly.

"How did you know it was me and not one of the other ladies?" she wondered. "By ear?"

"In your case not really," Dave chuckled. "You smell different."

Pippa was taken aback. "I'm smelling?"

Dave laughed out loudly. "I didn't say *that*. I rather would like to emphasize the word 'different'. As in perfume."

"But I don't use any perfume." Then it dawned on her. "Oh! So, that's what you meant."

"Indeed." He smiled. Then he changed the topic. "Do you have any fun plans for this Christmas Eve? Apart from going down to Town Hall tonight for the Wycliff caroling event?"

"Not yet," she sighed. "And I'm shopped out. I might check what little Heather is going to do. Maybe I can find a fun project with her."

"I don't think she needs that," Dave said. "I heard Abby and Aaron tell her that they were taking her down to the Maritime Center this morning and they'd take it from there."

"Oh," Pippa said and didn't know why this made her feel a little disappointed. "Well, I guess I'll come up with something else."

"If you want to keep me company later on, you are more than welcome to knock on my door," Dave said. "Abby has made me a jug of hot fruit punch. Non-alcoholic, for sure. It goes mighty well with the gingerbread I got from the German deli the other day."

"Sounds nice," Pippa said politely. Sitting in Dave's room and talking was not what she was able to embrace just now with her morning-active mind.

"See you later then."

"See you later, Dave." They passed each other, and Pippa stepped through the hallway into the breakfast room. Aaron and Heather were just about finished with their breakfast. Kathy and

Roger were busy, packing knitting needles and yarn into Ziplock bags as they were creating impromptu knitting kits. Abby was humming a Christmas carol in the kitchen. Grumpy Man wasn't anywhere to be seen.

The door of the room formerly assigned to Pippa opened, and she heard the young man Ramón's voice. Just as she was starting to help herself to one of the breakfast juices, Ramón arrived by her side.

"Good morning," he said politely, not looking at her though, but scanning the beverages nervously.

"Good morning," Pippa said.

"Would you know which tea helps with any tummy ache?"

Pippa looked up and found him staring helplessly at the collection of tea sachets presented in a beautiful basket next to the hot water jug.

"Is this about you or your young woman?"

"It's about Michelle," he said and sounded a bit anxious. "I think she is not feeling so good this morning, but she couldn't make up her mind about which tea she would like to have."

Pippa frowned and took a closer look at the sachets herself now. "How about fennel?" she suggested finally. "If it's just the tummy, that might help her. And if she doesn't like the taste of it – why not go for peppermint?"

Ramón smiled at her with a little relief peeking through the worry. "Thank you. I know my mother would probably have told me the same. I just keep forgetting things like these, herbs and healing stuff and so on." He grabbed two mugs, hung a sachet in each of them, and filled them with hot water. Without further words he turned around to fulfil his mission.

Poor boy, Pippa thought. He was probably the person with the very weirdest Christmas Eve of all of them.

*

Michelle had had nightmares all through the night. First, she had felt she was drowning. Then she had thought that somebody was trying to stifle her, and she had woken up with a gasp. Now she was just lounging on her bed, her back propped up against the headrest, and felt miserable.

"I wish this whole deal were over," she sighed. "I'm so sorry I kept you awake with my restlessness last night."

"It's fine," Ramón said. He was pale this morning. Two nights in the same bed with somebody tossing and turning surely hadn't helped him to get sleep. "Besides when it's over, it's only the beginning of something new."

"Don't I know?" Michelle moaned. Then she suddenly turned pale and sat up. "Ouch."

"Are you okay?" Ramón pulled a fresh T-shirt over his head and then slipped into his sneakers.

Michelle panted, then she breathed normally again, and blew a strand of hair from her face. "Yeah, I'm fine. It's just my

219

back that is acting up a little this morn... ouch!" She gripped her belly and looked at Ramón with alarm. "This really hurt."

Ramón was at the door instantly. "Do you need a doctor? Do you want me to call a doctor?" He was pale, and his eyes were wild.

Michelle had to laugh. "No! Don't! It's not due, and I'm just a bit squeamish after last night's dreams. It'll be over in a moment."

"What if not? What if it *is* the baby?"

"Then there will be time enough to get to the hospital." Michelle felt she had to comfort Ramón more than herself. "You said that they have started clearing the main roads. That probably means that soon everything will be back to normal."

"What if they don't have a hospital?"

"I think I saw a sign near where we parked your car."

"Oh good." Ramón really looked relieved. Michelle almost congratulated herself though she felt less and less confident by the minute. The pain in her back was increasing, and so was the pressure on her abdomen. "Want me to get any breakfast for you?"

There seemed to be some new kind of awe in his eyes. The possibility of Michelle having a child and truly giving birth soon had suddenly come home to him with a vengeance. Up to now it had been something that was not anything he'd had to deal with. Yes, she had become bigger by the month, and she had started waddling instead of being her old light-footed self. She had

had a couple of mood-swings. But the baby had been sort of an abstract bulge. Now that Ramón was sharing not just a room, but the same bed with her, the changes in Michelle became even more apparent. There were changes every day. If he were honest, the past 24 hours had been nerve-rackingly different with her not moving out of the room, pacing like a tigress in front of the window or the fireplace, barely touching any food he brought her.

"No breakfast, thank you." Michelle closed her eyes and sank against the headrest again. Ramón was about to slip through the door when she called out, "A cup of tea would be nice though." She looked at him pleadingly.

"What kind?"

"Anything herbal. Except ginger. – Oh, and no rosehip either. – And maybe not chamomile either."

Ramón stood on the threshold, impatience spreading over his face. "Can you make up your mind?"

"Anything decaffeinated." Ramón nodded and closed the door behind him. Michelle closed her eyes again. Had she started to become a burden to her friend? Not being able to decide on something as simple as a cup of tea – really?! "Ouch!"

This time the pain had felt as if it were cutting right through her back bone. Michelle whimpered. It couldn't be the baby yet. It was not to come before New Year's. But how much did a baby know about scheduling?! Not even grown-ups with all the calendars, alarm clocks, and wake-up calls in the world managed to be on schedule. Though, to be honest, they usually

221

would be late whereas her baby seemed to feel a little more urgent on showing up.

Michelle hugged her belly. She slowly slid off the bed and managed to get to the window. The view of the few wintry bushes in the yard and the snowy roofs of Downtown was gorgeous. A ferry was lying at the ferry dock. A few cars were parked in the waiting lines. Yet, no ferries were leaving Wycliff or arriving here. A helicopter was circling above. Michelle thought she was able to read the name of a Seattle TV station on its bottom. Well, with being cut off from the outside world Wycliff had probably made it into the news day before yesterday already. She just hadn't felt like watching television. She had so many different things on her mind.

Just imagine her baby was coming here of all places! She cringed. She couldn't make a mess of this gorgeous little room. There were other guests around, too. She couldn't start yelling and screaming in a Bed & Breakfast. The absurdity of the situation hit home, and she laughed. "Please, my little one, can you wait until I can safely be somewhere else?" Michelle whispered to her belly and stroked it softly.

It struck her then that no matter where she'd be, there wouldn't be a place that wouldn't be embarrassing. If it happened at Ramón's family home – how awfully disturbing would that be?! Or back at the dorms in Portland? Or in the middle of the road?

It occurred to Michelle that birthing came probably *never* at the right time or in the right place when it started, and that it

222

always meant one or the other awkwardness. You had to be able to rely on the people around you to do the right thing. She had read about cab drivers who'd delivered babies by the roadside on the way to a hospital. Or policemen, firemen doing their thing. Would Ramón be able to handle the situation? Would he be calm enough to get her to a hospital?

Another cramp, this time in the tummy. Strong, but not as painful as the one before had been. Maybe it was a false alarm after all.

Well, Ramón was probably capable of way more than she was still willing to credit him with. He had been willing to take her to his family over the most festive of all holidays, Christmas. And he had been able to find them a room. And hadn't he just asked her whether he should find her a doctor?! She had her answer right there. Ramón was the most solid man she could imagine. For a moment she wished he had been the baby's father, not that jerk of her ex. But Ramón would probably not even have let such a thing happen –getting her pregnant and leaving her in the lurch. Why was she centering her thoughts around Ramón all of a sudden, anyhow?!

The door knob turned, and a light kick of the foot opened it wide enough for Ramón to step in, two steaming mugs in his hands. He set both of them on Michelle's side of the bed. "I brought you two different flavors," he said with an impish smile. "After you couldn't decide, I thought I'd better make sure that at least one flavor was better than the other." Michelle playfully punched his right upper arm, then winced. "Hey, is that the thanks for my chivalrous act?" he teased. Then he became sober. "How's the baby?"

"I don't know," Michelle gasped as a new streak of pain passed through her abdomen. "Maybe you can ask her that in a few hours."

"What?"

"I keep thinking of the baby as being a girl," Michelle said.

"I was not asking about that. It doesn't matter to me whether it's a boy or a girl." Ramón stared at her in disbelief. "Did you just say 'in a few hours'?"

Chapter 18

December 24, 01:00 p.m.

"Let's see whether they can figure us out," Charlene giggled, and tossed her burgundy-colored pashmina shawl over her shoulder. She saw Dave in his usual seat by the fire place. "Hi, and aren't you looking cozy in that rocking chair of yours?! All toasty and Christmassy."

"Well, I've been called Santa Dave by our little girl. Might as well act the part," he chuckled.

The sisters laughed. They usually had great fun together. But this year somehow beat it all. Maybe it was these extraordinary circumstances that had changed their original plans so much. Maybe it was because just one of them had made a change, and the others had followed suit as in a domino effect.

This morning, right after breakfast, they had decided to go have some fun in Downtown. Naturally, they had left all their gifts for each other at Charlene's house in Steilacoom. They had decided they'd get one gift each to have a traditional Christmas after all.

"We can't have a landslide or two ruin our Christmas," Starlene had stated. And her sisters had agreed.

Off they had walked towards the bluff. The air had been smelling of snow.

"I hope it won't start snowing again, today," Darlene had said. "It's nice to have a white Christmas, for sure, but I'd love to have Christmas dinner at Charlene's rather than anywhere else this year."

"No such thing," Charlene had said. "I had intended to take the turkey out of the freezer when we came home from our outing. It will be a solid block of ice when we get home."

"It's still in the freezer?" Starlene had asked aghast.

"Sure," Charlene had said. "There'd have been time enough. Now it doesn't matter – it won't happen." She had almost slipped on a patch of hardened snow and barely managed to steady herself at the railing.

"I do smell snow, too," Starlene had said after a while as they had been carefully descending the staircase down the bluff. "I wouldn't mind a few flakes tonight, mind you. Since we are still stuck."

"Do you think they know anything new at town hall?" Darlene had looked at her hopefully.

"We could go there and find out," Charlene had suggested, slipping again.

"What kind of silly shoes did you put on this morning anyway?!" Starlene had giggled. "Or are you just faking this?"

"These are my best winter boots," Charlene had protested. "They are not silly. These stairs are silly. They should have an elevator to Downtown."

"Sure," Darlene had said with a tinge of sarcasm. Then she had started to giggle as well. Soon the three sisters had been standing on the stairs and just given way to a gale of laughter to the utter bewilderment or amusement of other people passing by.

"We need to get you some more sensible shoes," Starlene had suggested. "Christmas gift from me and Darlene. What do you say, Darlene?"

"Great idea," Darlene had nodded.

They had finally reached Back Row without further slipping and walked towards Town Hall. The building had been locked though, as it was Christmas Eve and working hours had finished very late the night before. Mayor Thompson had worked on the phone with his staff until almost midnight and given everybody the morning off.

"There is an information board," Charlene had pointed out. They had walked over to the end of the building, and Darlene had started scratching the ice from the protective glass, so they were able to see what information there was.

"It doesn't say anything new," Starlene had said, a little disappointed.

"Well, ladies," a male voice behind them had said. "Rather nothing said than nothing done, right?"

They had turned around and faced a white-haired gentleman with the most incredible blue eyes in a movie-star-like face. Starlene had fluttered her lashes at him, Charlene had gaped, and Darlene had stroked back a few strands of hair behind her left ear.

"We are working on it, believe me." He had smiled. "Clark Thompson, by the way. I, umh, I'm the Mayor of Wycliff. Looks like you belong to our involuntary guests?"

"Involuntary, but not unwillingly," Starlene had said and flashed him a smile.

"We are staying at *The Gull's Nest*," Charlene had added. "So, we are really comfortable."

"Good. Well, you will have to stay another night definitely, but we hope that at least one road will be dug out by tomorrow night. It might take a while longer for the trains."

"Oh, we are here by car," Darlene had hastened to reassure him. "To be able to get back home would be wonderful indeed." Charlene had nudged her, and she had blushed. "This is nothing against Wycliff at all, of course."

Clark had laughed. "I totally understand. Well, ladies, I hope you enjoy today – maybe I see you at 'Caroling at the Town Hall' tonight?"

"Definitely!" Charlene had gushed. "We are looking so forward to this."

Clark had doffed an invisible hat at them and walked on. The three sisters had looked at each other and sighed. "What a handsome man!"

"Isn't he the one who suggested to build an oil plant here?" Charlene had ventured.

"Oh my, you are right!" Starlene had said. "And his wife got kidnapped and all that …"

They had stared after him in silence. "Just as well that he's married," Darlene had shrugged. "That way we won't have to decide who gets to be his first date." And she had given her sisters a big, comical wink.

They had cheerfully walked towards the yacht harbor to see the boats some of which were decked with spruce wreaths and red bows, others with Christmas lights. They had entered the Harbor Pub to have an eggnog. Then they had walked up Main and found a store that sold shoes, amongst other clothing items.

"Look at these," Starlene had exclaimed and pulled a pair of purple suede boots from a shelf. "Aren't these just gorgeous?!"

"Wonderful!" Darlene had breathed. "This color! And the soft material!"

"Yes, and ever so practical to replace what boots I'm wearing," Charlene had laughed. "Girls, I thought we were looking for something practical. Not elegant show pieces, but some boots a logger would want to wear on an icy path. I mean, *you* told me I needed boots that don't make me slip. I'm pretty sure, these won't just make me slip in this weather, but these stilettos will get me in trouble with every crack in the pavement."

Starlene had placed the boots back on the shelf. "I just said they are pretty – and they are. But, of course, you are right. This weather calls for something way sturdier."

In the end, they had found some pretty, low-heeled black leather boots that ended in a furry cuff just under Charlene's knees and sported a glittery buckle above the ankle.

"Quite unusual, indeed," Darlene had stated. "Though I'm not sure I like the combination with your light-blue leggings. It looks somewhat ..." She had searched for a befitting word and failed.

"True," Starlene had said. "They are infinitely cute, but they simply don't go with what you're wearing."

"Well," Charlene had conceded. "I might want to look into a different color ..."

After an hour, Charlene had ended up with an entirely new outfit, and Darlene, who had admired another pair of boots, had found herself overhauling her wardrobe as well.

"You know," Charlene had said when they had finally emerged from the store again, their former attire stashed in fancy paper bags, "I feel like I'm not really done yet. I have changed so much, I'd love to do some final touch-up to my new me."

"Let me guess," Darlene had said enthusiastically. "A date with a hairdresser?"

"That is if they can squeeze us in yet ..."

They had been lucky. Though the two hair salons on Main Street didn't take any walk-ins on Christmas Eve, the tiny one on Back Row did.

When the triplets had emerged after another hour and a half, they had looked at each other conspiratorially. "Let's see whether anybody guesses who is who," Starlene had said.

"Fun," Charlene had agreed.

"Anybody who thinks we are individually different, even though we are triplets, will find us out," Darlene had been convinced.

"I doubt it," Starlene had said briskly.

"Let's wait and see," Darlene had said. And they had returned back to *The Gull's Nest* in high spirits.

The first person they ran into after their return was Pippa who threw her hands into the air with a surprised gasp. "Oh, my goodness! How fun! You are looking so nice. But how is anybody to know who is who now?!" And she looked cluelessly from one triplet to the next. "You are Darlene, right?" she asked one. But the sister shook her head and smiled mischievously. "I give up!"

"You shouldn't," she heard Ronald's voice from the hallway. He had just decided to be a bit more companionable and give it a try by joining the other guests in the lounge by the fireplace. "I'm pretty sure you will be able to discern them sooner or later."

"Later might be too late," Pippa sighed in mock despair. "We all might be on our way home when the penny drops." She turned to the sisters. "This is so not fair!" She laughed. "But my, you *are* looking stunning. Each one of you!"

"Thank you," one sister said, who wore a very elegant black coat and boots and sported a brand-new, platinum-blonde pixie haircut. "I hope I won't long for my old looks. It will take a while to grow back a neat bob, you know ..."

"I love my new haircut," another sister said. "It will be so much easier to style every morning."

"I got to get used to mine," said the third sister. "I just thought your pixies look good on you – so I had them cut my hair in the same style."

"And that makes you, the last one who has just spoken, Darlene," Dave stated from his rocking chair by the fireplace.

The three sisters were totally stunned.

"That's true. But how did you figure it out?!" Darlene exclaimed. "You can't even see how different we look. Are our voices that different?"

"I'd have guessed all the same," Ronald chuckled. "Because you seem to be the most conservative of the three of you. And there is still a tad of green on you whereas your sisters have stepped entirely outside their box."

"Well," Dave said," I couldn't see the colors, of course. But I remember Darlene saying yesterday that she loved her greens and that she pretty much stuck by her guns. And here she tells us that she had her hair cut into the same style as her sisters and that she still has to get used to hers. Which doesn't sound like an entirely convinced decision she made. Right?"

"Caught," Darlene said. "But you make it sound more serious than it is."

"Well, you love your sisters and try to conform to them pretty much as you did before. This time not with a color scheme but by ways of a haircut. That's not all wrong. As long as you are happy with it," Dave said.

"And it suits you really well," Ronald added and blushed, not used to complimenting anybody after such a long time.

"Look at you," Pippa teased. "And can't you be a charmer after all!"

"Don't try me too hard," he grumbled, but there was a new twinkle in his eyes that belied his grumpiness.

At that moment, a door in the hallway was flung open, and Ramón rushed out of his room, panic in his face. He approached the group in the lobby with fast steps and opened his mouth to speak. But his voice failed him.

"Are you alright, dear?" Pippa asked. Then she paled. "Oh my! It is about your girl, right?"

Ramón nodded. "Michelle ... She hasn't been herself all morning. But now it really looks like she is about to give birth."

"Well," Dave said. "Then we ought to get her an ambulance and send her off to the hospital."

"There is no way," Ramón said.

"Why?" Starlene asked and raised her eyebrows.

"She says it's too late."

"And ... is it?" Pippa scoured his face.

"She says she didn't want to go to the hospital. She doesn't have the money. But I think she definitely needs a doctor. I mean, how can you not want to have a doctor when you are giving birth?!" Ramón looked around the group frantically. "So, what do I do?"

"Calm down first," Dave said quietly. "We have a doctor in the house."

"No," Ronald said firmly.

"Oh yes, we do," Dave insisted. "You know everything that needs to be done."

"I told you I don't have a license anymore."

"Neither do cab drivers, fire fighters, policemen, and other people who help out when a woman gives birth."

"It takes more than just cutting an umbilical cord."

"Agreed," Dave said. "And I will make a phone call to get a doctor over. Or a midwife. Anybody with the appropriate certificates, instruments, and whatnot. But, for heaven's sake, Ronald, get yourself over to that girl and honor your learning."

Ronald looked at his hands. They were trembling. He looked from one face to the next. All eyes were upon him.

"You can do this," Pippa finally said calmly. "Nature will help you. And your confidence will be back once you are in the process of helping. I'll heat water." She turned to Dave. "Would you know where Abby keeps fresh towels?"

"At the back of the hallway, there's a walk-in closet."

"Good," Pippa nodded. "Ramón, you better sit down before you faint. Starlene, would you mind calling the emergency line for St. Christopher's?" In a jiffy, Pippa had set everybody busy. Darlene and Starlene went outside to clear a parking spot for any vehicle that might pull up at the curb – be it an ambulance or the private car of a doctor. Dave was talking to Ramón to settle his nerves. Starlene was passing information to the hospital responder. Pippa was filling pot after pot with water and heated them on the stovetop.

In the middle of it all, Abby returned with Aaron and Heather. She quickly grasped the situation and turned to Aaron. "I'm not sure it's a good idea to have a kid witness the situation."

"What situation?" Aaron asked her, somewhat caught off-guard, as he was still relishing the past hours they had spent together downtown. Abby just nudged him with her elbow. At that moment they heard a loud moan come from the direction of the hallway. "Oh, this … yes. Well, what do you think we should do?"

"Could you run another errand with Heather?" She looked a little exasperated. Did she really have to come up with an idea how to keep his daughter from overhearing a woman in labor?!

"Well, you could go down to the Community Center and let Kathy and Roger know that we are about to have a birthing at the house." Pippa suggested from the kitchen.

"Do you need their help?" Aaron asked.

Abby looked at him, rolling her eyes. "Can you just get Heather out of here, please?"

"For how long?"

Starlene finally hung up. She joined Abby and Aaron. "The doctor is with another birther at the hospital right now. But they are dispatching a midwife towards here. She should be coming within half an hour."

"Half an hour?!" Ramón said aghast from the corner where he was sitting next to Dave.

"Keep calm," Starlene said. "Dr. Ronald is with Michelle, and he knows what to do apparently. Right Dave?"

"Indeed, he does," Dave confirmed. "He is a gynecologist. Michelle is in safe hands. And the midwife will be of great support when it comes to delivering the little mite."

Another moan from the room at the back of the hallway. "Aaron ..." Abby gave the man by her side *the* look.

Aaron was startled out of his thoughts again, then he grabbed Heather's hand.

"Where are we going?" Heather asked.

"Want to have some knitting fun with Kathy and Roger?" he asked with faked cheerfulness. He'd have preferred to stay at the house but saw the necessity of getting his daughter away from the situation.

"Sure," she said and smiled brightly. "I might knit a shawl for the baby."

"What do you know about any baby?" he asked.

"Come on, Dad," Heather was giggling. "I know that sound from all those movies on TV. The pretty lady from room number 2 is having a baby. And you want me to be away while she does. So, let's go to the Community Center quickly. I want to have that shawl finished by the time the baby is here." And she pulled Aaron to the front door with enthusiastic urgency.

Chapter 19

December 24, 01:00 p.m.

Kathy and Roger had started out to the Community Center first thing in the morning, right after breakfast. They had spent the evening before packing more knitting kits, and they had stuffed as much yarn as possible into a suitcase that Abby had lent them. They would sell the kits and offer free knitting classes for all the stranded people that wanted to join.

"Because knitting gets your mind off worries", Kathy had told Abby. "Maybe not for long, but certainly for as long as you have to concentrate on your stitches and your pattern."

Abby had looked surprised. "As in therapy for the soul?"

"Yes," Kathy had smiled. "But also from worries such as about temporarily non-available ferry schedules, not being able to go home, not giving your kids the perfect Christmas for once."

"That is wonderful," Abby had exclaimed. "I wish I could come along."

"You don't have any worries yourself, I hope," Roger said with a gentle smile.

Abby frowned, then shook her head. "Actually, I think my problems were solved only last night. Thanks to little Heather." She bit her lips and thought she'd already said too much.

"Heather," Roger said and couldn't subdue a quiet chuckle. "She is something else, isn't she?"

238

"Without our grown-up inhibitions," Abby nodded, "but with a lot of empathy and insight. I'd love to see how she will come out once she is an adult herself."

"Probably wonderful," Kathy said. "Thank you for supporting us with this suitcase!"

"You're welcome," Abby had smiled, and Kathy and Roger had ventured on their walk, laden like a small caravan.

At the Community Center, they had already been anticipated by a group of eager little knitters from the day before, but also by some grown-ups who apparently had caught the needle-crafting bug as well. Whereas the former could hardly wait for Kathy and Roger to open the suitcase and be done with offering their kits or just more yarn, the latter were a bit shyer in their approach, reluctantly made their choices, and looked a bit embarrassed that they knew so little about what the kids had grasped with such seeming ease.

When they finally had grouped around The Sock Peddlers, this corner of the building became the quietest of all. You could have heard the dropping of a stitch if there was one. Every once in a while, somebody raised a hand to signal they needed help with their project. But as the patterns were kept simple and the color changes were in the yarns themselves, even the least capable knitters emerged from the knitting class with a sizeable item that they showed around proudly and couldn't wait to finish later in the afternoon when another class would be offered.

Another group of people was sitting by the fire place in the Community Center's lobby, listening to an author reading from her latest novel. It was a Christmas story about a fictional town on the shores of South Puget Sound, and though most of the listeners were female, one or the other curious male had also seated himself in the group and was listening. Every once in a while, there was a comment from the reader's audience, and she obviously enjoyed the interaction. It felt like in her own childhood when there had always seemed to be some reading aloud going on in her family. Now, these stranded guests of Wycliff had bonded temporarily when she finished her reading after an hour.

"Your small-town – is that Wycliff?" asked one lady, as the reader had to drink a sip of water to keep her voice moist. "Or is it Steilacoom?"

"It's any town you want to make it," answered the author. "It's just a place in my mind. In your mind it might look entirely different. As long as it works for *you*."

"Is it true that you write real people into your stories?" asked somebody else.

"Does it make you feel uncomfortable?" the author asked.

"No, I find it's fun. It gives the story a different vibe. Could you read some more, please? We've got so much time on our hands, stranded as we are. I for my part would love to hear some more."

As the other people in the audience confirmed the wish, the author nodded with a smile. Then she continued reading. The fire in the chimney was crackling merrily.

Caroling sounded from the music room at the other end of the Community Center. The fitness room was filled with an impromptu yoga class, and people did a pretty good job of knotting their limbs in spite of their everyday clothing.

Meanwhile, the fragrance of soul food invaded every nook and cranny of the building, as the commercial kitchen was opened up for Hope and Destiny and their staff of volunteer helpers. They had decided on two dishes only, a meat and a vegetarian one, as they wanted to feed as many people as possible with as little effort as necessary. While one group was baking batch after batch of rolls to go with the stews, Hope commanded a brigade that was responsible for the creation of a cabbage and potato one-pot dish, to be served with an optional smoked sausage. The other was a classic chili con carne that was put together by Destiny and her group.

Busy as the cooks were, there was lots of laughter all around. And Hope and Destiny exchanged happy smiles, as their labor of love was accepted and supported so gladly. Every once in a while, a little wistful frown crept over Hope's face though, and finally, Destiny managed to get to her side.

"What's up, sis'? Not all happy?"

Hope made a little sigh. "Is it so obvious?"

"Well, probably not for everybody else. But I know you too well not to notice."

"It's not really anything."

"Not really, huh?" Destiny rolled her eyes, and Hope had to laugh.

"Okay, yes, but it is too silly even to talk about."

"Girl, I'm not leaving my side of the kitchen to talk about nothing." Destiny stood arms akimbo and glared at her sister. "Just talk it out and make it better." Hope swallowed and looked in the direction of the door. It dawned on Destiny now, and her face relented. She let her arms sink. "You have a crush on that firefighter, right? It's not one-sided after all?"

Hope nodded lightly. "He doesn't know where we are today."

Destiny patted her sister's shoulder. "Listen, if he feels about you the way you feel about him, he'll find you."

"And if he doesn't?"

"Maybe he simply has other duties to fulfil and will have to wait a little longer. There are a thousand reasons that can deter a man from a woman's side."

"But what if …?" Hope left the rest of her thought hanging in the air.

"Oh, but I saw how he was looking at you, sis'. No doubt that he likes you."

"You think?"

"You better stir those potatoes, girl. I smell something burning."

"Oh no!" Hope lifted the lid of the pot nearest to her and started stirring frantically. Then she called out, "They were not burning!" But she only saw Destiny's shoulders quake with a chuckle as she wound her way back to her station.

"A chef better stick with their tasks", Destiny called back. "Keeps some silly minds busy."

"Silly!" Hope muttered. But she knew that Destiny was right. They needed to do their job thoroughly. If they pulled it off to the delight of their guests, their reputation as a restaurant would be made. And that would be a gain of which they hadn't even thought when they had set out on their cooking expedition at the Community Center in the first place.

In the early afternoon, shortly after lunch in the big dining room, classes and other entertainment continued. Little Heather fairly danced into Kathy and Roger's knitting class and tugged on Kathy's sleeve. "You wouldn't guess what's happening up at *The Gull's Nest* right now!" she whispered urgently.

Kathy looked down on the little girl with questioning eyes. "I hope it's something good."

"We are going to have a real Christmas baby!" Heather squealed. "Just like in the story."

"I should hope not," Kathy frowned. "I hope that everything will turn out way better for these people than in the Christmas story."

Heather pondered that, twisting her hands. "You are right," she admitted finally. "And, after all, they are not in the garden shed either."

Kathy bit her lips, suppressing some jolly laughter. "No, and I guess, today we wouldn't even know what to do with frankincense and myrrh anymore."

Heather nodded. Then she said, "But I know what they could do with." She pointed at her knitting needles. "I have started a tiny little shawl for the baby."

Kathy took the little girl into her arms. "You are such a kind being. But you know, we better make something different. A shawl is not for babies, but a cap would be ideal. And I'll help you with it. Actually, you could crank the knitting machine, and I will start along with some baby shoes in the same colors."

"Couldn't we all help out with something?" Heather asked hopefully. "They will need so much more for the baby than just that."

At that point, one of the adult knitters had overheard part of the conversation and turned to one of her neighbors. The group became a bit unruly. Kathy didn't notice as long as she was helping Heather to start the first row on the circular knitting machine, but then she looked at the group. "Do you have any questions?"

Roger turned around at that, wondering as well. He had been instructing a group of children how to cast on stitches. He sought Kathy's eyes, and she gave him just a wondering shrug.

"Actually, it's more of a suggestion," answered the lady who had started the slight unrest. "I apologize, but I couldn't help overhearing that there will be a newborn somewhere in Wycliff tonight. And your words about the gift of the Magi made us wonder whether not all of us could make this knitting class so much more meaningful if we contributed to a baby wardrobe. It's doable, if everybody just did parts, I think."

Kathy's eyes started gleaming. "Why, this is a wonderful idea. And very generous of you. But if anybody would prefer to knit something different, please, feel free to do so."

"We already agreed", said the lady, and a look into the eager faces around her were confirmation enough. Soon, busy quiet set about this part of the room, and the needles were clicking frantically as row after row emerged under ever more skillful fingers, creating patches for blankets, shoes, little sweaters, caps, mittens, and even a knitted kitten.

Nobody watched an unobtrusive, stout lady walk in, pass by, and slip into the room where the choir was rehearsing. Nobody in the choir paid her much attention either, except the conductor, Wycliff High's music teacher. His eyes grew wide, and she shot him a warning glance, while placing the tip of her index finger onto her lips. He looked back at her in an irritated, disappointed way, but nodded shortly before resuming to note down something in his sheet music.

"Let's make tonight extra-special with some beautiful traditional hymns from all over the world," he suggested. "I'm sure that there are a lot of guests from other countries in Wycliff tonight. Any suggestions?"

"'Silent Night' should be a given," somebody said. "I guess it's from Germany."

"Not quite," the conductor said. "It's actually from Austria. But you are right – the original is in German. Is anybody able to sing the first stanza in German?" He looked around, saw a hand rise, and nodded with a big smile. "Your solo tonight, Ma'am. The choir will be humming the accompanying chords. Further suggestions?"

"Isn't 'O Holy Night' originally a French song?" a gentleman asked. "Would that be an option? I know my mother used to love it."

"It's a bit of a challenge in such a short time," the music teacher said. "I'm sure some of you would be up to it, but I'd like everybody involved."

They discussed the program until they had come up with five international carols. Then they decided to leave the rest to a sing-along activity with the Wycliffians and Wycliff's voluntary and involuntary guests. They began some warming up exercises, during which the conductor nervously sought eye contact with the lady who so badly wanted to stay anonymous. Was he doing all the right things? She ignored him, though, and simply played along.

He heaved a big sigh. He couldn't be that wrong in his attempts to get the choir sound right if La Strega herself joined in and seemed to have fun. If she didn't want to be fussed over, he would respect that. He had a hunch that, for once, she just wanted to enjoy herself incognito. Didn't a star have the right to be as human as everybody else? Still, he felt a knot in his throat that almost choked him. How much he wanted to acknowledge that there was a musical legend among them on this special day!

Meanwhile in the commercial kitchen, the clattering of pots and pans had ceased. Everything had been cleaned away, and for a short break the counter tops and all the stations were gleaming again. Hope and Destiny looked at each other with big grins.

"That was quite some success," Destiny said.

Hope nodded. "I'm glad though that Oberlin Church and the Catholic church will step up tomorrow and take over for Christmas dinner. I'm pretty wiped."

"Everybody seems to put in something," Destiny said. "This town is really special. I had heard a lot about its Christmas spirit, but I think you have to have seen and experienced it yourself to believe it. I mean, look at how it has taken over everybody!"

"M-hm," Hope made and looked a bit forlorn in the big kitchen.

"Hey," Destiny said and wiggled her eyebrows. "Mr. Right will show up, I'm sure. You just trust the Lord because He knows when the right moment will be. And I have the feeling He wants you to feel your best when that moment comes. Not now with both of us steaming with the kitchen heat, our hair all askew, and none of us looking like the Queen of Sheba."

Hope laughed against her will. "You are right. I should better concentrate on timing tonight's dining shifts. And what we should offer. Let's check our pantry and go from there."

Meanwhile up on the bluff, everybody left at *The Gull's Nest* was busy preparing for the arrival of a new baby, while waiting for the midwife to arrive. It was a calm business because Ronald commandeered in a quiet, unhectic manner, though he felt very nervous about the situation. Sure, everything would work out as it should; you didn't unlearn a natural process such as birthing. But what if there were complications – and he without a license? Pippa caught his eye at one of these worrying moments and raised her brows.

"You alright, Ronald?" she asked.

He caught himself and gave her a crisp "of course". Pippa nodded and went her way again.

Ramón meanwhile was sitting next to Dave, clasping and unclasping his hands, his face all white.

Dave sensed his unrest. "Calm down, my boy. Even though it might be Michelle's first birth, she's not the first woman in this situation. It just sounds dreadful, but imagine a hospital with a few birthers at the same time."

Ramón laughed, desperation on his face. "I rather not. I mean, imagine that. It's …. I mean … how does a woman stand this? How do they survive this? It sounds awful."

Dave nodded. "That's one of the miracles surrounding birth, I guess. That the mother survives and another life is added to our world. None of our doing, really. It's all in our Maker's hands. We can just help along a bit. Or sit by and wait it out."

Ramón frowned. "I wonder whether the guy who left her knew what he was doing to her."

"Why wonder about him now?" Dave asked. "Is he even worth it? He probably didn't think beyond his own pleasure."

"Son of a gun!" Ramón exclaimed. "I hope he will pay for it."

"She can make him, of course," Dave agreed. "And she should go for child support. Other than that – what will her future look like?"

Ramón shrugged. "She's pretty much on her own right now. Her parents have told her not to reach out to them."

"That might have been a rash decision they are ruing by now," Dave pondered.

"Could be. Do you think she should call them once it's over?"

"Don't you think it might be even nicer if somebody gave them a call while she's still in labor? So that she doesn't have to make that decision herself once she holds her little one in her arms?"

"I'm scared," Ramón admitted. "They sound so different from my loving family. So cold and calculating. What if they have their minds set against Latinos as well? They might not welcome my call."

"Then it would be their loss not to appreciate the friendship of a fine young gentleman who sees so caringly to a young lady who is in distress." Dave cleared his throat, then turned his head towards Ramón with unseeing eyes. "You placed yourself on a white horse and have donned a shining armor this far, young man. Now it's time to face the dragon."

Ramón laughed sheepishly. "Well, so be it. After all, what could they do to me, right? It's just a phone call, and I'm not the one who has been doing wrong by their daughter."

"That's the spirit, Ramón!" Dave applauded. "And if the outcome is contrary to what I expect it will be, then you have spared Michelle a heart-breaking moment."

Chapter 20

December 24, 02:00 p.m.

It never rains, but it pours. In the middle of Dave's serious conversation with Ramón about Michelle and her baby's future, in the middle of the bustle between the impromptu birthing room and the kitchen the doorbell rang, and Abby rushed to open. Outside stood a lady heavily bundled up, big carpetbag in hand, with flushed cheeks either from the cold or the effort to make it through the snowy outdoors.

"Did you call about an imminent birth?" she asked.

"Are you the midwife?" Abby countered hectically.

"I am."

"Well, please, come in. I'll show you the way." Abby stepped aside and let the lady enter.

"How far is she gone?"

"I have no idea." Abby blushed. She felt embarrassed to discuss such intimate details with a stranger, in front of Dave and Ramón at that. "The doctor will be able to tell you."

"The doctor? There is a doctor here already, and you are giving me a call?"

"He's not licensed in this state." The lady puffed and put down her carpetbag. Abby quickly added, "In fact, his license has run out. So, we wanted to make sure that everything is lawful and so …" She faltered.

The midwife relented and slipped out of her coat. Abby took it and hung it on the clothes rack by the door. "It's the last room on the right."

A loud yelp from the back of the house would have indicated as much to the midwife, who hoisted up her bag now and walked towards that door. Abby sighed with relief. At least Michelle was taken good care of now.

At that moment the phone on the reception desk rang. Abby lifted the receiver without even checking the number on the display.

"*The Gull's Nest*, Abby speaking," she said automatically.

"I just wanted to wish you a Merry Christmas, Abby," a male voice said. Abby shrunk as if struck. "I know, it's been a while. And we parted in sort of a … well, anyhow, I thought we are still friends and all that."

This is just what I needed on top of it all, Abby thought sarcastically. Aloud she said, "Are we though?"

She took the phone with her, went to her own room, and closed the door. Then she sank into the armchair by her fireplace.

"I know, it must be a surprise to you."

"Surprise, indeed, Hank. You've got the nerve to call!" At that moment, Abby had totally forgotten that only a couple of days ago she had intended to drive all the way up to Seattle and visit her ex-boyfriend, Hank, to try and persuade him to return to Wycliff. "What makes you think I even want to talk to you."

"Hey," Hank said and sounded a bit wounded. "We both agreed that it was the best way for us to separate back then. Don't say you didn't want me to leave."

"I didn't," Abby said. "I mean, I did."

Hank laughed nervously. "That's what I've always found so endearing about you, scatterbrains. Anyhow, back then you said I should leave. And so, I did."

"Well, there was a female reason in Seattle, as far as I remember," Abby countered. "You didn't think you'd get away with two-timing me, did you?"

"But you had less and less time what with your business," Hank complained. "I felt left in the lurch, and I needed somebody for comfort."

"Poor you," Abby said, rolling her eyes. "Well, you obviously got more than just comfort from her. So, what makes you call now?"

Hank sighed. "Always straightforward, right?"

"Always."

"Well, I … I know you are snowed in in Wycliff. And there are those landslides. Saw it on TV last night at the sports bar around the corner."

"What of it?"

"I had thought of coming down for a visit over Christmas. But that is off for now, of course. It rather looks like it might be New Year's Eve."

"And what makes you think that I am good with that?" Abby asked.

"Well, we have been good with each other for years, and I thought I could move in again. Just as an old friend. Maybe with benefits if you want."

"What?!" Abby held the receiver away and stared at it aghast. His voice was going on and on, and she didn't hear a single word, as thoughts rushed through her mind and made her dizzy. Then she held the receiver to her ear again. "What did you say?"

"I know, it's short notice. Grace threw me out last night. I have been able to find a hotel room close-by, so I didn't have to lug my stuff more than a few blocks through the snowfall. But do you have any idea how much a hotel room in Seattle is during the Christmas season? It's costing me an arm and a leg. So, I thought, good old Abby has that cozy Bed & Breakfast over in Wycliff, and she's got a golden heart."

"Yes," Abby said, and a wave of rage rose in her. "Of course. And there was always breakfast on the table and some decent dinner. And everything was taken care of by me."

"Yes, right?" Hank said cheerfully.

"You must think me an utter idiot," Abby said and felt ice-cold inside all of a sudden.

"What?"

"Do you think I am so lonesome and needy that at the first hint you would like to return I'd say 'yes' and 'please' and open my doors for you? You have some cheek that you think you just need to call and tell me what a cozy place and 'golden heart' I have, to make me forget everything that happened. That you betrayed me after all these years. That you left me for somebody else." She swallowed. "You know, Hank, you are a lousy mite, and I surely do pity you. You even lied to me when you told me you had an apartment of your own in Seattle."

"I didn't lie. I really had one. But do you have any idea how much ..."

"... an apartment costs in Seattle?" Abby felt like punching somebody. "As a matter of fact, I do, and I couldn't care less. So, you moved in with that woman, and now she has tossed you out. Good job. I wonder what you did this time. Or maybe, I don't wonder at all. Maybe she simply didn't have such a 'golden heart' as 'good old Abby' did, overlooking all your whims and forgiving you your lack of support when it came to my business."

"But ..."

"No but," Abby said firmly. "You listen to me, Hank. There won't be a meeting between the two of us. Not anywhere. Ever. Don't even try to call this number again." Then she pressed the disconnect button.

She dropped the receiver to the floor and yelled from the deepest depth of her heart. Somebody rushed to her door and threw it open.

"Anything happened to you?" Pippa asked worried.

Abby opened her eyes. "I'm alright," she said calmly. "I just needed a good cleansing of my system."

255

Pippa grinned. "You surely outdid our birther next door."

Abby blushed. "You wouldn't guess with whom I was on the phone right now."

Pippa laughed. "Well, there are only two possibilities, actually. The lottery to tell you that you have won the jackpot. Or an ex-boyfriend of yours to hook up with you again. Judging from the anger in your shout, it was the latter."

Abby had to laugh. "You are so right. You know the human soul, Pippa. I wish I were as wise as that. How do I get there?"

"Easily," Pippa said. "You just wait until you are older and your ex-boyfriends don't call you anymore."

Abby grinned. "I'll be out in a moment again. Just let me get some big breaths."

Pippa nodded and left her, closing the door softly. Abby buried her face in her hands, sagging. Life was a roller coaster sometimes. But she had finally managed to step off its madness.

Pippa, meanwhile, joined Dave and Ramón because she was not needed in the birthing room for now. "It looks like a lot of things are wrapping themselves up today."

"Well, they better," Dave said.

"How do you mean?"

"Well, it's Christmas Eve. If things aren't wrapped up by now …" He chuckled, and Pippa burst into laughter.

Ramón bit his lips. "I guess I better make my phone call now. Is there any place private? I mean, our room is not an ideal location for ..."

"Use mine," Dave said. "24."

"Thank you," Ramón said and rose, retrieving his smart phone from the coffee table. "Keep your fingers crossed for me." He left the cozy sitting area by the fireplace and made for the stairs.

"Why keep fingers crossed?" Pippa wanted to know.

"He's calling Michelle's parents," Dave said.

"Oh." Pippa nodded. Then she leaned back into her armchair. "I wouldn't want to be in his shoes."

"Well," Dave said. "It's the difficult tasks we take on that make us grow."

Ramón's feet grew heavier and heavier as he reached the top of the stairs and walked towards Dave's room. Michelle had given him her home number a while ago. That had been when she had still had some hope that her parents might relent towards her and her situation. Only – they hadn't. And she hadn't talked to them in over a month now. What would he, a perfect stranger, tell them? Would they even hear him out?

He gently opened the door and entered the almost bare room Dave lived in. Dave, the Santa-look-alike. Santa Dave, as little Heather called him. He seemed to have what a lot of blind people accomplished – a fine hearing that went beyond mere sound waves. The listening kind that finds the nuances of thought and emotion. He had sensed the fear that Ramón was battling. But he had sent him on because he also knew that some things had to be done.

"Coward!" Ramón scolded himself. Then he stood by the window and gazed out across the snowy gardens, the rooftops of Downtown, the gray sea, the hazy shades that were islands out in the Sound. With a sigh he pressed some keys on his phone and listened intently for his call to go through.

"Hello," a gruff voice said on the other side.

"Hello," Ramón stammered. "Is this the Taylor residence?"

"And who wants to know this?"

"Uh, sorry …" Ramón wiped his hand across his face. "This is Ramón Desoto."

"Should I know you?"

"No. I mean, yes."

"Listen, I don't have any time for silly pranks or requests for money. It's Christmas Eve, and that means family time in this country, Mr. Resoto."

"Desoto," Ramón corrected. "Mr. Taylor, this is about your family." He briefly paused. "It's about Michelle."

"Michelle?" A female voice in the background asked frantically. Then he heard hands change a receiver and the woman's voice was on the phone with him. "Did you say Michelle? How is she? Where is she? And who are you?"

"Calm down, woman," Mr. Taylor said to his wife.

Ramón pictured him looming over her. "I'm Ramón Desoto, a college friend of Michelle's."

"A college friend?" Michelle's father snorted. "Michelle seems to make the oddest choices of late."

The receiver was muted with a hand apparently, but Ramón was still able to overhear Mrs. Taylor's words. "This is not about Michelle's friends or choices; this is about *her*. Now, please, let me talk to this young man."

Ramón heard some uncouth words about strangers calling over the holidays, probably scrounging off his daughter's bank account, before Mrs. Taylor was on again. "I'm sorry for this," she said gently. "Are you still there?"

"I am. And I am sorry for intruding on you in this way. It's not usually my style. But I wanted to let you know that Michelle is … She is having her baby right now." Silence. "Mrs. Taylor?"

A big, dry sob. "Oh, my baby! And she is all alone in this!" Another sob. "Where is she anyhow? Can I get there?"

"First of all, she is in good hands, I believe. She is with a doctor and a midwife in Wycliff in Washington State right now."

"Washington? Why? Why not in Portland?!"

"Umh, it's a long story."

"I will listen."

"Well, Michelle and I have become friends in the past months. Not the kind your husband may think of. Umh. I knew she would be alone at the dorms over the holidays, so I invited her

259

to come along and visit my family in Renton instead. Only, we never made it that far because of the snow."

"Which hospital is she at?"

Ramón almost coughed. "Not a hospital, Mrs. Taylor. Everything happened way too fast to go there. She's at a nice Bed & Breakfast place with me."

"Oh my God," the woman moaned. "How horrible!"

"Well, just rest assured that everything is being done to make her as comfortable as if she were in a hospital," Ramón consoled her though he had no inkling what a hospital would be doing in such a situation. "I just thought I'd let you know. And whether she would be permitted to … umh …" He faltered, then mustered courage again. "She told me that Mr. Taylor had told her that she needn't ever come home again. But I thought since she is having his first grandchild right now, you might want to know and maybe even want to see her and the baby after all."

"Oh, of course we do!" Mrs. Taylor exclaimed. "We will come right away."

The receiver was changed over again, and Mr. Taylor was on the phone once more. "Listen, Mr. Redondo."

"Desoto."

"Well, yes. Listen. Of course, we will not come right away. And you tell that girl that she should be glad that …"

The phone must have been wrested from his hands for Mrs. Taylor was on again. "Don't listen to my husband, Mr. *Desoto*." And she made it a point that she had heard Ramón's last

260

name right. "This is all silly male pride about not losing face and retracting words that were said in anger. Of course, our little girl always has a home here. I have been missing her voice so badly over the past months." She sobbed. "And to know that this is such a tough day for her, and I cannot be there ..."

Ramón didn't know how to react. So, he scrambled on. "Is this what I can tell her?"

"No." Mr. Taylor said in the background.

"Stop it, Jackson!" Mrs. Taylor told him off. Then she said to Ramón, "Yes. Of course. My husband will get over it and accept that there is currently no husband or male parent in the picture. Tell Michelle that I will try to travel over as quickly as possible."

"I will," Ramón said. "Though it might take you a while yet. We are snowed in. And they don't know when Wycliff will be connected with the outer world again."

"I will find a way," Mrs. Taylor was convinced.

Mothers always think they do, Ramón thought to himself. And somehow, against all odds, they actually do. Mostly. Aloud he said, "I'll make sure to tell her as soon as I'm permitted to talk to her."

"Is she still in?"

"Yes," Ramón said and overheard a loud yelp of pain again from below just at that moment.

"Was that her?" the voice sounded worried.

"No," Ramón lied. "That was on TV. Sorry." Why should he add to the woman's anguish?

"Oh," she just said. "Well."

"Merry Christmas, Mr. and Mrs. Taylor," Ramón said because he had run out of things to say.

"Merry Christmas, Mr. Desoto," Mrs. Taylor said. Ramón was almost about to hang up on her when she added, "Oh, and Mr. Desoto ..."

"Yes?"

"Thank you for being such a friend to our daughter. I'm sure she knows what she has in you."

Click.

Ramón looked at the receiver, incredulous. He had done it! He had rebonded Michelle and her family. He, a stranger. No, not a stranger anymore. Michelle's friend.

Another yelp of pain from below, then a tiny meowing sound.

"Madre mia," Ramón said under his breath and turned towards the door. Then he exclaimed, "Madre mia, the baby is here!" And bounded out of the room.

Chapter 21

December 24, 02:00 p.m.

"Sorry, we are out of Weisswurst," Sabine told the lady in front of the deli counter at *Dottie's Deli*.

"But I ordered them well ahead of today," the lady said with an upset look at the display. "Are you sure you didn't wrap a package for me and put it into your walk-in cooler?"

Sabine nodded. "Absolutely sure. I have looked. There is not a single package with your name on it!"

"But what am I going to do now?!" The lady asked. "It's such a Christmas tradition in our family. Everybody has been looking forward to this for months."

"Can you, please, make up your mind, lady?" somebody in the line asked impatiently. "You are not the only one having a special dinner tonight. And we want to be home in time for church, too."

"Well," the lady at the counter said, turning towards the line and, not seeing who had spoken, addressed all of them. "If you are such Christians, you might be a bit more empathetic." Nobody answered her back, but some people looked away. Some were rolling their eyes. One just said, "Oh, please ..."

Sabine suppressed a smirk. "I'm truly sorry about the sausages. Maybe I may cut you some slices of our liver cheese?"

"Nobody in our family eats liver."

"Well," Sabine said. "It's just a silly name for a veal loaf. It's got as fine a structure as cooked liver, I guess, but there is neither liver nor cheese in it." The lady eyed the loaf that Sabine pointed out in the counter. "Actually, it might even be quite similar to the veal in the Weisswurst, just a bit differently seasoned. It's another shape, too. And you simply pan-fry it."

The lady sighed. "I guess I will have to make it do."

"How much would you like then?"

Another long sigh. "Eight slices, about half an inch thick?"

Sabine nodded and set herself to work.

Dottie's Deli was crowded this afternoon. It seemed as if everybody had left buying groceries until the last minute and as if it was the last opportunity to buy anything at all. Behind the deli counter, even Julie, Dottie's journalist daughter, was helping out at the slicers. Dottie and her business partner and best friend, Pattie May, went dizzy with stuffing goodies into totes and tapping numbers into the cash registers. There was no time for any chit-chat with the customers. Everybody just wanted to be done with today's work and go home.

"Why do we make Christmas such madness each and every day, I wonder?" said one of the customers as Dottie was trying to fit one more item into the lady's cloth tote, gave up, and pushed it into one of the store's totes.

Dottie had no answer other than "Merry Christmas", thinking that this lady herself was adding to the madness by shopping at the very last minute.

"How long will you be open today?" asked another customer.

"Three. Another hour to go," Pattie May answered irritated. "Bummer, did I already add this box of chocolate to the bill or not?"

"You didn't," the customer said, and Pattie lifted her gaze from the cash register to the customer, surprised by such honesty.

"Angela," she said with a smile. "Merry Christmas!"

"Merry Christmas to you," Angela Fortescue said, her heavily made-up face beaming.

"Why, you are looking great today! It's twenty dollars and seventy cents."

Angela nodded and handed over some bills. "Keep the change," she said. "And Merry Christmas to you." She grabbed her tote and gave Dottie a tiny wave, too.

"Goodness, that lady has changed," somebody in the line muttered more to herself than anybody else.

"Well, I guess designing all these wonderful cloth totes and bags has brought some meaning to her life," another customer in line said.

"I heard that her daughter has returned to her after years of separation," another one said. "Of course, it could just be a rumor, but …" she left the rest unsaid.

"Little Florence?" an old woman said. "Oh my, wouldn't that be a Christmas surprise to her?!"

On and on the chatting and gossiping went, and the shop door kept opening and closing continuously, letting new people into the warmth and letting out customers with totes crammed with German groceries. Dottie's team was working unremittingly, but their Christmas cheer was wearing thin in this last hour of business.

Outside, on snowy Main Street, Angela Fortescue was probably the happiest person in the world right now. At least she thought she was. How her little world had changed in a relatively short time! Not only had she helped found a cottage industry business that gave women of little means some extra money on the side. She had found new friends in doing so, one of them being Mayor Thompson's wife, Thora. They were designing all kinds of environmentally friendly shopping totes, but also handbags. Their totes were selling in almost all of Wycliff's stores, and *La Boutique* sold a line of their high-end evening handbags. She had been debt free for months after years of penny pinching and even being able to save up a little. And on top of all this, her long-lost daughter, Florence, had finally returned home.

"Merry Christmas, Angela," somebody called from across the street and started approaching her.

"Why, Thora!" Angela exclaimed. "I have just been thinking of you and how much our friendship has changed my life." They hugged, totes and all.

"You are looking wonderful today," Thora said. "As if you were beaming from the inside!"

"And so I am," Angela smiled. "I feel like I have received all the Christmas bliss there is in the world today."

"What happened?"

"Let's have a quick cup of coffee at *The Lavender Café*," Angela suggested.

Thora looked at her watch nervously. "Okay, but just a quick cup. Clark will be home in half an hour, and I have promised him to read over his Christmas address one more time."

The unequal friends, one so much older and always outfitted a bit overly youthful and over the top, the other in her mid-forties with dark short hair and a no-nonsense attitude, walked towards Back Row.

"You remember I told you about my dreadful marriage? I mean, it was my own fault. I should never have pretended to Thomas that his cousin Johnny's child was his own. But when one is young and foolish ..."

Thora nodded. She remembered the story Angela had told her. And how Thomas had divorced her, sending little Florence back to her natural father. How Angela had reached out to Florence in letters that finally were returned with a letter from Johnny, who told her to stop writing, as it upset his wife receiving letters in their home that were written by a former love of his.

"But how did she find you?" Thora asked as they entered the cozy place that was fragrant with coffee vapor and the sweet scent of vanilla and gingerbread.

A waitress approached them hastily. "You know we are closing in half an hour?" she asked anxiously.

"Sure," Thora said. "No worries, we'd just like a cup of coffee and one of your lavender cookies each, and you can boot us out on the hour!"

The waitress smiled. "I wouldn't be like this under normal circumstances, but today ..."

"... is Christmas Eve," Angela said. "Of course, it's your good right to close punctually. As it is any given day, I should think."

The waitress led them to a tiny table in the back of the room and quickly wiped off a few crumbs with a napkin. "I'll be back in a moment," she said.

"So, again," Thora asked. "How in the world did she find you? I mean, you haven't heard of each other in how many decades?"

Angela sighed. "I have stopped counting them. Well, imagine that Margaret called me from *La Boutique* yesterday and said she had a customer there who'd like to meet me about a special bag design."

"Did she know it was Florence?"

"She had no clue. Well, she gave Flo my address and sent her over. You can't believe how shocked I was when I opened the door!"

Thora shook her head in wonder. "I can't even imagine. So, you recognized her immediately?"

"What with Johnny's eyes and Italian looks and that tiny birthmark over her left upper lip? I thought I'd lose my mind!"

The waitress came with two cups of coffee and a plate of cookies. "The extra ones are on the house because it's Christmas," she said cheerfully. Thora and Angela thanked her profusely.

"So, Florence came in, and it felt so weird. I was half ashamed of how poor my home must be looking to her compared to what it was like when she was sent away as a child. On the other hand, I'm so proud of what I have achieved over time."

"And it *is* beautiful and cozy, Angela. No need to be ashamed of anything in it."

"Well, we sat down, and we just looked at each other for a while because I was so flabbergasted, and she must have been, too. To think that, after all these years, you are able to embrace your own child again and yet, you can't because she's become a stranger!" Angela's eyes teared up.

"That's awful," Thora muttered.

"It is. It was. But ..." Angela pulled herself together. "In the end she rose and embraced me, and it felt so heavenly good and right. And it was as if all the decades fell off and it was just the two of us again. Like we were way back when – only without the lies and pretenses and fears."

"Beautiful," Thora breathed. Then she nibbled on one of the glazed lavender cookies.

"Well, she told me that she was passing by Wycliff on her way up to Seattle. A business trip, she said. And she remembered the town and simply wanted to see once again where she had spent some years of her childhood. She said she had never thought that I might still be living here."

"Then how …?"

"Flo recognized the design of one of the handbags in Margaret's store as mine. She remembered that I had sewn an additional little pocket underneath one of my pompadours because it made so much more sense to have a bill or a credit card handy in a jiffy instead of having to rummage through the bag's inside. So, she asked Margaret who the designer was and never gave away that I was her mother."

"What a coincidence," Thora marveled.

"I don't believe in coincidences," Angela said, her eyes shiny. "I think it's divine providence."

Thora nodded and sipped from her cup. "So, you caught up on all the time lost?"

"Yes and no. I mean, how can you catch up on everything in so short a while?! I showed her my home, and we went through my photo album. So many memories. So much time lost." Angela swallowed hard. "In the end, it became dark, and she said she had to go because she was living up on the bluff and didn't want to climb up there in the dark."

"Will she be back?"

"Oh yes! We are going to spend Christmas together. She'll come to dinner after the Town Hall Caroling tonight. And though she will have to stay at *The Gull's Nest* because I simply cannot accommodate her in my tiny home, she promised she'd be with me all of Christmas Day."

"Does she have any family of her own who is waiting for her?"

"Oh no," Angela said. "That's the only sad thing. She never married for fear that everything might turn out as bad as Thomas' and my marriage. Or as tainted as Johnny's because she felt she made her step-mother really unhappy by her very existence."

"That is truly sad," Thora said. "I mean, taking it out on a child."

"She insists that her step-mother didn't. But that her happiness seemed sort of decreased by having her as a reminder of Johnny's life before their marriage."

"Silly. Pretty much everybody has what you'd call 'a life before'."

"Not everybody is strong enough for every situation," Angela said quietly and smoothed out a wrinkle in her cloth napkin. "Anyhow, there is no family waiting for her. So, I can enjoy her to the full and without the bad conscience of stealing her from anybody."

"Oh, I hope you will have as lovely a Christmas as can be, Angela," Thora gushed and stroked her friend's hand.

"It will be, I'm sure," Angela smiled.

"You said she was on a business trip?"

"I did. But you know, I don't even know what she's doing. I never asked her. I was just so incredibly happy to finally have her back."

"That's certainly more important than anything," Thora chuckled.

"Oh, but rest assured I'll ask her tonight," Angela said. "There is so much to catch up on."

"I bet," Thora nodded and smiled.

"Ladies," the waitress approached them again.

"Oh, alright," Thora said and crammed the rest of her cookie into her mouth. Then she took out her wallet. She swallowed the cookie down with a sip of coffee. "It's on me," she said to Angela, shoving a bill onto the table that exceeded the due amount by far. "The rest is for you," she smiled at the waitress. "Merry Christmas!"

They left behind a happily beaming waitress as they stepped outside again. Winter dusk was setting in already. "See you later at the Town Hall Caroling," Thora said and hugged her friend.

Angela just hugged her back and nodded. Then she plodded on towards her home to prepare for her cherished visitor.

When Thora was passing the post office on Back Row a few minutes later, she bumped into a man who was trying to get a glimpse into the dimly lit basement of *The Soup Cellar*.

"Trying to get a bowl of soup?" she asked. The man unfolded to his full length. "Oh, it's you, Pascal!"

"Yeah," he said and looked a bit bewildered. "As a matter of fact, I am wondering where the ladies from the establishment below are. I have cleared their stairs for them and just strewn another light layer of sand. But they haven't been in for the past 24 hours." He put on a long face.

"You mean Hope and Destiny?"

"That's them."

"Haven't you heard that they are busy cooking and serving food over at the Community Center? For all the stranded tourists?"

"Are they?" Pascal's face lit up. "Oh, that sounds like their golden hearts alright!" He quickly marched off, then turned around once more. "Thank you, Thora!"

"Merry Christmas!"

"And to you!"

Thora shook her head with a big smile. "And if there isn't some love story in the making," she said to herself.

Pascal quickened his pace. A few minutes later, the Community Center came in sight, and the warm lights from the windows painted yellow puddles on the snow outside. Pascal stomped off the snow from his heavy boots before he entered through the front door.

The lobby was crowded with people, some sitting by the fire place, others inspecting the Christmas tree decorations. Pascal moved on quickly. He already smelled something savory in the air. That must be tonight's dinner batches getting prepped in the commercial kitchen.

He peeked around the corner and saw Hope chopping herbs. Destiny was carrying a heavy pot of water from a sink to a station when her eyes caught sight of him. She blinked, then she set down her pot. She walked to her sister's side. "You know", Destiny said, "I think I forgot something over at *The Soup Cellar*. Let me fetch it quickly. I'll be back in a few." Then she grabbed her coat from a hook, walked out of the kitchen, and winked at Pascal as she was passing him.

He blushed. Was it so obvious? He felt all these tiny butterflies inside. But – would he stand a chance?

Pascal picked up his courage and stepped inside the kitchen. Hope was humming under her breath, chopping away in utter concentration. But somehow, she must have sensed another person in the room, for suddenly she looked up from her task.

"Pascal!" she exclaimed, and a huge smile broke over her face.

He let out a big breath of relief. This Christmas might be different from all his former ones. He walked up to her station.

"I've been looking for you at your restaurant. I had no idea you were doing this." He swept his arm over the scene – the stations in full preparation of another feeding of the five thousand. Then he rounded the counter and stood right next to her. She looked at him with shining eyes.

Pascal had no idea whether he was looking love-struck. He didn't care. "Do you mind?" he asked, pulling a branch of mistletoe out of his pocket to hold it over them. Then he simply enjoyed Hope's soft and tender lips.

Chapter 22

December 24, 03:00 p.m.

Michelle felt absolutely exhausted and exhilarated at the same time. Little did she care about what went on around her yet. She was holding this tiny bundle of life, this utterly perfect miracle in her arms. The face all red and wrinkled, a tiny button of a nose, the cutest bud of a mouth, and these mini-fingers, all perfect with their tiny nails. How had this all grown inside her? And how could her parents not want the little boy? Just because they disliked that there was no father who was willing to take his part in the child's life?

"I will always be there and protect you," she whispered, and the little bundle moved, the face stretching into a big toothless yawn. "I love you with all my heart."

Ronald and the midwife were moving around the room, putting things in order.

"It's a wrap," said the midwife cheerfully. "And it was an easy one at that. Not always the case with a first one."

Ronald nodded. "Thank you for coming over and being such a support."

"You know," the midwife said. "In the paperwork you are giving me all the credit because legally you have to. What with your out-of-state license expired ... But honestly: You should go for a Washington license and practice again. It's a shame a wonderfully empathetic doctor like you should be lost to patients!"

Ronald blushed. "Thank you. I feel … a bit overwhelmed right now." He was looking at his hands, and they were shaking. "I guess I'm not used to all the adrenaline anymore that comes with a birth." He turned to Michelle, who was talking to her little boy in the softest voice that a new mother would find for her baby. "What are you going to call him?" he asked.

"Noel," Michelle said.

"What a beautiful name," the midwife approved. "Will you also bestow him a middle name?"

"I don't know yet," Michelle smiled and was searching the door with her eyes. "Does Ramón know already?"

Ronald chuckled. "I suppose everybody who is inside the house knows that by now we have a new guest at *The Gull's Nest*. And they are probably bursting with curiosity. Would you want me to ask Ramón in? Do you feel up to it?"

Michelle nodded. Ronald opened the door only by a crack and pushed his head into the hallway. His eyes found Ramón as he was nervously pacing to and fro in the lobby.

"Young man," Ronald called. Ramón whipped around. "Somebody wants to be introduced to you."

Ramón eagerly rushed towards Ronald. "Is she alright?"

"Everything went just fine," Ronald smiled. The midwife appeared behind him now and squeezed past him into the hallway. "You can go in now. But only for a couple of minutes. She needs to rest." He opened the door for Ramón, stepped outside, and closed the door behind the young man.

Abby had fixed a coffee tray for the midwife and Ronald, and they sat down, gratefulness, exhaustion, and wonder mingling in their faces. Every birth was such a miracle in itself. A life had come into being without any human determination as to that there *would* be life. It was or it wasn't. In this case, the baby had developed in all the healthiest ways, and the mother had birthed it, and they had only had to lend a helping hand. No complications whatsoever. Well, according to what Ronald knew, the complications would be coming up in the shape of the girl's parents and the baby's father soon enough.

"... you know?" The midwife's voice was droning through his thoughts.

"Excuse me, what did you say?"

The midwife smiled at him with kind eyes. "I said that there was going to be an opening at the hospital next year. They will post the position by summer when their residential gynecologist is retiring. You could see to your license and then apply, you know?"

Ronald scratched his brow. "I'm not sure whether I'm up to it."

"Well, you certainly were in there," the midwife said and nodded in the direction of Michelle and Ramón's bedroom. Then she emptied her cup. "At least give it a thought, will you?"

Ronald nodded. "I will."

The midwife rose and gave him her hand. "It was a pleasure working with you, Dr. Hoffman."

"The pleasure was all mine," he answered courteously and rose, shaking her hand. "Merry Christmas to you!"

"Merry Christmas," she smiled. "See you back in Wycliff soon." She went for her coat and hat, then closed the front door behind her. Ronald was still standing.

"Well, there you go," Dave said from his rocking chair by the fire. "I'm not the only one who tells you to return to what's your obvious vocation. Even a position at the hospital is going to open. There is no coincidence in life."

Ronald sighed. "I guess I have to make up my mind whether it's ready for spontaneous decisions or not."

"You know, when the big guy upstairs hands you an opportunity that might save you, you better grasp it with both hands."

"Maybe I need to rediscover my faith first."

"Well, you just helped deliver one of His miracles. What's not to believe in?"

Ronald bit his lips. "I hear you," he sighed. "He gives, and He takes. I guess His taking is sometimes harder to accept than the way we take His giving for granted." He went for the front door and slipped into his coat. "I'll take a walk for a while. I'll be back in time to take you down for the Town Hall Caroling." Opening the door, he welcomed the cold air that hit his face. Maybe it would clear his mind and help him make a decision.

Meanwhile, in the birthing room, Ramón was cautiously approaching Michelle and the tiny bundle in her arms. He was literally walking on tiptoes. He smiled at his friend nervously.

"Come here," she said softly.

He went to her side and stood there, helplessly. "Are you okay?"

"A bit sore," she said, her voice still hoarse. She fussed with the blanket that was wrapped around her boy-child. "Meet little Noel!"

"Noel?"

"As in Christmas?"

"Nice!" He bent over and looked at the tiny face and the thin streaks of baby hair covering its head. "He's so … tiny!"

"Well, he was big enough to make me feel I was ripping apart," Michelle chuckled, then moaned. The baby opened his eyes. "Want to hold him?"

"I …" Ramón stared at her doubtfully.

"Come on," she encouraged him. "Noel is not made of sugar." Ramón bent over and dug his hands underneath the bundle. "Just support his head with one hand. There you go!"

Ramón gazed at the little boy in wonder. The little boy stared back. "He's looking at me!" Ramón gasped. Then he quickly handed the bundle back to its mother. He exhaled when she took over again. "This is incredible!"

"Well, he is pretty real to me," Michelle said with a smile that came from a source which seemed to light her face in a way

Ramón had never seen before. "But my little guy needs a male role model in his life, too." Ramón looked at Michelle questioningly. "You have been such a great friend all these months and especially these past days – kind of a real hero. Would you …" Michelle swallowed. "Would you be Noel's godfather? Please?"

Ramón's eyes widened. "You want me …"

"You'd be perfect. I know this. You would teach him decency and responsibility. Just by being around every once in a while. Just by being you."

Ramón cleared his throat. "If you really trust me to be good enough for this …"

"More than good enough, for sure!"

"Well, then … Yes." He touched one of the baby's hands with his index finger, and the baby's tiny fingers grasped it and closed tightly around. "You are my new godchild," he whispered softly. "I hope we will be great friends, little one."

Michelle smiled. "Thank you," she whispered, then closed her eyes. Ramón carefully removed his finger from the baby's tiny fist. Then he tiptoed towards the door. The news about Michelle's parents could wait. Let the mother and her baby get some rest first.

"How is she?" Darlene asked Ramón when he returned to the lobby.

"How is the little boy?" Charlene wanted to know.

"What's his name?" Starlene asked.

Ramón shook his head as if waking from a dream. "The little boy is beautiful. His name is Noel. And Michelle is doing fine – she just fell asleep." He slowly let himself down into the corner of a sofa. "I'm his godfather now."

"Oh, how wonderful! Congratulations," Abby said. "That must be some great experiences you will be making."

"Well," Ramón admitted. "I have to get used to the thought first and then figure what I'm supposed to do. I mean, I don't even know whether he will like me."

"Ah, come on," Starlene chided. "What's not to like about a fine young gentleman like you?"

"I'm a Latino."

"That's racist. Children don't know about ethnicity unless they get it from their parents."

"Or grandparents," Ramón said darkly. "Michelle's father might not like me in the picture."

"Well, that's his loss," Darlene said. "Very obviously, the baby's natural father doesn't show half the responsibility and kindness that you do. So, stand tall, young man! And I hope that man gets taken down a notch or two."

"Yes," Charlene agreed. "If Michelle has decided on you, who would even dare to diss her?! Let's face it: You have been the only male person in the little one's life so far. All the other ones have backed out. Now there's some character in that!"

Abby came out of her kitchen with a tray of warm cookies. "Anybody want a bite before we are all headed to the Caroling?"

Ramón happily grabbed a cookie and bit into it. His eyes lit up. "Delicious!"

"Thank you," Abby smiled. "Somehow when I'm nervous, baking is my last resort. It helps me to take my mind off things. I don't know how that happens."

"Oh, because of all the precise measuring and timing you have to do, dear!" chimed Starlene. "Nothing better than doing something productive that needs all of your concentration."

"Especially when it's as rewarding as a delicious cookie," Charlene agreed and bit into hers.

"So, what was the outcome of your phone call earlier on?" Dave wanted to know from Ramón.

"Well," the young man smiled brightly. "It looks like at least Michelle's mother is totally on her side. Her dad though is still wary about the baby."

"Well, he better take the little boy as a fact," Starlene said. "He is his own flesh and blood, too, after all."

"It's a pity how old-fashioned behaviorism sometimes counteracts humaneness," Darlene sighed.

"So, what's going to happen?" Abby wanted to know. "I mean, you are welcome to stay until Michelle is well enough again. But what are the plans after that?"

"Her mother said that they were coming as soon as possible," Ramón said.

"Well," Dave chuckled. "Then be ready to encounter them rather sooner than later and be prepared for the stand-off with the grandfather."

"Shush!" Charlene said. "Don't make it sound as bad as that. I'm pretty sure that everybody has enough politeness in them to deal with the situation gracefully."

"I should hope so," Ramón said. "I will definitely have to tell my family they'll have to wait a bit longer for me, though. I can't let Michelle stay here on her own even though I know she is in good hands."

"What will Michelle do after she is healed up enough?" Abby asked softly.

Ramón shrugged. "She was talking about hoping to be permitted to keep the baby in the dorms and take him into lectures, so she can finish her degree. But she'd also have to take on a job. I don't know whether that will work out for her at all."

"Couldn't her grandparents take the little one?" Starlene asked.

"They are living down in Texas. That's way too far out of the way," Ramón said. "A child belongs with their mother is all that I know. Or at least close enough so they can see each other more often and bond."

"And the other grandparents?" Abby asked.

"When there is no natural father accepting his responsibility, I doubt that his parents are willing to take on any."

"Chips and blocks," Dave agreed. They all fell silent, eating cookies and listening to the fire crackling in the fireplace.

"Have you heard the news yet?" Pippa, who had gone upstairs to her shared room for a while, had returned to the lobby and burst into the pensive quiet.

"What news?" Dave asked.

"There is a rumor that a famous opera singer has been stranded in Wycliff."

"Really?" Starlene asked and raised her eyebrows. "Is there a chance to know who he is, where he has found accommodations, and whether it's possible to get an autograph?"

"It's a she," Pippa said. "It's La Strega. They don't know where she is staying, and so we don't know whether she would be willing to sign any autographs for anybody."

"Imagine that," Dave chuckled. "La Strega stranded in Wycliff. And she was to appear at the Christmas gala that I wanted to listen to on TV this afternoon while you are all caroling down by the town hall."

"But you were going to come with us, weren't you?" Pippa asked. "We wouldn't want to leave you up here all by yourself."

"Well, I wouldn't have been all by myself," Dave corrected her. "Michelle and the baby are here. And if my guess is right, their young protector will stay at *The Gull's Nest* as well.

But I appreciate your offer all the more as La Strega was the one incentive of listening to the gala anyhow. Now that she's not singing, I might as well carol along with all of you. Who will be standing in for her, by the way?"

"Oh, one of these child prodigies. I forget her name," Pippa said. "They appear one moment, are predicted to do great, and as soon as they are a bit older, they vanish again. I wonder what happens. Maybe they are fed up with all the big hoo-ha that went on while other children were enjoying all the fun stuff. So, they decide it's *their* turn now."

"La Strega," sighed Starlene. "That woman has one of the most powerful voices ever. I mean, whenever she opens her mouth, she manages to give me the goosebumps. I just wonder why she is stranded in a town like Wycliff. What was she doing around here?"

"Oh, I can see that. She might just have wanted to have a break for herself, too. As far as I know, she has had a huge concert tour around the States, and the gala in Seattle was to have been the last event this year," Dave replied. "Wycliff is simply a tourist magnet all year around, but especially during the Christmas season. And even La Strega might have had a curiosity for something as simple as a Christmas small-town that coincidentally would have been just a short detour. If we hadn't been cut off by this historic snow storm."

"Oh my, she must be totally distressed by this! Imagine she would have had this TV show with all these other world stars.

And instead she is stuck in a small-town with normal people like us. What a disappointment for her!"

"I don't think that she's disappointed," Dave said.

"Ah, come on," Pippa protested. "Instead of listening to her colleagues' pitch-perfect musical gift and performing herself, she might only be listening to the off-tune humming and droning of Wycliffians and stranded people at the town hall or in church. Not that there isn't one or the other talent among these amateur musicians here. But it will be a far cry from perfection for the ears of a La Strega."

"It's either *a* Strega or of *La* Strega," Ramón put in quietly. "Not two articles." He grinned impishly.

"True," Pippa laughed. "I should have known better as the well-read librarian I am, right? Anyhow, I think it can't be fun for her to be stranded like this."

"On the contrary," Dave chuckled. "I think she is having the time of her life."

"How would *you* know?" Starlene asked, and her sisters bent forward curiously in their seats.

Dave shook his head, and his face was gleaming with mirth.

"You know because you have heard where she is …," Pippa suddenly burst out.

"Where?" Darlene asked.

"Yes, where?" Even Ramon was curious by now, though he had never heard of La Strega before.

"I mustn't tell," Dave said. "She seems to prefer to be incognito. But I have a hunch that by tonight the entire town of Wycliff will know who she is and where she is staying."

Chapter 23

December 24, 04:00 p.m.

Downtown Wycliff's businesses had closed their doors. The winter dusk had slowly sunk on the Victorian streets, and fewer and fewer people were seen hurrying through the snow towards home or a place where they were invited. Behind quite a few windows, one could glimpse decorated Christmas trees. And the one in front of town hall was shining in all its glorious 40 feet height.

Across, in the Community Center by the yacht harbor, people started gathering in the non-denominational chapel room for an early Christmas Eve service. Pastor Clement Wayland of Oberlin Church hadn't discussed it long with his wife, Sophie.

"I know, it will have to be some very swift dinner, dear," he had said. "The seven o'clock candle light service at Oberlin is a given. And I want them to be able to enjoy the Town Hall Caroling before as well. But I want to offer all these stranded people some special Christmas joy, too. So, it's better I make my way over now instead of waiting until much later. Their Christmas is disrupted enough as it is. There are children there – they must not be kept up overly long."

Sophie had nodded. "Does Wycliff know what a wonderful pastor they have in you?"

He had rolled his eyes. "Sophie, Sophie, this is not about personal vanities. This is about being a shepherd, a spiritual guide in a rather disheartening situation."

"But you don't even have a piano player down there to accompany any church hymns."

"Oh, I heard they have formed an impromptu choir at the Community Center – which means that Wycliff High's music teacher might be available."

"Does he know already?"

"No. But he will," Pastor Wayland had said cheerfully. "Perk up, Sophie, it will be a wonderful opportunity to practice Christian charity."

Sophie had given him a hug. "If I weren't already married to you, I'd marry you all over again, Pastor Wayland. Make sure you stay warm."

He had hugged her back and left the vicarage. Oberlin Church next door had been decorated with pine branches and red bows, and they had strung light chains through some of the bushes that made the snow on the branches glitter like a thousand diamonds in the dark.

Pastor Wayland picked his way carefully across patches of black ice. A danger that came with melted snow that was refreezing, he thought as he made his way into Downtown. He should see to it later that his congregation would have sure footing on their way to and from the candle light service. Meanwhile, he needed to figure what he would tell the people at the Community

Center. He didn't want to preach tonight's Oberlin sermon already – that seemed like laziness to him even if nobody picked up on it. But also, the Oberlin congregation was in a different situation from that of the tourists and workers who had been stuck away from home for the third day in a row now. Hopefully, they'd soon be delivered.

When Pastor Wayland entered the Community Center, the air was filled with the smell of cinnamon buns and something savory that was being prepped in the commercial kitchen. The lobby was packed with people, and he nodded to them.

"If you feel like it, I'd like to offer you a Christmas Eve service," he said cheerfully. "Anybody who wants to celebrate the birthday of our Lord with me, please, head over to the chapel room."

He hadn't expected anybody to follow him at once, but he heard someone say, "Now that is something I hadn't expected down here. Indeed, we aren't forgotten even by the church."

"No, you are not," Pastor Clement turned around. "And why would you say 'not even by the church'?"

The older woman who had said this was blushing now. "Well, I haven't had much good experience with my church in my hometown. When my husband was really sick last year, they didn't once ask how he was. But when he passed away, they wanted to do a memorial service with all the bells and whistles. I said they should have been there when he needed them, not when it wasn't of any use to him anymore."

"I'm sorry," Pastor Clement said. "Well, maybe you come along and find whether I might help you find some comfort in the service."

She nodded doubtfully, but rose and followed him.

It took a while until word had gotten around that there would be a non-denominational Christmas service at the Community Center. In the end, though, the chapel room was packed, and there were even people in the hallway who tried to stand as close as possible. The music teacher of Wycliff High had settled in at the piano, turning the stool until it was comfortable for him and discussing the hymns they'd sing. And then, Pastor Clement rang a dinner bell he had borrowed from the kitchen, and the service began.

There were quite a few kids in his spur-of-the-moment congregation. A few workers from a road construction crew had kept together, standing out in their bright orange and yellow overalls. A group of senior out-of-towners who had been driven over for a day's outing was visibly exhausted by the extended stay. Some younger couples didn't seem to mind but took the entire ordeal as an adventure, more or less. What a challenge to talk to this mixed congregation thought Pastor Clement.

But when the first hymn was sung, he simply started reciting the Christmas story as written by St. Luke. The children's eyes grew rapt. Some of the grown-up's faces started looking wistful. Everybody seemed to have their own connection with the ancient words, their own memories of childhood, of family, of love and loss, of darkness being lightened. The next hymn was sung with even deeper emotion. The piano eventually went quiet, and silence settled over the room. Except for a few suppressed coughs and feet shuffling, Pastor Clement didn't hear a thing. He cleared his voice.

"This is supposed to be the night of all nights. Christmas Eve. The birthday of Jesus Christ, our Redeemer. How many centuries after the night of his birth as we have just heard about? Every round birthday is celebrated big time. After people become a hundred years old, each and every year is celebrated like the wondrous gift of life it is. And here we are celebrating a birthday of over 2000 years, and Jesus lives. Are we celebrating Him even big enough?"

Pastor Clement was looking around and found some bewildered looks, some pensive ones, some even amused. "*We would if we could*, is what some of you are obviously thinking. *If we were at home and could do everything as usually. But instead we are stuck, relying on what we are being handed.* Of course, this is not what any of you – or us Wycliffians – had anticipated. They call it Snowmageddon on the news already. We are cut off from the world. It is dreadful. And you are not where you planned to be. Some of you are missed by their loved ones. Some of you just want to be home. You miss your tree, your fluffy duvets, your jammies; you cannot prepare your Christmas dinner as usually. You won't have gifts tomorrow because they are wrapped somewhere underneath the tree or maybe still in some secret place only Santa knows about."

One of the kids started bawling now. "I know, kiddo," Pastor Wayland said. "It's not fun to be here under these circumstances. But Santa will probably be just a little later for you, right?" The kid's parents winked, and the mother turned to the little one and consoled it quickly.

"Think of the shepherds back then. They were out there in the wilderness, in the dark, in the cold. There were robbers in the wilderness, and shepherding was dangerous business. These shepherds themselves would have to have been pretty tough and rough people. And here they are invited to enter a barn in which a child has been born. It's a moment of physical warmth. Imagine the cattle whose body warmth had heated the room somewhat. But this little boychild was born under the roughest and toughest circumstances they could imagine. Probably worse than they remembered from their own homes. A manger with some hay for a bed. Probably swaddled in Mary's shawl that usually served as a head scarf. No food. No women who might have served her as midwives or comforted her during her labor. I imagine how fearsome it must have been to be invaded upon by a horde of ruffians when she had just born her child. Joseph must have been equally daunted until they realized that these shepherds came to worship."

Pastor Clement looked around the chapel room. The people in the back were pressing in even more closely so as not to lose any of his sermon.

"That was baby Jesus' first birthday. A miserable occasion. Maybe the shepherds gifted something – a piece of bread here, a slice of cheese there, or some dried fruit if they had brought any of that along. It's more than two thousand years later. How do we celebrate His birthday today?" He searched the room. "Is anyone of you receiving a car for Christmas?"

"Here!" a young man said proudly.

"Or diamond jewelry?" A couple of other hands rose. "Or the Disney figurines from the latest movie? A vacation in the Caribbean or in Hawaii?" Each of the questions had been answered with happy smiles and raised hands.

"Nothing wrong with that," said Pastor Wayland. "These are wonderful gifts. And though you may not get them at the time you had originally planned for, you will receive them. All these wonderful gifts will be waiting for you when you come home. And then you can still celebrate." He paused and looked around. "But what will Jesus get on *this* day? It's *His* birthday after all. You may be inconvenienced a bit today and maybe tomorrow, until you arrive at your destination. But what have we prepared to give our Lord *today*?"

Some of the congregation's faces looked stricken, some downright upset. Others nodded pensively.

295

"Come to think of it, this so-called Snowmageddon has turned out to be a real blessing to Wycliff at this time of year. Because we are all learning to make do in our isolation from the outside world. To make do, to share, to be patient, to make use of our individual gifts. You have been stranded where you didn't want to be. But it is not a barn, and there are cots for everybody. There is food and warmth. There is no fear of being assaulted by assassins from an unknown wilderness. Creature comforts – they are all seen to and more. And the people in Wycliff have been sharing – bedding and clothes, they have been donating soap and shampoo. There have been people around serving wonderful meals to all of you. Others have seen to your mental wellness in entertaining you with stories, teaching you how to knit, relaxing yourselves with yoga. I heard a few of you will gather at the Caroling later on and regale the Wycliffians with international Christmas hymns and carols. These … these are gifts that really count."

Pastor Wayland smiled. "This is what Christian love comes down to – not the material gifts in themselves, not the celebration of ourselves, but the care of one another in spirit. The sharing of skills. The feeding of the crowds. But there is more. It's not a one-sided situation. Your compliments, your encouragement for the people who come here to try and make you feel better, your effort to come up with a gift of music to the town, your accomplishment of a graceful attitude in a situation about which you are not happy, but which none of us is able to change – this is what is also a gift to our Lord."

Pastor Wayland folded his hands. "I have heard on the news this afternoon that there are working crews out there who are slaving to get through to us. To remove the snow and the soil from the landslides. They are working now as we are celebrating in this town. Isn't that a gift?! There are people at the police station, the fire department, the hospital who take care of all of us within the town limits of Wycliff, not asking whether it would be better to sit down with their family instead. But just caring. On Christmas Eve. Isn't that a gift?!"

He looked around the room once more. "You will get yours tomorrow. It's not *your* birthday. And Jesus has little use for diamonds, cars, or plastic dolls. But we can make his birthday a good one in considering what we *can* give him. The ancient Greek Christians called it agape. The love of God for man and of man for God. As we are seen to by ourselves and by one another, let's try to make this a birthday that is worthy of our Lord Jesus. And maybe we can make it work even beyond this once-a-year-party on which we mostly give to ourselves. Because I think that is what Jesus would like best."

He paused. Then he stepped aside and signaled the music teacher to start the next hymn. The rest of the service went according to the usual liturgy, and in the end they all stood and sang "Silent Night".

"That was a mighty feisty sermon, Pastor," the older woman from before told him as he was about to leave to prepare for the later candle light service in Uptown. "I wish we had somebody like you down in my hometown."

Pastor Wayland took off his glasses and rubbed them against his shawl. Then he put them on again. "Maybe they are not bad either. Maybe they are just not good for you. Not everybody is the same. Be patient. Trust in God – you will find what you need." He nodded towards her. "Merry Christmas, Ma'am."

"Merry Christmas," she breathed. His back was already turned on her, and he walked outside. He could glimpse people starting to gather by the steps of Town Hall. The nativity scene under the tree was illuminated by some strategically clever positioned spotlights that created a cozy light but didn't blind anybody. Some town hall windows were decorated with garlands and bows, artificial candles lit inside.

As Pastor Wayland walked up to the crowd, he wished he could linger and just be part of it, no specific responsibilities on Christmas Eve for once. But he had promised himself to strew the sidewalks around Oberlin Church with some more sand to make it a safe walk for his congregation. A few people in the crowd recognized him, waved at him and either called "See you later, Pastor!" or "Merry Christmas, Pastor Wayland!" He waved and hoped they didn't see his slight misgivings on his face. Ah, hadn't he just preached about foregoing the little things to do the bigger work for God? Was the joke on him after all?

298

The group from *The Gull's Nest* had set out together and walked downhill carefully and slowly. It was the first time in a couple of years that Dave was headed towards the Town Hall Caroling again, and the joy was written all over his face. Little Heather was skipping along on the hand of Aaron on one side, Abby helping Dave on the other. The three sisters were walking ahead, chatting in merry anticipation. Ronald and Pippa were walking behind, mostly in friendly silence, but pointing out particularly atmospheric decorations behind snowy window ledges. Kathy and Roger made up the rear, arms linked, faces glowing with cold and joy. They had brought a lot of people happiness today, and they were filled with their own gratitude for this.

Their group found a spot near the steps of Town Hall, though there was already quite a crowd. Abby waved to Izzy Watson, whom she spotted across by the nativity scene along with her friend Bill Smith. Dotty McMahon was there with her husband, Luke, the Wycliff Chief of Police. And now, there came Clark Thompson out of Town Hall, accompanied by his wife, Thora, and delivered a short speech, wishing everybody a Merry Christmas.

"Thank goodness, he's not one of those politicians who find it oh so correct to say 'Happy Holidays'!" muttered Angela Fortescue under her breath.

Dave, who had ended up next to her, said, "Well, there are people who celebrate Hanukkah, too. Or Kwanzaa ..."

"True," Angela conceded. "But they wouldn't be here, singing Christmas carols under this tree."

"Probably not," Dave agreed.

Now the impromptu choir from the Community Center was forming on the Town Hall steps, and Florence, who had been spending the hour before at Angela's home and was standing next to her, pressed her mother's hand. "I'm joining them now," she whispered.

"Enjoy the singing," Angela replied. "I know, you loved to sing as a kid …"

Florence threaded her way through the people and found her place in the front row of the choir. The music teacher of Wycliff High turned towards the people and announced the first carol, "Il est né" from France. It was followed by "Oh Sanctissima", a hymn originally from Portugal, the Ukrainian Carol of the Bells, and the ancient Latin "Oh come, oh come, Emmanuel".

"And what would a Christmas caroling event be without our all-time favorite, 'Silent Night'?" the music teacher asked. "Tonight, our ears will receive an extra special treat."

He lifted his arms to start conducting the song, Florence stepped out front, and the choir reshaped its line. Then they began humming a few chords before Florence's rich soprano set in.

"I'll be darned," Angela muttered, staring at her daughter in disbelief, her mouth agape.

"La Strega," Dave whispered, eyes running over with sheer tears of emotion.

"Who?" Angela asked.

"La Strega," he repeated.

Angela laughed out, but suppressed it quickly. "That's my daughter, Florence!" she protested.

"Your daughter is La Strega," Dave said, wiping away his tears. "Florence Piccolini is the legendary opera star La Strega, the sorceress, who casts a spell over everybody who hears her sing."

"I'll be ..." Angela stared at Dave, then back at her daughter, who was now into the second stanza, backed by the soft harmonic humming of the choir.

"La Strega?" whispered Darlene to Dave. "Are you sure?"

He nodded. "I knew I recognized her voice whenever I heard her laugh. I was sure when Pippa brought the news that La Strega was stranded in Wycliff."

Pippa stood thunderstruck. Tiny Wycliff had received a musical Christmas gift that the Seattle Christmas gala would have to do without today.

Chapter 24

December 25, 09:00 a.m.

"Santa was here, after all!" Heather was squealing with joy when she came down the stairs in *The Gull's Nest* on Christmas Day. There were wrapped boxes underneath the tree in the lobby, and the tables were decorated with Christmas cookies. Heather snagged one at their table and pushed it into her mouth.

Last night, they had had a dinner of Weisswurst and Wieners with optional mashers and sauerkraut, or with potato salad that Abby had prepared for everybody who had wanted to dine at the Bed & Breakfast. The room was fragrant with bacon, fried sausages, and eggs now, but also with an underlying remaining whiff of sauerkraut, and the powerful scent of pine. The radio was on in the kitchen, and Heather walked over to wish Abby a good morning.

Abby was busy setting out Danish pastries and cream cheese, cutting up honey melon, and distributing coffee into diverse china pots. "Will Santa have brought anything to the kids at the Community Center, too?" Heather asked Abby.

Abby frowned. "You know, I think Santa has a lot of good helpers in Wycliff who saw to that." And she was right, for the church congregations and the Wycliff Kiwanis had already taken care of that problem and sent a Santa with a pile of gifts over to the Community Center.

"… is finally going to change for the better," a voice from the radio said.

"Shhh," Abby said. "The news!"

"As working crews have been continuously clearing the roads into Wycliff, there will be one-lane traffic possible past the affected areas. Train traffic will have to wait a while longer, as the tracks need to be inspected for damage. Road traffic is anticipated to be back to normal within the next couple of days, as weather conditions improve."

Abby switched off the radio. "Good news," she said cheerfully. "You will be able to go home today."

Heather pouted. "I don't want to go back. I like it so much better here. With you and Santa Dave and all the others."

"But everybody else will be going home, too," Abby reminded her and stroked the little girl's back, taking her into her arms, finally. "Besides, you can come back all the time. You will just have to ask your daddy."

"But it won't be the same," Heather sighed.

"No," Abby agreed. "But that is what life is all about. Constant changes and little adventures down the road. Just imagine, if there hadn't been all that snow and the landslides, we'd never even have met."

"True," Heather said. "Still."

At that moment they could hear a door in the hallway open and Michelle's soft voice saying something. A few moments later

Ramón entered the breakfast room to fetch some items for Michelle. "Good morning!" he said cheerfully.

"Good morning," Abby said. "And good news, too. Traffic is coming through to Wycliff again, and the weather is getting better."

Ramón frowned. "I'm not sure that melting snow makes me feel better about the weather," he said, glimpsing out of the window. "The snow is turning into gray slush already, and underneath the trees there are these drippy wet spots. Icicles are falling from the roofs. I actually prefer the winter wonderland we enjoyed until yesterday."

"Even though you were shoveling out so many people and you must feel your muscles now?"

"Ah, that goes with real winter weather," he said. "Excuse me now. I must get some food to Michelle. She needs it to feed the little one."

"But Noel can't eat what you put on the tray," Heather protested.

The adults laughed, and Ramón prodded her nose with his finger. "No, of course not. But Michelle needs to eat well in order to be able to nourish her baby. One day you will understand."

Heather's eyes grew wide. "Oh," she just made. "Oh …"

The three sisters came downstairs now, laden with wrapped parcels. "Here come the three Magi," Starlene announced with a big wink. One of the parcels on her arm threatened to tumble down. "May we enter our little Christmas child's room?" She looked at Ramón with questioning eyes.

"But!" He was lost for words for a moment. Then he nodded, opening the door with his shoulders, tray in both hands, and trying to make enough room for the cheerful trio. Out of mere curiosity, Heather followed, so did Abby with Aaron. Ronald heard the commotion in his room and popped out, still binding his tie that he had donned for the occasion of Christmas Day. Kathy and Roger slipped out of their room, arms filled with wrapped bundles that they swiftly placed onto each breakfast table. Then they returned to the group, still some gifts in their hands, entering to see Michelle and Noel. Upstairs, Pippa and Florence had heard the unrest as well, and they quickly made themselves ready to join the other guests of *The Gull's Nest*.

In the middle of it all, the doorbell rang, and Abby had to forego watching the unwrapping of a car seat, a bottle warmer, and a fold-down changing table that the three sisters presented to Michelle for the new-born baby. "We thought it might be more useful to you than gold, myrrh, and frankincense," Charlene joked.

When Abby peered through the windows, as she was approaching the front door, she saw a very fashionably dressed lady and an elegantly dressed gentleman standing behind a smaller, very dark-haired lady in a more colorful, but nonetheless very tasteful outfit, waiting in the melting garden.

"Oh my," Abby pressed her hand to her mouth, because she had a sudden hunch whom she was going to face. "All at once," she sighed. Then she opened the door, putting on a cheerful smile that she wasn't feeling at that moment. "Good morning. And won't you want to come in, please? You must have had quite a trip!"

"Half as bad," the lady in the colorfully embroidered coat said. "Besides, a mother will do anything to see her child on Christmas Day."

"See, Jackson," the elegant other lady chimed in. "That's exactly what I told you, too. Now, where do I find my little Michelle, please?"

Abby wordlessly pointed towards the hallway. The two ladies swiftly stepped in the direction, while the gentleman was still hovering in the doorway. "And don't you want to come in, too, Mr. Taylor?" Abby ventured. "I'm sure you'd love to see your brand-new grandson, as well."

He stepped inside, finally, and took off his hat, turning the rim in his hands. "A grandson, huh?"

"A darling little boy," she smiled sweetly. "And such a wonderful Christmas gift to all of us in this house."

"I'm sure it must have caused you a lot of trouble. Some damage even," Mr. Taylor answered gruffly, but not entirely unfriendly. "If I can write you a check …"

"Please, Mr. Taylor!" Abby exclaimed and shook her head. "Come along and meet Noel."

"Is that what she called him?" he asked. Abby nodded. "No middle name yet?"

"I'm sure that will be mended as soon as the grandfather has connected with the baby," she smiled. Then she added bravely," And with the mother …"

Mr. Taylor gave her a stern look, then he nodded briefly. "May it be so. It's Christmas, isn't it?"

"It's more than just Christmas, if I dare say so," Abby ventured. "It's a family future under one roof."

He looked at her curiously. "Are you one of those meddlers?" he asked. "Those women who are constantly putting their oars into other people's life, while their own boat is running in circles?"

Abby sighed. "Touchée," she said. "I was until yesterday. But I guess, I'm moving on from now."

He nodded with a quirky smile, then he followed his wife in the direction from which exclamations and cooing sounds came through a doorway into a bedroom that was jammed full with strangers. Except for his wife, of course, and his daughter, who held a whimpering little bundle in her arms and was looking more beautiful than he had ever found possible.

Their eyes met and held each other. Then Michelle held out her baby son to her father. He stepped over wordlessly and took his grandson into his arms. He peered into the tiny face, his stern mien melting. Then he looked at his daughter. "Noel, huh?"

Michelle nodded. "Noel Jackson," she said quietly.

Jackson Taylor's knees suddenly felt a bit wobbly, and he had to sit on the bedside, cradling little Noel in his arms. "Thank you," he swallowed. Then non-sequitur, "I know it can't have been easy."

"It wasn't," she admitted. "But then it was." She motioned for Ramón to come closer. "This is my friend Ramón, Father. He has taken care of me in the kindest way possible for the past months. I have asked him to be Noel's godfather."

Jackson Taylor passed his grandson over to Michelle, and rose. He held out his hand. "I appreciate what you have done for Michelle," he said. "And in a way for us."

Ramón shook his hand. "It was a joy and an honor," he said. Then he bravely added. "And so much more."

Mr. Taylor scanned his face, then nodded. "We'll see about the 'so much more'."

"Sir," Ramón only said.

"Jackson," Mrs. Tayler admonished.

It was Pippa, who had sense enough for the sensitivity of the situation and started whispering to the other guests to leave the room to the Taylors, Ramón, and his mother. Once she closed the door behind all of them, she said," Let's hope for the best because I think the crisis is over."

"Let's hope for it, indeed," Ronald Hoffman replied. "Christmas spirit is fine enough, but will it outlast what the young people are facing?"

"Oh, don't be such a Negative Nelly," Dave scolded him. "Of course, these people are all in their right senses. It sometimes simply takes encountering what you are prejudiced against –

everything will be fine. I'm pretty sure that Ramón will get his 'so much more' one way or another. They are all so young, and life is full of possibilities."

"Come to think of it and apropos possibilities," Starlene changed the subject. "I think I have had my funnest Christmas ever, so far." She was beaming at Abby. "You are a wonderful host, you know?"

"Totally," Charlene was gushing. "I so enjoyed it, even though it was so not what we had planned for." She looked at Darlene questioningly. "What do you think, sis'?"

"Oh, apart from a Christmas turkey sitting still frozen in somebody's freezer ..." She was looking at her sisters totally sober; then she burst into laughter over their stricken faces. "I've had the time of my life at *The Gull's Nest!*"

"So, what with everything else we have changed over the past days, I think we could change our little tradition into a new one as well," Starlene stated rather than asked her two siblings. "I think, unless Abby has other plans for next year, we'd love to stay at your place over Christmas again." The triplets were beaming now. "Could we make the booking right now?"

Heather tugged on Aaron's sleeve. "Could we do this, too?" she asked with big hopeful eyes.

"Is this really what you want?" he asked carefully.

"It would be my only Christmas wish," she begged.

Aaron chuckled. "We'll see about that. In the meantime, we might just as well ask Abby whether she'll keep her Bed & Breakfast open over the holidays."

"Indeed," Roger put in quietly. "We enjoyed it very much, too. Kathy and I have discussed this last night, and unless you decide to close *The Gull's Nest* over Christmas and do something totally different ..."

"We'd love to book the same room again," Kathy completed his request.

"I'd like to book the room I'm at, again, too," Pippa said. "And I'm willing to share it with whichever lady guest would need a bed in town, as well. Will you be open, Abby? Please?"

Everybody was turning towards Abby now. She looked into the faces which had been those of utter strangers only a couple of days ago but now had become those of friends. Her eyes teared up, and she smiled with joy. Her voice trembled a little as she answered, "Of course, *The Gull's Nest* will be open for you over Christmas next year! How could I not do this?! I mean, this is really something to look forward to."

"Yippee!" little Heather shouted, and the adults laughed. Then she frowned. "But how about Dr. Hoffman?"

They all looked at Ronald now. He harrumphed. "I ...," he began. Then he grinned. "I might come over to visit with you folks, but I'm not booking for now." Their faces all fell. "Now, don't pretend I had been such good company, for I know I haven't. Apart from that ... This gentleman here," he laid his hand on

Dave's shoulder, "and Michelle's midwife persuaded me to look into a Washington license in my field and to apply for a position at St. Christopher's Hospital here in Wycliff." He looked at Pippa. "I might take up residence in Wycliff, and if so, I'd like to invite you all over for Christmas dinner next year."

They all started cheering and talking at the same time.

The hullabaloo woke the tiny bundle in room number 2, and it started to scream in protest, while its grandmother and its godfather's mother were desperately handing it to and fro between themselves to soothe it.

All of a sudden, an angelic voice came from above, singing Brahms' lullaby. The baby stopped mid-scream, seemed to wonder, and started closing its eyes.

"La Strega?" Jackson Taylor asked astonished. "Never knew she made any a cappella recordings."

"She didn't," Ramón said quietly. "It's her alright. She has a room upstairs."

"You know her?" Jackson Taylor said in wonder. "Could you introduce me?"

Ramón chuckled. "Sure, I could. She is a very reclusive lady, though. Unless she has some competition as to voice volume, apparently."

Mr. Taylor laughed and patted the younger man's shoulder. "I guess, we'll leave the women folk to each other for now. Do you think the landlady has a glass of something stronger than tea to toast my little grandson?" And putting his arm around

Ramón's shoulder jovially, he led him out of the room. "Sherry or Port or so?" were the last words the ladies overheard before the door closed behind them.

*

The sound of dripping water was filling Wycliff. It sounded like merry brooks ran in the sewers as the snow melted, and turned into slush. A snow plough slowly ran along Jupiter Avenue, piling up the heavy masses to the curbsides. People were seen pouring out of the Community Center with their Christmas shopping and surprise gifts from caring Wycliffians. The Park & Ride lot in the Harbor Mall was emptying, and the ferry tooted its horn as it announced the first trip out of town today.

Pippa stood at the railing with Ronald, looking back as the town of Wycliff became smaller and smaller. "Would you like to share my Christmas dinner?" she asked Ronald. She turned her head and looked into his eyes which had gained a new shimmer of hopefulness and content.

He suddenly pulled her into his side. "I better," he said. "I was just thinking I better try your cooking before you make Christmas dinner over in Wycliff next year."

"I never offered ..." Pippa gasped. "Did you just say this?!"

"I never qualified for charm school for obvious reasons," he admitted. "But you might teach me how to graduate with honors. Would you help me, please?"

Pippa slightly nodded and smiled. "Then just let's start over the last part."

"Before I asked for your help in the charm department?"

"Before you asked me to cook Christmas dinner next year."

"What did I do?"

Pippa looked at where he had placed his hands. Then she rearranged them until she found herself in a hug. "This is how one starts," she said.

"But there is no mistletoe," he said with a quiver in his voice.

"Adults don't need mistletoes," she said hoarsely. "They just need courage." And then she kissed him.

Recipes

The Soup Cellar's Squash Bisque

1 Uchiki Kuri aka Red Kuri aka Hokkaido Squash

water

Knorr chicken bouillon powder

pepper

dry white wine

sour cream

chopped pistachios

Scrub the squash clean, cut it up, leave the skin on, seed it, and put it into a big pot.

Add some water and boil for approximately 20 to 25 minutes.

Let it cool off, then puree it.

Add a cup of water.

Add bouillon powder, pepper, and wine, until desired flavor intensity and thickness are reached.

Serve with dollops of sour cream and pistachios. Serve baguette or other breads as a side.

Options: If you cannot purchase a Kuri squash, any other winter squash will do. Just prep the squash as you would usually, then continue with boiling.

Abby's Weisswurst with Potato Salad

4 weisswursts (white sausages/veal sausages)

flour

butter

4 midsized potatoes

vinegar

1 onion, finely chopped

bouillon powder

Dijon mustard

canola or sunflower seed oil

either 1 small cucumber, four stalks of celery, or two bell peppers
(no matter what color)

Boil the potatoes in their jackets until soft.

Meanwhile mix to taste vinegar, onion, bouillon powder, mustard,
and oil in a bowl.

Wash the white sausages and roll them in flour.

Melt some butter in a pan and fry sausages in it at medium heat
until the flour coat becomes golden brown on all sides.

Skin the potatoes and cut them into small slices into the bowl.

Stir and let cool off.

Add either peeled and sliced cucumber, sliced celery stalks, or
cubed bell pepper.

Serve sausages with sweet mustard or with cream horseradish.

Options: If you prepare the potato salad with cucumber, add fresh or dried dill to the vinaigrette. If you make it with celery, add celery seeds. If you make it with bell peppers, add a crushed clove of garlic.

Abby's Cinnamon Buns

2/3 cups butter

3 ½ cups flour

5 tsp. baking powder

1 ½ tsp. salt

1 ½ cups milk

¼ cup Crisco

1 tsp. cinnamon

¼ cup sugar

2-3 tbsp. brown sugar

Mix butter with the dry ingredients, then slightly kneed.

Roll into squares.

Melt Crisco, brush it onto dough.

Spread cinnamon & sugar mix on top.

Roll up the squares and cut the rolls into slices of desired thickness.

Bake at 180 degrees C (355 degrees F) for 20 minutes on middle rack.

Acknowledgements

Let me thank all of my friends and readers for their incredible support, especially those who make the effort to write reviews on the internet, be it on their Facebook pages, their blogs, on Amazon, Goodreads, or similar.

My story was inspired by my sweet fellow writer and soul sister, Sandra Windges, who has published two adorable advent calendar stories for grown-ups over the past years. I wanted to surprise her with an advent calendar story of which she didn't know the plot. And by Marianne Bull, cherished Jane of all trades at the Steilacoom Historical Museum, who has supported my book signings and sales over numerous years. As she loves unusual advent calendars – well, here you go, my dear friend. This one is especially for you!

How could I not write *The Sock Peddlers* (https://thesockpeddlers.com/) into my story, Kathy and Roger Johansen, who are caring friends and have hosted countless events with me reading to a group of knitters, crocheters, and drawing artists? I hope you like your appearances.

Special thanks to Dieter and Denise Mielimonka, who read and edited a draft of my manuscript. It's wonderful to get honest and constructive criticism. They are also the source of the wedding cake episode.

Thanks to all my writer friends who have been extremely supportive of me, especially Anjali Banerjee aka A.J. Banner,

Sandra Windges, Dorothy Wilhelm, D.L. Fowler, Marshall Miller, and Peter Stockwell.

To my friends Karen Lodder Carlson (https://germangirlinamerica.com/) and to Pamela Sommer (https://www.thegermanradio.com/) my special thanks – you are simply priceless!

Ben Sclair, editor of The Suburban Times (https://thesubtimes.com/) in Lakewood, WA – if it weren't for you and your wonderful medium, marketing my books would be so much less fun.

My biggest supporter, quietly keeping in the background but facilitating so many of my ventures, is my husband, Donald. If it weren't for him, none of my writing would happen.

Susanne Bacon was born in Stuttgart, Germany, has a double Master's degree in literature and linguistics, and has been working as an author, journalist, and columnist for over 20 years. She lives with her husband in the South Puget Sound region in Washington State. You can contact her at www.facebook.com/susannebaconauthor.

Made in the USA
Columbia, SC
07 May 2020